# IN THE CARDS

MYSTERIOUS CHARM: BOOK 5

CELIA LAKE

Cover design by Augusta Scarlett.

Created with Vellum

# ALSO BY CELIA LAKE

**The Mysterious Charm Series**

Outcrossing
Goblin Fruit
Magician's Hoard
Wards of the Roses
In The Cards
On The Bias
Seven Sisters

Find a complete list of all my books at celialake.com/books.

Sign up for my newsletter to be the first to hear about future books and learn about fascinating bits of research. Happy reading!

## ABOUT IN THE CARDS

**Family brings out the best and worst in all of us.**

Having survived tuberculosis, a family scandal, and a dangerous magical drink, Laura is ready for a quiet visit to a beautiful home on a remote island off the coast of Cornwall. She finally has a chance to meet more people near enough her age, and begin to build her own connections in the world. It's more than past time.

Galen knows his mother wants him to marry, and soon. Laura seems more promising than the other young women who have been invited to stay. But there are things in his family and in the house he doesn't understand. Even his best friend Martin's investigative skills as a journalist haven't helped. When one of the other house guests is murdered, Galen, Laura, and Martin have to work together to protect the innocent and make sure the murderer is caught. New alliances are forged, old bonds are renewed, and nothing is quite what it seems.

**Uncover the murderer and explore the twists of romance in the Isles of Scilly in 1925.**

# ONE

## NOVEMBER 1925 AT A LARGE PARTY IN WILTSHIRE

Laura finally found a corner of the terrace. The party was large, with many more people than she had been expecting, and she could feel the flutters of anxiety again. Too many people pressed around her, wanting too many different things, and Laura wasn't sure whether what they wanted was a good idea for anyone involved. She kept hearing snatches of conversation, people beguiling other people to drink, eat, be merry, and all of it made her more and more unsettled.

Now that she had a chance to catch her breath in a more protected position, she could begin to pick out the little groupings. Seeing people move from place to place brought to mind her brother-in-law's comments, as he was coaching Lizzie through some of the formal social events they had to attend.

He had said people would make their own groupings. In a group of mixed age you could expect a group of older folks tutting over the foibles and miseries of youth. You could expect a cluster of bright young things, usually in the midst of the dancing floor, certain they were going on to rule the world. Or that they would at least comment cynically about it over their drinks.

Somewhere around the edges, there would be the more interesting people, the ones with particular hobbies or passions or intrigues. That's where he spent his time. Well, with Lizzie, now, who had taken to his hobbies of diplomatic conversations and occasional investigations like a fish to water.

They had just left on a belated honeymoon, though, and were no help here. Laura had got the invite on the strength of Lizzie's marriage. She was too old to be much threat to the daughters just coming out, and too young to cluck over things with the aunties and grandmothers. The War had taken many of the men who might have been her age. It left her with youngsters, or people long since married off, usually with two or three children walking and talking by now.

Even with all of that, it was better to be at the party than home alone. Here, she might meet someone interesting. In fact, she'd already been asked to a house party in a fortnight out on an island off Cornwall.

A smaller gathering, Madam Amberly had said; half a dozen people, with a larger party on the Saturday. She was pleasantly lost in thought about what that might be like, if it might lead to something more, to friendships at least, when she heard someone calling across the terrace.

"Laura? Laura Penhallow?"

It was a young woman she'd met at one of the many parties Lizzie and Lord Carillon had thrown, trying to rehabilitate the Penhallow name a bit. He had hoped that if people knew the two sisters, met them as people, the shadows of their father and uncle would fall on them a bit less heavily. It was hardly their fault, after all, that that last doomed expedition had lost many people a lot of money. It was hardly their fault that they had been orphaned by it, either, but Laura had no particular faith anyone would care about that part. They had not cared so far.

It had mostly been a failure. Oh, people were pleasant enough to both of them, and they weren't excluding Lizzie now. It would be too awkward to be too cold to His Lordship's wife, after all. But there was a difference between the big public invitations and the private ones, the ones where you actually made friends.

She nodded and waved a little. "Psyche, over here." Psyche Donovan was from one of the better-off families, but her family had mostly earned their money by being clever and good at magic, rather than the more distasteful approaches that Laura now wanted to give a wide berth. Psyche was very earnest, very fluttery, and prone to having her nose in a novel of some kind, but she also had a kind heart. Laura had found that more rare in these circles than she liked.

"Did you know? There's a fortune teller. Do come, I don't want to go by myself. That's a lovely dress, is it from Meaning, in town? The pale blue, it really brings out your eyes, and that edging, it looks so sharp. Quite the mode! But you still haven't bobbed your hair. Though it is a lovely colour, that gold, nothing like mine."

Laura smiled. "My sister would have my head. And I'd miss it. I fought too hard to keep it long for years." The nurses had kept wanting her to consider cutting it, to make it easier to manage. Now it was pinned up fashionably, though, with the help of one of the maids at Ytene. "I'm not sure what I think of fortune tellers, but I'll come along, at least."

Psyche grinned, and reached for Laura's hand, tugging

her along like a rather speedy tugboat pulling a larger ship through a harbour's traffic. They went off into one of the smaller drawing rooms along the right side of the first floor.

Laura's first impression was that someone had worked to set quite the spooky mood. There were dim charm lights glowing in the corners of the ceiling and throwing shadows everywhere. Streamers of fabric in deep reds and purples and blues draped at angles from the ceiling like a sketch of a tent, sparkling with other charms that made the colour ebb and flow.

In the centre, at a round table, sat a woman, her hair tied back in a scarf, wearing a rather dated dress. It was nearly Victorian, though it was rather less modest around the decolletage than that usually implied.

"Come in, come in. Which of you shall I read for first?"

Psyche hung back, suddenly shy. Laura glanced at her and said, "My friend was curious. Can you tell me more about..." She paused, looking for the diplomatic phrase. "Your approach?"

It earned her a chuckle. "An open mind but a cautious one, I like that. Did you by chance study divination in school?"

Laura blinked. "No, ma'am." She almost offered something more - that she'd left school before the years it was an option, that she wasn't sure she'd have taken it anyway. "I've known a few people who read cards, though."

"Then you may know something of these. I use a French deck, an ancient deck, the Tarot de Marseilles. Not so old as the Sforza or some of the Italian, nor so drenched in Albion's magic as the Howard, but it is a good friend, a helpful friend. Come, sit." The woman had a slight accent, one Laura, with all her experiences in Europe, couldn't quite place, with a faint hesitation between words. And the fact she was using the Marseilles deck, common in France, but less so in Albion or other parts of Europe, that was also curious. It made Laura worry that there was some trickery here.

Laura paused for a moment before sitting. "Is there a fee?"

"Most cautious and practical!" It seemed to delight the reader. "No, no, I read here by arrangement with our hostess, a little space away from the noise and the strutting of young men and the grumbling of old ones."

That made Laura smile, and Psyche bumped her with her hip. "Go on, you go first."

"Come, sit down here." The reader gestured at the chair across from her. "Your friend may stay if you wish, or I will read for her next if you prefer a private reading."

Laura frowned, sitting down and letting her skirt settle. She didn't really believe it would turn up anything she wanted hidden.

"Psyche, do stay, it will be more fun that way." Besides which, an overture towards friendship was a precious thing, and worth encouraging, even if Psyche was a bit silly sometimes.

The reader beamed at them. "Now, then, you should take these cards, spread them before you, and then draw the cards and place them here, as I tell you."

Laura nodded, and begin to spread the cards in an arc, keeping them close enough to her side of the table to reach them easily.

Psyche settled down in a chair beside her, peering at the backs. "They're beautiful. Mistress. Um. What should we call you?"

"I am Madam Bertilak." It was like she was giving a gift. Laura frowned, considering the name, unable to pin down the half-remembered story it evoked. Then the woman gestured again. "Find your cards, dear one. Begin there, move right to left, as the sun passes over the earth. Face up."

Laura could just hear her sister's likely lecture on how that wasn't how it worked at all, but she did as instructed, placing five cards.

"Your foundations, the distant past." Madam Bertilak indicated the card on the right. "The recent past. The present. The near future. The more distant future, prone to change." Her finger moved from card to card.

Laura nodded. That seemed sensible enough, if one thought bits of card could tell you anything. She leaned to peer at the cards, brightly coloured.

"The Magician. It can indicate a lingering illness, especially of the lungs. Something where there is a certain amount of - how does one say it?" Madam Bertilak paused, tapping the table with a fingernail. "Show. Smoke and mirrors. Performance. There may also be real skill, but it is hidden behind the show."

Laura frowned, and shook her head, the image of several of the doctors she had met at various sanitaria suddenly dominating her thoughts. They had smiled, shaken hands, and charmed her mother. None of them had much to offer except the usual; the endless fresh cold air, the surgeries to inflate or deflate the lung, the specific foods. Their insinuations that if something did not work, it was a flaw in her, not in their treatment. She shivered, suddenly cold, and the reader glanced at her.

"An uncomfortable past, my dear? I am sorry, but you have had a bad time of it, haven't you? This is the Eight of Cups, and I find it often in the readings for young women, betrayed by men. Betrayed in the heart, you say, not just in the body."

Laura frowned, and said, "Psyche, would you be a love and fetch me something to drink? Wine, or - if they have a mulled wine, or cider?" Ordinary wine would be safe enough to drink, and she might be able to recover by the time Psyche got back.

. Psyche bobbed up, apparently oblivious to Laura's deeper agitation. "Oh, of course, and a shawl? You seem to be taking a bit of a chill."

"That is so kind, yes. My shawl's in the cloakroom, here's the token."

She waited until the younger woman had left, curling her arms around herself at her waist, willing the tension out of her shoulders without success.

"They cut close, then?"

Laura had been looking down the cards, but she looked up, to meet Madam Bertilak's eyes, which were a curious blue-green. The expression was kind enough. A real kindness, not the false kindness Laura had long since learned to recognise. Like fake kind doctors.

"Rather, yes, madam." She paused. It would give too much away to explain, at least yet. "The next card, please?"

"There is a gift here." She tapped the second card again. "A sign - there are plenty of cups, to be filled. You may take things away from what you have learned in this betrayal. And I am sorry for it. You seem a kind woman."

Laura ducked her head, but said nothing.

After a few moments, Madam Bertilak went on. "The next card, ah, that is - you have had many changes in your life, yes? This is the Wheel of Fortune, it explains itself, the way that life changes, swinging us up and down, up and down. You have been down, here, so perhaps now it is time for up."

Laura looked up and smiled, more hopeful now. At least

this one had not cut so much like a knife. "That would be welcome, yes." She peered at the card, which had a much starker image than the more expected Howard, with its red and white roses and the background of a great battlefield. This was a mechanical and tumbling creature, fate like clockwork, and it seemed a rather differently ordered world. She was not at all sure what to make of it.

"This, oh, goodness." The woman tutted over it. "This card, it scares many people. It is Death, you see, the reaper who comes for us all in our turn." A skeletal figure, holding a scythe, grimacing, with parts of bodies and heads strewn on the field at his feet.

Laura peered at it and then took a breath. "I've seen enough of death that - what I feel is more complicated than fear."

The woman raised an eyebrow and said, "A most unusual young woman even in these times. Mature for your years and wise. But you should not fear for yourself, for see, this last card?"

She indicated the last card, on the left, "Les Amoreux. The lovers. In this deck, it is about choice. You see that it is a young man, with two women. One older and wealthy, but the look on her face, perhaps she is not so kind? And the younger, gentler, beautiful, but not near so well dressed. He must choose. But see, there is Cupid, with his arrow, a sign from the heavens about which way will bring blessings."

"And you think that is for me?"

"Ah, but the other cards, in your past, those have been true enough, yes?"

"You said..." Laura paused, trying to gather her thoughts. "You said this was only a possible future."

"Yes. You will have to live a little longer to find out. My

advice to you, wise young woman, is to think carefully about what you choose, how it will last."

Laura was about to say something else, when Psyche came back with a mug of mulled wine, and a shawl. She was glad of the excuse to give her seat over, and fuss about warming herself up.

Madam Bertilak took a shrewd look at her, and gathered up all but the last card, with a "Here, see, there is a fine card to end on."

Psyche's eyes widened in delight, and she said "Is there someone you're interested in, Laura? There are rather a lot of men tonight, for a change." Laura smiled, and let the chatter wash over her, until Psyche settled down and shuffled and drew her much less distressing cards.

# TWO

## THURSDAY AFTERNOON, NOVEMBER 19TH, IN THE ISLES OF SCILLY

A week and a half later, Laura found herself standing by the portal in a circular paved courtyard cut into the slope of an island. This was not the Cornwall she knew. The gate of the portal was made out of white stone, and at a few places she could see moss establishing itself. A broad path led up toward the house, but she could see no one at all.

She and her uncle and father had sailed to a number of the other Isles of Scilly, but never this one. For years, the great house that went with this courtyard had been boarded up, or used for only a few weeks over the summer for select guests. Now, though, the Amberlys made their primary home here. One of so many changes since the War, so many places had been abandoned or turned over for War work, and now they were opened up again.

Laura had asked about the family, but hadn't been able to learn much. Cassian Amberly had inherited the family properties as a second son, very unexpectedly. His wife, Parnell, came from one of the Third Families, the ones who had come over to England with William the Conqueror.

They had two sons, Julius and Galen. Julius had been a recluse since the War, not that anyone could blame a man for that, really.

Gossip was, that was why the family was here. With the newly added portal, the rest of the family could visit elsewhere easily enough, and they could bring supplies in even if the seas were rough. They were rough right now, with the choppiness of the coming winter, grey and cold, and they would only get worse. Magic could make the house cosy and warm, if there was enough money for specialists. Judging by the look of the house, money was not in short supply.

The place was gleaming in the autumn sunlight, all white stone and whitewash, and quite modern. Laura thought it was Romanesque revival, done in the 1860s or so. Why Romanesque, she wasn't sure, except that perhaps it reflected the Norman roots somehow.

It rose up, crowning the hill with a decided tower, and wings spreading out at right angles at the base. Quite large, one might say excessively so, for an island that had such a small area of land in the first place. There might be a decent kitchen garden and chickens, maybe even a few sheep or goats, but she didn't think the grazing would run to cows. It made them awfully dependent on the portal, she realised, if the seas were too rough for boats.

She turned, looking to see if anyone was coming to meet her. She had a trunk and was not terribly pleased about leaving it. The day was clear, and she could see across to Tresco, at the northeast, and the larger St Mary's to the southwest, but there were clouds that suggested there might be mists or even storms coming.

"Ahoy, the traveller!" She heard a voice calling down, someone coming down the path. Two someones. One was tow-headed, one of the shining blondes, sharply dressed in a jacket and slacks and a deep purple vest. The other was dark-haired, trailing behind, wearing rather scruffier clothing. It wasn't the cut or the fit, precisely, but a sense of wear around the knees and elbows. Despite their differences, they came rushing down as if they were a pair of horses pulling as a team, wheeling and moving together.

"Beg pardon, we didn't realise the portal had started up. Galen Amberley, of course, in case you've forgotten. This is Martin Taylor. We've been friends since school. He's here to fill out the numbers a bit." He had the upper class drawl Laura had got used to from her brother-in-law. It was a voice that assumed the world lay before him, ready to be taken up, or at least provide him all the amusements he might want.

"And because Galen gets tremendously bored at these things. Can't do without supervision." Martin's voice was a bright tenor, somehow sharper. Well-educated, but like his clothes, not quite of the same cut. There was a twinkle in his eyes that Laura thought promised good humour, at least.

"Is this your trunk? Do you mind a charm on it? Martin's quite good with that one that makes the thing not so blasted heavy."

Laura nodded. To her surprise, Martin didn't make a move to do the charm, but stuck his hands in his pockets, as if waiting for something.

Galen glanced over, then laughed. "Martin insists I play fair, even if Mother won't." He didn't continue, however.

Laura let the silence draw out for a good fifteen seconds, then said, amused, "I presume there is more to it than that rather opaque sentence?"

Martin grinned at her. "See, I said she'd prefer it."

Laura just raised her eyebrow. "I can stand here all day. Your mother might worry though."

"Oh, it's Mother who's the complication. And Father. They're looking to marry me off, and Martin insists you be warned before you're thrown into the fray. Have the walk up to collect yourself for the challenge ahead."

Laura blinked. "That's rather bold."

"He's the bold one." Galen gestured at Martin. "He was a Boar, at school. He is supposed to charge boldly."

Laura snorted. "I've never thought the house selections were all that." She eyed him up and down. "I suppose you're Fox?"

"A hit, a very palpable hit!" Martin crowed.

Galen looked amused. "Well, I make it easy." He had a deep amethyst ring, matching his vest. "At your service for charismatic plotting, yes."

"So long as it's charismatic." Laura felt a bit off balance, and she was retreating to the silly pleasantries that had kept her safe for long enough. She did not like the undertow here, being thrown into the water with no idea what Galen or his parents were plotting. But there was nothing for it now but seeing if they'd tell her, unless she wanted to storm off in a snit to an empty house.

"And you?"

She shrugged. "I was in Seal House, but I left school after the third year. Health reasons, now sorted out." Her tone was brisk, the no-nonsense explanation they'd settled on, she and Lizzie together. She didn't wear the aquamarine her mother had given her, but she kept it safe in her jewellery box.

"Pity. I'd love to find out a few of their mysteries." Martin was not moving, still.

Laura frowned, not sure how to take that. She knew few enough of the house's magics, and even if she did know, she did not like the idea other people could demand them.

There was no way to answer that that wasn't prickly, so she didn't.

Fortunately, Galen moved things right along. "Anyway, Mother is hoping dreadfully that you'll find me of interest. I want to say that of course I won't press, but we do want to show you a pleasant time. And you have to admit, there's not a better view in all Albion, now, is there?" There was quite a bit of pride in his tone, as if he'd laid the whole thing out himself.

Laura had to smile. "Nor a number of other places. I did a bit of travelling."

"Oh, did you? Where? Come on, Martin, we've done the fair thing."

She did not want to rush into answering personal questions. "Is your mother going to be awful?"

"Oh, no. She's subtle about that kind of thing. Just, she won't make a fuss if we wander off together. Which is good for you, because the other people she's invited are a bit dull or total unknowns, but American, so probably a bit brash."

Martin chimed in, "And at least one is probably both."

"You do not make this sound appealing, you realise."

Galen shrugged. "Gorgeous views, balmy temperatures, and we are delightful company, if we do say so ourselves." He seemed entirely comfortable speaking for the both of them. "And the party tomorrow should be grand. Mother always arranges a fantastic spread, and there'll be more people."

"You always think with your stomach." That was Martin again.

"You're the one lurking by the buffet table; don't come over all innocent. When people aren't making you dance. He doesn't care for it," Galen added to Laura.

"Is there a reason? You seem deft enough?"

"Oh, never felt entirely at ease with it. I don't come from Galen's sort of family. I'm more likely to have a pen in hand than, well, a lady's hand." His voice sounded breezy but with an edge to it, as if he'd practised how to make it sound good.

Laura looked him up and down. "Not a scholar, you don't have the right hunch to your shoulders. And I somehow don't see you as the impoverished novelist, in a garret. You're far too sociable for that." He definitely was better built than the average impoverished writer.

Galen laughed, and clapped his hands, the sound echoing against the rock of the courtyard. "She's got you there." It made him seem younger, buoyant.

"Journalist. All staff pieces so far, nothing with my name on it, but I aspire to people running away from my questions in time."

Laura snorted. "What kind of journalism, then? I hope nothing of that..." She paused, not sure how to finish the sentence.

"Oh, I know you had a horrible time with the gossip rags. Nothing like that. I want to do proper investigations. Figure out things that are going wrong and improve them. Shine a light on them, if that's not too utterly aspirational of me."

Laura considered. "That has a certain potential nobility to it." It made her think a bit better of him. If he asked questions because he wanted to improve matters, that was better than prying for no good reason.

Martin bowed and then said, "We should take your trunk along. Sorry we don't have a footman handy, Galen's mother has them working on something for the party. And Jacobs, the butler, overseeing."

Galen added, "And as I said, she thinks the more time

we have alone, the better. Quite scandalous, really. I hope you don't mind."

Laura shook her head. "Not if this is how you intend to go on. Amusing, not tedious."

"Oh, you seem like a nice sort, and not dull."

She contemplated for a moment, then said, "I must be a fair bit older, though? I don't remember either of you from school."

"You might not, even if we'd been there at the same time. We were rather wrapped up in our own things. I'm twenty-four and a half. Martin's three months my junior. You?"

Martin cuffed him on the arm. "Idiot. Don't ask a lady her age."

"It's been in the papers, so I can't imagine why it should be secret. Thirty-one." She paused, then added, smiling. "And going on three-quarters of a year. If we're being precise."

"In the papers?" Martin waved his hands over the trunk, then nudged Galen, picking up one of the handles. They lifted it easily now and turned to lead the way up the broad path to the house.

"My sister married Lord Carillon this fall. You can't imagine how many of the pieces about her included the line 'Among her attendants was her younger sister, Lorelai Penhallow, a spinster of thirty-one years'."

"It seems rather dull. To be defined by that."

"It is, rather. But there are - well. The War. As everyone says."

Martin glanced at Galen, and said, "Galen's brother had a bad War. They don't talk about it. So you don't put your foot in it, asking. 'I hope the family is well' is fine, that sort of thing, but asking after Julius directly gets awkward."

Galen didn't say anything for a moment, navigating a bit of a rise in the path. "He was injured. You - he keeps to himself. The back wing, the upper floor. No one goes there but the servants who tend to him, and sometimes Mother and Father. And Blythe."

Laura swallowed. "Not you?" She could come back to the other people, but that omission meant something, she was sure.

"Not often, no. I don't think he likes me to." His voice got quieter, the way people did when they didn't want to admit something they found difficult.

"Siblings are hard." It came out of her before she could stop herself. "My sister and I had a horrible way of rubbing each other wrong for a long time. We're a good bit better now."

# THREE

## THURSDAY AFTERNOON

"I'm glad that worked for you." Galen hoped his voice didn't sound as false as it felt. He glanced at Martin, wanting some reassurance. He felt like things had got off to a wobbly start. Then, as a peace offering, he asked, "Would it help to know the plans?"

"Please, yes." If his mother were going to round up possible brides, at least Laura was not an awful prospect. Thus far, any rate. They'd only just met properly, but at least she wasn't looking at him like she was making a lengthy list of all his flaws, or analysing the size of his bank accounts from his cufflinks. And she was neither making him do all the talking, nor chattering away and not letting him get a word in edgewise.

"We'll bring this up to the house, to your room, and there's a maid who'll be looking after you. I'm sure you want to unpack, or freshen up, or whatever you do, yes?"

Laura smiled. "Journey by portal's not nearly so messy as by train - the soot will go everywhere! But I do appreciate the chance. Especially if I'm meeting your parents, and I assume that happens sometime in here?"

"Oh, yes. When you're ready, the maid will show you how to get to the parlour, and we'll introduce you round. Our other guests aren't here yet, I think. They were coming through in an hour or so."

"Other guests?" Laura sounded curious, and he certainly agreed with Martin that it was awfully rude to drop her in the middle of it without proper warning.

"Two are family. Silvia and Attis Tipson. Aunt Silvia is my father's sister."

"That's a usual sort of thing. What sort of people are they?"

"Oh, Uncle Attis was a Healer. He's retired now, though he sometimes consults. He can go on and on about old cases, but mostly he's rather pleasant."

Martin snorted. "You like him because he gives you money every time he visits. Started with small coins, he's up to larger sums, now."

"And he listens to me, and he treats me like I might have a brain in my head." It was an old argument, and he didn't mind Martin teasing. Even if he didn't want to get into the muck about it with a near-stranger. Besides, if she took some sort of offense to it it would be better out soon before anyone got attached.

"And Silvia - um. Is there a proper form of address for them?"

"Oh, Healer Tipson and Madam Tipson, that's what they prefer. Old-fashioned, you know. A lot of the family is. I think that's actually why Mother is interested in you. She keeps complaining about the young women, and how terribly awfully modern they are, dancing and drinking and high hemlines, and bare shoulders, and all that." He paused, then said, "Oh, goodness, I suppose someone should have warned you. About what clothes to bring."

Laura shook her head. "I've a number of dresses with bare shoulders, but wraps or - you know, those long flowy translucent things to go over them. We were doing a lot with my brother-in-law's extended family and larger social circles, and most of them are still quite traditional. Or paranoid. It's sometimes hard to tell the difference."

Martin blinked. "Paranoid?"

Galen and Laura started talking together, and he grinned, and waved a hand. "I'll let the lady explain." Besides, the trunk was getting a little harder to carry, and being out of breath wasn't attractive.

Laura smiled back, then said more seriously to Martin, "There's a whole set of things you can put on someone's skin, potions and alchemical things. Even poisons. Fussy to make, and expensive, but they exist. So among a certain circle, baring skin, especially shoulders and arms, is a sign of trust or, well, grand stupidity. Not a thing you do casually, either way."

"I'd not heard it put quite like that, but you're right," Galen said. He then added, "Aunt Silvia's actually supposed to know quite a lot about that sort of thing. So if you do get curious and want three-quarters of an hour lecture on the topic..."

Martin shook his head. "I do not understand your sort of people, Galen, and I'm fairly sure I never will." He seemed about to make some other comment, but instead said, "Keep going about who will be here. You didn't explain Blythe."

"Oh, I always do that." Galen felt himself flushing, he kept feeling one step behind. "Laura, she is a companion to my mother, she's in her late forties or so. Fetch and carry, overseeing things, whatever household direction mother doesn't care for. She's a distant cousin, no money, no family, nowhere to live. And she honestly seems to like Mother and Father."

Laura nodded. "That's not so common, I gather. But you implied others?"

"There are two I haven't met yet. A brother and sister, born over here, but they have been in America for ages. About your age, maybe a bit older? Thirties, anyway. Senara and Basil Wilson. Father came across them in some business arrangement he hasn't explained and invited them up for a visit."

Martin frowned. "Not very like him."

"No, and Mother was furious, but he just set his jaw and said he had his reasons, add two more to the count. It was just supposed to be people who would sit around the drawing room, not need entertaining, except for you, Laura."

Galen had given up fighting with his mother about it. He felt he could perfectly well find his own wife, if his parents didn't keep insisting he be on the island most of the time. And yet his mother kept asserting most young modern girls wouldn't do at all. It had left them in an uncomfortable detente punctuated by awkward visits. Laura, at least, didn't seem in the mode of the ones his mother had tried so far. She had an unspoiled quality to her, which might have been what appealed to Mother. Besides her connections to a landed lord, which might also be a factor.

Laura considered, then counted out on her fingers. "Your parents, me, you, Martin, Blythe, Healer and Madam Tipson, and the Wilsons. So ten all-told? And we're the youngest?"

"Exactly. They will encourage us to go wander off and ramble, or whatever it is young people do that is not noisy or annoying. The older folks will sit around and do whatever it is they do. Croquet or watercolours." Galen grinned. "There's not a lot to do here, but the views are great, and it's a good-sized island to ramble around."

"Are there seals?" Laura sounded very earnest. "I'd not mind that, if you need an outing."

Galen laughed, broadly. "Oh, we have many seals. Seabirds, too, and some rather nice plants, besides the gardens. It's not really the proper season for gardens, even though it's warmer here than the mainland of Cornwall."

"That's where I'm from. Lanyon, out on the northern coast, so rather more chilly, sometimes."

"So you have a sense of how this is different. This isn't where I grew up, mind. When I was little, up to part way through school, we were living in Cumbria, there's a big old family estate near Carlisle. We're not lords of the land, that's other bits of the family, but we have quite a nice estate." He'd not been able to spend time there in far too long, and he missed the horses and long rides along the lanes and edges of the field, and something other than the sea, as beautiful as it could be.

Laura paused, then said "And this?"

He wondered for a moment if she'd spotted how unhappy he felt here at times, how penned in. "Better for my brother, the sea air. And I suppose if I marry, I could move back there." He couldn't keep the wistfulness out of his voice.

"Maybe you can introduce me to the land up there, sometime?" Laura's voice had turned shy.

Galen smiled. "Do you ride? That's one thing we can't do here, and I miss it terribly. Not fox-hunting, I can take or leave that, but being out on a fine day, nothing between you and the world, and the horse having opinions."

"I didn't for quite a while, but I've picked it up again.

My brother-in-law's got rather a lot of horses, he's breeding them for pavo, and for use in the New Forest. So I've picked up more, just visiting there."

"That must be interesting, seeing how it's done? I've done a bit of training, but it's the kind of thing you have to stick to, and I've never been great at that." Martin raised an eyebrow at him, but Galen figured if Laura wanted a steady man who diligently made progress on things, she should find out now he wasn't that.

They had got up to the main house now, and Galen gestured. "This is the usual entrance, of course there's a kitchen door and all that, and one off the library, but it's usually locked. Father doesn't like risking the damp getting into his books."

Laura paused and said, "Can I catch my breath? You both too, that was a fair hill! And - is that a conservatory on the side there?"

Galen glanced at the house, where the glass walls took over from the stone, then nodded. "I think they built it as an orangery, but it's got other things in it now. Very pleasant, even in bad weather, and Father had some really clever chap make sure the glass was all resistant to breakage. We do get bad storms through here and there, and we're right on top of the hill, no buffer from things thrashing about. It's charmed to keep a proper temperature, too."

He was watching Laura carefully now. He did like how she was taking a moment to take in the whole place, the tower, the wings, the conservatory.

"How's the house laid out?"

Martin murmured, "No reason we couldn't give her a tour, once she's freshened up? We can go wait in the upstairs sitting room."

Galen snorted. "That's true. How about this, we take

you up to your room, let you settle, and then we'll give you a tour before subjecting you to Mother and Father."

Laura nodded, opened her mouth as if to ask something, and then said, "Right. And do tell me if there's somewhere I shouldn't go, or whatever. I'm not so used to houses like this. Besides the obvious, like the family wing."

"Lord Carillon's got a huge place, doesn't he?"

"Several." Laura's tone was dry. "Mostly he's at Ytene, of course, he's the landed lord there, the obligations. That's why they didn't go off on honeymoon until a few weeks ago, they had to do the harvest rituals with the village."

Martin rocked on his heels a little. "What sort of honeymoon, then?"

"Oh, Italy, mostly. A bit of time in Greece. He has some connections there, from earlier travel. And Lizzie - that's my sister - she's been to northern Europe, but not so much there. They want to go out to Egypt sometime, and he did rather a lot of exploring in South America, but that's sort of, sort of," She broke off.

Galen said, quietly, "That's what happened to your father and uncle, yes?"

Laura nodded. "They were exploring, trading, the goal was to bring back more plants, medicinal ones, that kind of thing? Only they disappeared, and no one knows what happened. A lot of people - they lost money, investing, and they're very cross, but it's difficult." She stopped and swallowed hard. "Sorry. We've only just met. I shouldn't go on."

Galen glanced at Martin, who was better with this sort of thing.

Martin shrugged minutely before saying, "Well, I'm sure no one will fuss here. That's the useful thing about Americans, they know a totally different set of gossip. And for all Galen's mother's other challenges, she's quite insistent on making people feel comfortable. Even me, and I'm quite the young radical hothead by most reasonable standards."

Galen let it go. It wasn't nearly that simple, but his mother had invited Martin, continued to invite Martin, and that was what mattered most. "Come on, let's get your trunk upstairs."

# FOUR

## THURSDAY AFTERNOON

Getting the trunk up the central stairs took more effort than Martin wanted to admit. He needed a pause to catch his breath, and once he and Galen had set the trunk down to the right side, he said "To the left is the family side, and the right is for guests. The right side of the hall is for the ones they especially like, the best views."

Laura blinked. He rather liked how she didn't say the first thing to come to mind. He couldn't abide women who babbled. "Who else is on this end?"

"I'm on the family side, upstairs, across from Galen. I've stayed an awful lot with them over the years, I think they decided it was better than us tromping through the hallways at all hours." If sometimes grudgingly.

In fact, he had the distinct impression that if he hadn't been needed to make up the numbers they might have tried to keep him away this time. They did seem to labour under the illusion that their son would manage sufficient boldness to get himself married if Martin weren't there. Martin was none too sure. Galen did well drawing people out socially, doing all the casual social things with people, but he trusted Martin's ability to read their deeper intentions far more than his own.

Galen grinned. "Something like that. Also, it's easier to raid the kitchen stores from that side, there's a back staircase that goes straight down, but we don't let on to Mother about that."

Laura nodded. "And who else is along here?" She looked down the hallway.

"The Wilsons, I expect. And I think the Tipsons this time, too?" Martin wasn't sure about that. "You're this room here, just down the hall." He gestured at the door on the right, and then he and Galen hefted the trunk for the last stretch.

"Aunt Silvia prefers the view off the family wing, she asked Father about it specially, I believe." Galen said. "She made quite a fuss about it, actually. She insists the view of the sea is much better, something about the angles and the light." He pushed open the door, revealing a room decorated in pale greens.

"Here, quite modern, since we did the renovations recently. Your own en suite, through here, though the maids know how to make the hot water behave, and I haven't the foggiest. Bed, closets, a little sitting area. If you want to be sociable, there's a parlour along on the end here. Or any of the public rooms downstairs, of course."

Laura glanced around. "Could you fill me in a bit more up here? I mean, I feel nervous about being overheard, asking silly questions."

Martin waved a hand at Galen. "How about you go off and let your parents know we'll be down in a couple and see about some tea?"

Galen laughed. "That's me sorted. You tell her all the

things someone like me won't think to. Good idea." He swept a half-mocking bow, and went out, closing the door behind him.

"Sit, please. The chairs are quite comfortable. Not like some older estates, with poking springs everywhere. How about we talk for a little, then I can take you down. Save the tour for later."

It made Laura laugh, and he liked how her eyes crinkled up. "You have a broader experience than the Amberlys, then?" There was no comment about the tour, which meant he'd guessed right that she'd rather have a breather.

"Oh, quite. It's handy to get on with people from school."

"You seem - closer than a lot of school friends?" She sounded a little uncertain, now.

He'd heard that tone before, people who wondered if he and Galen shared a bed as well as everything else. Explaining how they really were, that was more complicated. They'd made agreements, he and Galen, about when they'd share certain things, and when they wouldn't. "More shared interests than it looks like."

"But you're not from one of the Great Families."

"Goodness, no. Fifth Families. You?"

"My mother was First Families, my father was Fourth. Cornish, you know?"

"So you're familiar with working for a living." He approved. It was good for people to know what that was like.

"Actually, not so much." He could see her begin to bunch up her skirt in her hand, folding and unfolding the cloth. "I was ill for quite a while. Nearly a decade. All better now, they promise. But I couldn't work. And then I got a job, and it all went..."

She paused, searching for the right word, like she wasn't used to talking about it. "Sour. I guess that's the right term. I've done a little secretarial work since, for women dealing with planning family weddings, or events, but nothing terribly steady."

Martin tilted his head. "But you'd like something steadier?" He wasn't sure what to do with her visible discomfort, other than not press further.

Laura paused, her hand stopping. "Well, I suppose that depends on how this visit goes. Some other things. Lizzie's made it clear I don't need to work, precisely. But I'm not sure I'm cut out for being a spinster aunt in the Women's Auxiliary or arranging flower shows or whatever."

"There's quite a lot of other possible good work out there, you know. Depending on your skills. You ever considered nursing?"

He was startled to see her shiver, visibly and violently. "No thanks, ta. Spent enough time in hospital." It came out before she could stop it, from the way she pinched her lips together immediately afterwards.

Martin changed the topic, promptly. "So, what you can expect. Galen's mother obviously wants you here. But you seem the sort of person who understands it's seeing if you're possibly presentable as a spouse to the man likely to inherit."

"His brother's as badly off as that then?" The tone made him wonder if she'd heard some of the wilder rumours, that Julius needed to be confined for everyone's safety. There was no way to ask.

"Rather. I've never met him. Galen and I didn't get close until our second year, and Julius was already fighting by then. Then he was in hospital, and they were fixing this place up. Then they got him here, and he stays away from people."

Laura frowned. "That seems awful all round." Then she bit her lip. "I won't pry. Just. Seems awfully lonely for him."

"The Amberlys - his parents - go up there almost every day, one or both of them. And Blythe, too. I can't tell if Galen hasn't wanted to, or they've told him not to, but either way, he doesn't. I think they worry a bit about if Julius is all right. In the head, I mean. Considering everything. This is the sort of upper class First Families place where no one says things outright." Raising the possibility might draw her out about what she had heard.

Instead, Laura went somewhere different. She tilted her head, then said, "How on earth do you manage, then?"

It wasn't what he'd expected, that this turned personal so quickly, that she saw him that clearly. But at the same time, dissembling more felt wrong, like he was poisoning a well. Better, probably, to be honest. Within reason. "Galen's not so much like that, and I sit on my hands or bite my tongue a lot. They're not bad people, just tremendously insular and old-fashioned is the right word, really."

"Right." She considered. "I wasn't sure how to - what sort of place it was."

"The old-fashioned habit doesn't extend to formal chaperones, as you might have noticed. I'm no threat, I guess. Or if I am, you're not a suitable match for Galen, anyway. But cover your shoulders in your formal frocks, tone down the cosmetics, don't expect anyone to break out the latest dances."

"Even these Americans?"

"They are a mystery. I look forward to investigating it." He leaned forward, and he was sure his eagerness was blatant. "I'm not at all sure how they got invited. A big party, like Saturday, that would be one thing, but usually they don't ask a lot of people to stay. Galen says it was his father asked them, not his mother, and that's queer."

Laura snorted. "Well. Let me dig out a dress for tea. Are you the sort of man where if I wave dresses at you for the evenings, you can tell me if they're suitable? Or will you sit there and look baffled?"

"I work for a newspaper advertising everything from soap to towels to the latest labour-saving magical devices for the modern housewife. It also has a very thorough fashion section."

She laughed, and he liked how that sounded. And then he wondered why it mattered what he liked. Laura was meant for someone like Galen, never someone like him. "Right. I'm not used to having a maid, so I shan't wait. Let me take out a couple of things."

Laura retreated to where they'd set her trunk, then opened it, the two halves that opened up into a standing wardrobe. Martin whistled. "Now, that is posh."

"I've had it for ages, it was a present from my mother." Her voice got softer.

Martin coughed, unsure what to say, then decided to wait for her to offer him something less fraught to comment on. She rummaged in the trunk for a moment, then came out with three dresses.

One was a medium green with an inset piece in a darker teal and gold print forming a deep V neck. Martin thought the Art Déco stencilled roses around the hem in the same antique gold and deep teal were a particularly individual touch. The second was a pale green, the shade of flower stems in watercolour paintings, demure and proper. The third was a pale pink, with a skirt of trailing triangles of fabric, shading into deeper shades of rose.

He considered, evaluating them. "His mother will like the light green best, the pink is fantastic for tomorrow night, and I like the first one. Assuming you've a layer for over them."

She waved her hand at the packed stack of shawls. "That gives me a sense. I should change before I go down. That's the en suite?"

"Oh, I can step out into the hallway. It's no bother, I assume you're not one of those women who takes hours."

"Goodness, no, only for something exceedingly fancy. I enjoy looking nice, but my tolerance for preparation tops out at an hour." She waited a beat and then grinned at him. "There's a time and place for everything but keeping you waiting is not the time for me to dally. Besides, I should make my proper introductions downstairs."

Martin laughed. "No other questions? About the spaces?"

She shook her head. "I'm assuming I can ask the ones that will come up when I actually meet people. Oh. The staff here."

Not everyone would think to ask that. "Very loyal to the family, not that many of them, I try not to ask for them for anything complicated. The food's quite good, the cook trained in France, but I gather they're quite accommodating if there's anything you don't eat."

Martin waited, and when there was nothing else, he nodded and said "I'll be on the bench outside, when you're ready."

There was a pause of about ten minutes, during which he heard the pipes clank a few times, and then Laura appeared in the doorway. She was wearing a pale blue day dress, a sort of heathered blue with long sleeves and white details, that made her look about his age instead of most of a decade older. Her hair had been brushed, tidied, and pinned back so there were waves of blonde hair down past her shoulders.

He couldn't keep himself from whistling again. "You do know how to do the thing right, yes. Do let me escort you to the parlour, my lady."

# FIVE

## THURSDAY AFTERNOON

Laura was not sure what to expect when Martin led her downstairs. In other homes she'd visited, the parlours had been rather formal. Instead, he showed her into a room on the front of the house, under the family wing, that was comfortably decorated. There were plush broad sofas, easy chairs, a small fire against the chill of the evening, and half a dozen people standing around.

Galen was speaking to two of them. There was a family resemblance, but Laura couldn't tell if they were his parents or his aunt and uncle. He turned at the sound of the new arrivals and beamed at her. "Welcome! Father, may I introduce Laura Penhallow? Laura, you remember my mother, Parnell Amberly, and this is my father, Cassian Amberly."

His father made a slight bow over her hand, with a gesture at a kiss above it, very continental. His mother beamed generally. "Oh, that is a lovely outfit, Laura, just right for the afternoon. I do hope the room suits? If there's any problem at all, do let us know, we want you to feel comfortable and at home."

Laura knew her role here. "Oh, it's all most pleasant,

thank you, Madam Amberly. Such a delightful room, and of course, the views are spectacular. I do appreciate the invitation, and Galen and Martin have made sure I have everything I need."

Galen grinned at her, more or less over his mother's shoulder. "We expect our Americans momentarily. Here, may I introduce you to the others?" He offered his elbow, and she slipped her hand into it, allowing him to lead her to the two seated on a sofa by the large windows. "Aunt Silvia, Uncle Attis, this is Laura Penhallow. Laura, my aunt, Silvia Tipson, and her husband, Healer Attis Tipson."

Laura smiled, and said "Madam Tipson, Healer Tipson, a pleasure, I'm sure." The man blinked at her, then nodded, the nod of a retired man rarely bothered by his juniors, but approving enough in this case. Silvia considered, looking at Laura thoughtfully. "Rosalind - Porter, wasn't it? Married a Penhallow." She delivered the statement as if placing Laura would sort out her world.

"Yes, ma'am. Rosalind was my mother, and she married Hendrek Penhallow, my father. Perhaps you've seen my older sister, more recently? Elspeth, now Lady Carillon."

There was a little tutting. "Ah, yes. That made the papers." Silvia glanced from Laura to Galen, then to Galen's parents. "Nell will have her plots." It was clear that Silvia wasn't sure what she thought of this one. "Of a good family, though attenuated, even before the War. Only the two sons."

Galen leaned to say, "Mother's nickname with her more intimate friends is Nell, of course."

"What do you do with yourself, young woman?" That was Attis Tipson.

"I did some secretarial work, for a little, but gave it up for - well, to help my sister plan the wedding and the related festivities. A few other projects like that." That earned her a sniff, and Galen rescued her immediately. "Pardon, Aunt and Uncle, but I see Blythe's back, and I should introduce Laura around. We'll have much more time to talk."

As Galen led Laura away, she said, "Was it that I'm a Penhallow, or that I don't work?"

"Oh, Uncle Attis doesn't approve of idleness. I'm a great trial to him. Here, Blythe, this is Laura. Laura, this is Blythe. She knows where all the mysterious closets are, if you need anything, and don't want to ask Mother or the staff."

Blythe was a rather faded-looking woman, dressed in pale browns that more or less matched her hair. She bobbed, then looked Laura up and down, murmuring "Pleased to meet you. Galen, you did remember?" Laura couldn't figure out what she meant.

Galen snorted. "Already done, I promised," he agreed. "Is everything all set for supper?"

"The Americans arrived twenty minutes ago, they should be down before the gong."

Galen nodded, then said, "Let's circle back to Mother and Father." Laura gestured slightly. There was really no escaping the complicated small talk. She knew what the visit would involve.

Fortunately, once she got back to them, the Amberlys were much easier to chat with than the Tipsons. Parnell Amberly seemed to go out of her way to make it easy for Laura. As she got hints that Trellech and Carillon's estate in the New Forest were easy topics, and employment, apprenticeship and schooling were difficult ones, she guided the conversation with a smooth ease that seemed the elegant counterpoint to Galen's earnest claims of charismatic plotting.

The Americans did not appear before the gong rang to change for supper. When Laura was at the door of her room, she heard a buzz of conversation, and a maid being sent to fetch something from the rooms at the end of the hallway. She dressed herself in the pale green, applying just enough in the way of cosmetics to look bright-eyed and rosy-cheeked. All the outward signs of health, which were, at least, no longer entirely counterfeit.

There was a knock on her door, and when she opened it, Galen and Martin were standing there. Galen was rather striking in his formal black suit for supper. The longer jacket made him look rather older, and his deep purple waistcoat and silver cravat set the whole thing off.

He offered a small white flower she thought might be a camellia. "From the conservatory, they're just coming into bloom?" He was almost shy. "You look lovely, and Mother will entirely approve. We came to escort you down?"

"Let me tuck this in my hair, just a moment." They all heard a bit of noise at the end of the hallway, a burst of music. Laura frowned, but ducked into her room to look at the mirror and tuck the flower into the clip holding hair back from her face. She turned back to the young men with a smile.

Martin had moved enough that she could see he was less formally dressed. He wore a tunic and trousers rather than a full suit, in a deep blue that faded him into the background next to Galen's sharper colours. It was clearly a practiced set of costuming for him, and she wondered whether it was particular to spending time with the Amberlys or if he applied it in his professional life as well.

She slipped her arm into Galen's, and he led her down into a room she hadn't seen yet, designed for drinks before going into supper, with Martin trailing amiably behind them. One of the maids immediately brought around a small glass of sherry.

Madam Amberly lit up, seeing her come in. "Oh, don't you look lovely. And so thoughtful to escort her down, Galen, darling. Here, we're just waiting on our American guests."

As if on cue, there was a flurry of colour outside the door, and in swept a woman, dressed rather revealingly in bright red silk. Her hair was dark, in a scandalously short bob, and bounced. "Good evening, darlings. Oh, Cassius, this is really delightful, thank you so much for the invitation."

She strode over to Cassian Amberly, and kissed him, once on each cheek, her heels clicking. Everything about her seemed bigger and louder than could quite fit properly into the room's more sedate and somewhat faded air. If Madam Amberly had intended Laura to have pride of place as the evening's centrepiece, those plans were certainly entirely ruined.

She turned, holding a hand out to the man who had escorted her in, wearing a much more ordinary suit. American, not as sharply cut as Cassian or Galen or even Attis prefer. Presentable, not at all flashy. "My brother, Basil." She pronounced it with the long British A, but the rest of her accent was decidedly American.

Cassian looked stunned for a moment, then he held out his hand. "Senara, may I introduce you to my wife, Parnell. Nell, this is Senara Wilson. Basil, we're delighted to meet you. Make yourselves at home, we're just about ready to sit down to supper."

"Is there a cocktail? That's the horrid thing about America, these days, an utter lack of cocktails. Unless you have the right connections. Fortunately, we do quite a bit of travelling. And who are these other people, darling?" She moved with a sort of thinly controlled agitation, like she thought if eyes slipped away from her she might die of it.

There was an uncomfortable silence for a moment, then Parnell said, "You are very welcome, though I'm afraid you may find us a little - quiet. My companion, Blythe. Silvia and Attis Tipson - Silvia is Cassian's sister." There was a slight emphasis on her husband's name. "Our son, Galen, here, his friend from his school days, Martin Taylor, and this is Lorelai Penhallow, who is visiting us as well. You prefer Laura, don't you, dear?"

Laura nodded and did her best to pick up the conversation. "I do, thank you, Madam Amberly. I've been quite admiring the views." She paused, and then nodded to the American with, "Pardon, how do you prefer to be addressed?"

She appeared to be slightly distracted by Galen, but tried to cover it up with an airy wave of one hand. "Oh, Senara, honey, I'm not at all formal. Nell, this really is so quaint, one rarely sees houses quite like this where I come from."

Laura caught Parnell Amberly wincing. Senara moved forward to take the glass of offered sherry and stroll to the window. Seeing this, Laura raised her eyebrows at Galen, before she turned to face Basil. "Have you been to Cornwall before?"

He smiled at her, generously enough, a little tip of his glass, and she could feel his attention settle on her, measuring her up. Abruptly, Senara said, "Galen, do come be a dear, tell me what's out this window when there's light." Basil glanced after her, frowning, and neglected to answer the question.

Galen frowned, and his mother made a little sharp

gesture with her hand, indicating he should oblige. He nodded and walked over. A moment later, Senara had her hand on his shoulder, leaning on him.

Parnell said brightly, "Well, it's so good you arrived safely. I gather Senara has some business dealings with my husband? Do you normally travel together, Basil?"

Basil nodded, and finally spoke, with a clear baritone. "Usually, yes. We've a variety of interests, but they play well off each other." He kept his focus on his sister, watching her back as she peered out into the dark. Something in it reminded Laura of watching Carillon when his attention was on some plot, but she couldn't figure out why or what it might mean. "Senara thought there were some excellent business prospects, now we're branching out again. I came along to keep everything in proper order."

At that point, the gong sounded from inside the dining room, and the doors opened. Galen extracted himself and offered his arm to Laura, and Martin offered his to Blythe, leaving Senara paired with Cassian, Parnell with Attis, and Silvia rather uncertainly with Basil.

# SIX

## THURSDAY EVENING

Galen shivered once, when he got Laura's arm settled in his. She leaned closer to him and whispered, "Let me know if I can help."

He wasn't sure what to make of that. A woman, a woman he was supposed to be courting, offering that. It seemed wrong, somehow. Not that she didn't seem confident. Capable. Self-contained, even. He wasn't even sure she wanted to marry, she'd made light of being called a spinster in the papers. There were such things as dedicated spinsters, after all.

And she was nothing like Senara, who must be a few years older than she was. Senara had made him feel thrilled and also terrified. A woman like that wanted things, and he wasn't sure it was good for her to get them, without having the faintest idea why. He could not logic it, or fit it into patterns. Perhaps all Americans were like that? Or perhaps if he knew more of them he might be able to figure out how she was different, which would let him figure out what she wanted. Though really, Martin was the actual investigator of the two of them.

He felt Laura squeeze his arm, as he drew out the chair for her. His father had the seat at the end of the table, his mother at the other end. Laura had the pride of place, the honoured guest, at the right of his father, and he was next to her. Father escorted Senara to the seat at his left and then took his own place. The other chairs moved and scraped. Galen checked. Martin across from him, Blythe next to him, Basil to his mother's right, and Attis to her left. All very proper, if making the point that Laura was the most important guest, not Senara.

Senara had noticed, he thought, from the momentary frown on her face, before she said, brightly. "Now, who are you, dear? Very demure, your dress."

Laura tilted her head, offering an artlessness Galen hadn't expected from her. "Laura Penhallow. I had the pleasure of meeting Galen's mother at a small gathering a few weeks ago, and they were so kind to invite me to stay."

"Penhallow. Wasn't there a wedding, recently? Something in the papers when we were crossing. I rarely read the society papers, darling, but that was hard to avoid."

"My older sister, Elspeth, yes."

"Goodness, is she ancient?" Laura, rather to her credit, simply raised an eyebrow, as if thinking.

Galen frowned for a moment, then caught his mother's furious glance, a mix of annoyance at Senara and insistence that Galen not let the side down. It promised difficulties if Galen didn't keep himself under better control. He promptly turned his attention to focusing on Laura and being as pleasant about it as he could.

"Her husband does not think so." Laura was smiling, warmly and pleasantly. "Lord Geoffrey Carillon. He holds Ytene, I don't know if you're familiar with the land obligations in Albion? They're rather complex for foreigners, I've found."

Basil almost said something at that, and Galen's mother leaned in to say something Galen couldn't hear, a distraction.

Senara waved a hand, letting the light bounce off a rather gaudily large ring. "Archaic, honey. Utterly archaic." Now that she was no longer focused on him, Galen could think about her a bit more clearly, and wondered how much of her brash demeanor was deliberate distraction from whatever she was trying to get. He was quite certain she was trying to get something. Instinct, Martin would call it, probably.

"Some of us still keep the old ways. Besides, the land's beautiful. Unspoiled."

Senara snorted. "You've never seen a proper city, then."

Laura shrugged, delicately. "London, and not just the magical quarters. Berlin, once or twice, before the War. Vienna, the same. Though I spent most of my time in the Tyrol or the Swiss Alps." She paused, just a moment, then said, "I find I prefer that to the fuss and bustle of most cities. They're fun for a visit, but I can't imagine living there."

Galen reached under the table, pinching the flesh between his thumb and hand, so he didn't chortle aloud. Laura was saying every possible thing to win his mother's approval, without explicitly offending his father. Mind, she was likely offending Senara, but that seemed to be deliberate.

The other woman was looking at her, narrowing her eyes, and then she changed the subject abruptly. "Cassius, you didn't say your son was so handsome. And you, sweetheart, who are you again?" Galen couldn't decide just yet if that were another deliberate feint, or if she had given up Laura as useful to her goals. Whatever they were.

"Martin Taylor, a friend of Galen's since our school days." Now, Martin sounded utterly bored. Completely polite, but Galen knew that tone well, the one Martin used when he had no interest in that particular target.

Senara frowned minutely at him. Her charms clearly were not having much effect, as Martin was not paying the kind of attention Senara clearly assumed was her due. Martin was much the better man, Galen was very clear on this.

They were saved for the moment by the staff coming around to serve the soup. His mother had fussed over the menu and settled on something to show off the local fish and shellfish. They were beginning with a crab bisque, brilliantly prepared. Senara sipped at it, setting her spoon aside after having only a couple of spoonfuls.

Laura ate much more generously, he realised. He glanced down to see if his mother had noticed but she seemed to be trying and, remarkably, failing to draw out Basil, who was clearly a man of few words.

His father finally managed to wrest control of the conversation, asking the usual questions about the sea journey, about how Senara had found London during her stay. (Boring and tedious, apparently.) It wasn't at all clear to Galen what she did. She mentioned business interests, but he couldn't begin to figure out what they were. Manufactured goods? Printing? Medicinal supplies? Materia? He supposed there must be all sorts of magical materials available in the Americas that could not be got in Albion.

That carried them through to the soup being cleared away, and the sole being brought out, with a delicate dill sauce, and they tucked into that. Galen ventured a "This is delightful, mother," down the table.

It earned him a small nod, before his father inquired of Laura, "Did you catch a performance by Madeline Waters, when you were in Trellech?"

"The singer? Oh, yes, Carillon insisted. She was quite brilliant, I thought, a beautiful sense of musicality. Rather - building fancies in the air with her voice alone. He explained she uses some tricks of enchantment and incantation. Entirely within the legal limits, of course, but more than most can do."

Cassian snorted. "Oh, I suppose that's true. I heard her at the opera in London, just after the War. And her voice has only improved with age. Curious."

"I suppose one learns the - the particular timbre of the instrument over time, sir. Like one would learn the quirks of a sailing ship, or the lay of one's lands, or the prevailing winds."

Galen couldn't help noticing how nautical her references often were. He ventured to ask, "Do you like other music then? Or performances?"

Laura favoured him with a broad smile. "I'm afraid I've had a more limited exposure than I'd like. One of the places I stayed had an excellent string quartet, and I got quite familiar with that repertoire."

"Rather old-fashioned, isn't it? No jazz in your life?" That was Senara, clearly trying to find a way into the conversation.

Laura shrugged one shoulder. "A few parties, a year or two ago." She paused for a fraction of a second, just long enough for Martin's eyes to widen, as if in realisation of something. "I didn't care for the company, and I'm afraid it rather tainted my enjoyment of the music."

"Pity." Senara let the word draw out. "Jazz does a girl good."

The conversation was interrupted once again by the arrival of the roast and the fussing around serving it. Senara picked at her food again, the beef, the spinach, the tiny potatoes. Galen wondered if she were nervous, or if she were simply one of those women who appeared to survive on air and fancies. The conversation on their end of the table got quiet.

Galen could more easily hear the people down by his mother, some sort of rather terse discussion about a business matter. Basil was arguing it was very promising, and Uncle Attis was having none of the idea. Words like "margins" and "demand" were involved. Galen was left with the vague impression from his uncle's comments that Basil was trying to foist off some materia of limited utility on them. Surely if it was as useless as all that Father wouldn't?

Galen cast around for a better topic and finally offered, "Senara, Father said you've been in America for a number of years. Are you back in Albion for a while, or just a brief visit?"

She lit up at the attention, and said "Oh, darling, that rather depends on how we find things. But so far, it's been - promising, for our projects. I've got a couple of specific little things I'm working on. Very secret, yet." She leaned forward, as if hoping he'd ask.

He said, a little primly, "Oh, I won't pry," which earned him a smile from Laura.

Senara frowned, and then asked Martin, "I'm still not sure why you're here." It was rather more blunt.

"Oh, as Galen's friend. I'm a writer. I can work on things here, as easily as anywhere else." It was the blithe answer Martin gave when he didn't actually have a current assignment, but was hoping he'd get one soon. Especially one more exciting than standard reports on business or weather.

"Have I read anything you've written?"

That got the other stock answer. "Not that you'd know, yet, but I'll be making a name for myself. And getting my own byline."

Senara frowned, and then, finally, Galen managed to guide the rest of the meal into less complicated topics. When the ladies excused themselves to the parlour, Senara said "Oh, darlings, I'm exhausted, I should toddle up to bed."

His mother made the usual polite protestations, but she was clearly pleased not to have to entertain Senara further that evening. Galen was quite sure his mother and Silvia would be gossiping away within a minute. He could only hope it wouldn't be too tedious for Laura. Or difficult.

## SEVEN

### THURSDAY EVENING

An hour later, Galen and Martin presented themselves at the door to the withdrawing room, as the men returned from their drinks and, by the lingering smell, some cigars. "Mother, Aunt Silvia. We wondered if Laura might like a little walk outside, a breath of fresh air."

"Oh, goodness." Laura had been perched on a chair, making polite conversation with Parnell and Silvia, and she watched the expressions on Parnell's face. There was a rather doting fondness there, but also some pleasure at seeing Galen so attentive. She wondered, not for the first time, what other women had been presented for his theoretical approval.

"Laura, you mustn't get too cold. Do show her where the warm shawls are, Galen? And don't be too long? But I suppose it is a nice clear night." Parnell was dithering, there was no other term for it.

"Oh, if it's too chilly we'll come right back, I promise." Laura said, immediately. "Galen is quite thoughtful, a little fresh air would do me good. And it's not nearly as brisk as the Tyrol this time of year."

That earned her a beaming smile, and Galen extended his arm. "At your disposal, Laura."

He escorted her out toward the front door, Martin following along behind them. They paused briefly at a wardrobe set into an alcove. Galen drew out a cream wool shawl, rather enveloping, and then a purple one for him, and a red one for Martin.

"Here we go. And here's a lantern." He took something off a shelf at the bottom, and handed it over to Martin, who did something to it that made it begin to glow. "Shall we?"

"Thank you, kind sir." Laura kept her voice light. Clearly they were on good behaviour while they could be overheard.

Galen set off out the door, and along a curving path to the right, the opposite direction from the portal. "There's a pleasant walk along the ridge, and a place with benches and such, a bit down the way. Do you care for stars? We can turn the lantern off once we're there."

"I do rather, though they are not actually a necessity of mine."

The phrasing made Martin snort, behind her. "Are they a necessity for anyone?"

"Oh, yes. Father and Uncle Kenver got quite out of sorts without them. And Lizzie knew someone at school who was terribly wrapped up in astronomy. She didn't know if she was coming or going if it was cloudy for too many nights. She's teaching it now."

They walked along in silence for another minute or two, and then Martin said quietly, "Clear."

"I am so sorry, Laura. That Senara was so awful at supper."

It was enough to make Laura turn to face him. "It's not you who should be apologising. Good grief, you weren't the one being insulting every way intended, and half a dozen that might not have been meant." It came out more fiercely than she'd intended, and she immediately blushed.

Galen looked back at her in the lantern light, utterly baffled.

"Look, show me where we can sit down. Clearly neither of us will manage walking and talking about this."

Martin snorted behind them again and then stepped around Galen. "Let me go first with the light, mmm?"

They made an odd little procession. Further along the ridge, the path opened up into something flat, paved in stone that glimmered slightly in the lantern's glow. "Here, there's a bench, here, and one here."

"May I?" Galen inquired, after moving to let her sit at one of the benches.

"You are very well-mannered, Galen. Of course. Whatever is comfortable for talking."

"Well, comfortable for talking would be inside and padded, but no chance of that tonight without someone overhearing." Galen sounded a bit out of sorts.

Laura knew the signs well enough. This was a man, normally secure in his life, who had been faced with something unexpected, and teasing now would make thing horrid. She considered her options, then settled so she was angled toward him. She had all the little postures of attention and focus in the fall of her hand in her lap, the angle of her head inclining just so to listen.

"Can we - I feel sure I've missed something? Can we go back and start at the beginning? Who is Senara, anyway?"

Martin coughed, and Galen shook his head minutely. Martin subsided immediately. "Father said a little more, when we were having brandy and cigars. Uncle Attis asked, I guess."

"Madam Tipson was really baffled. And your mother made it quite clear the Wilsons were at your father's invitation, not hers, she'd only met them today. Not that that was much of an introduction, Senara said, what," Laura paused, thinking back. "You know, I don't think she ever actually said anything directly to your mother." It came out very sharp.

Galen blinked at her. "You sound offended?" He wasn't sure why, she could tell that.

"Of course I'm offended. It's a lot of work to have house guests. For the servants, but for someone hosting, a different kind of work. Figuring out what topics should be encouraged, what shouldn't. What foods to serve. What to wear to make the guests feel at home, or on guard, or whatever it is you want them to feel. There are dozens, hundreds of decisions there. Did your father spring the Wilsons on her?"

"No?" Galen's answer was hesitant and uncertain. Then, "Maybe?"

Martin murmured, just loudly enough to be heard. "Blythe told me he invited them after they invited you. Ten days ago?"

Galen blinked at Martin. "How..."

"Investigation, Galen. I do have skills." It was said lightly, but Laura realised something was very touchy there. She was sure when she saw Galen mouth something, perhaps 'Sorry', at his friend.

She took a breath, and said, "So. Who are they? Where are they from, besides apparently America?"

Galen frowned at her. "Wait. how do you know all that? About guests?"

Laura paused, trying to figure out how to answer that in

a way that was neither insulting nor too revealing. "I helped my sister hostess, oh, a dozen parties. No house parties, like this, mostly, but full evenings, like tomorrow."

Martin nodded. "So you're not from a family where you were taught that as a child?"

"Oh, no. Mother didn't do that kind of entertaining. Some of Papa's business connections, but usually they'd go out. Arrange a private room at the Explorer's Club or the Stream." She named the two clubs they'd used most often in Trellech.

"But Mother would choose the menu and make sure none of the guests were feuding or anything. Papa was hopeless at that." She considered for half a second and said, "A lot of men are. You're not, you don't have incentive to figure it out."

"And women do?" Martin sounded amused.

"We've only just met." She was stalling for time, she didn't want to explain this to them, how many things they apparently both missed, for all their deftness in other areas. People rarely took that well, especially men.

"And I - we - should not expect all your secrets?" His tone broadened. Definitely amused. That made it easier. He was good humoured, then, not prickly, by nature.

"Not the very first day, no." She could tease back, if he was like that. "I have to keep something in reserve."

Galen coughed. "I move we delay a discussion of your hostessing skills until at least tomorrow. The topic on the floor is the background of the mysterious Wilsons."

Laura laughed. "Well, for one thing, they've got abominable manners."

"What makes you say that?" Galen shifted a little, then she felt him reach to take her hand, letting her pull away if she wanted. She chose not to, turning her palm so he could slip his hand into hers. It seemed to reassure him, and she had no particular objection. It was endearing, actually, that he could let her see his uncertainty. So many young men of his class and background, they wouldn't let that show at all, certainly not to a near stranger.

"Senara was rude to your mother. Someone with manners would have thanked her for hosting them, and especially at short notice. She'd have got your father's name right, goodness. She'd have not demanded cocktails first thing. She'd not have taken you off to the window."

Galen ducked his head. "I knew I shouldn't let her, but I wasn't sure how to how to say no? Especially after Mother indicated that I should."

"The thing with people like that," Laura said, choosing her words carefully. It wouldn't do to insult him. "Is that they set things up to make you feel you're the wrong one. When in fact, they're being rude and dismissive and awful. And then you find yourself all turned around, and it's even easier for them to do it the next time."

There was a long pause, which Martin eventually interrupted. "Some experience of that type, then?"

Laura nodded, then moved to tuck her hair up under the shawl, so it wouldn't blow in the wind so much. It gave her time to think. "More than enough, yes." she agreed.

"You were brilliant with her. At supper. All her being nasty, saying you hadn't travelled, couldn't possibly know." Galen's voice was warm, full of admiration.

Laura smiled at him. "Ta," she said, deliberately being less formal. "You were saying your father said more?"

"Yes. Senara and Basil are in some sort of business. Import-export, I think. Materia, maybe? He was really unspecific about it. Father does some of that, and there's some particular plants here, on the Isles of Scilly, that we harvest. There's a particular kind of fish scale, and a couple of rare birds and butterflies, and so on. Uncle Attis didn't care for the deal, I think he thinks Father's being cheated. Basil was pressing rather hard, apparently. Father made him shut up fast."

"Can your father give them rights to that kind of thing?"

"Oh, Merlin, no. He's not Lord of the land. But he knows Lord Trewithgy well, and could recommend the deal. We're the only major magical family actually in the Isles, I think. I mean, there's some who are fishermen and crafters, but not with the connections to arrange something like that?"

Laura frowned. "But are there unique species here? I suppose that's a question for our walk tomorrow. Go on. So your father invited them, at short notice? So they could have a chat about it?"

Galen nodded. At about that point, they heard a voice, coming along the path. "Master Galen? Martin? Miss Penhallow?" It was Blythe. "Madam worries about the weather turning, will you come along in?"

"Coming, Blythe." Galen called out, and then stood, offering his arm to Laura. "We shouldn't worry them."

# EIGHT

## THURSDAY EVENING

When the three of them returned to the drawing room, Madam Amberly immediately shooed the young men off. "Go enjoy yourselves, do. We'll see to Laura. Sit here, Laura, dear. Do you play Tarrochi?"

Laura did. Negotiating that, however, was a trifle complicated, so she delayed settling into the game by saying, "I do, Madam Amberly, but only some of the variants. It's not so common here as on the continent, that's what I was told. All sorts of different rules. I'm most familiar with Call the King, I think that's how you say it in English, Tappu, that's the Swiss version, and the Jeu de Tarot."

"You have travelled, dear. How are your other languages?"

Laura settled down at the indicated chair, to settle in to play with Madam Amberly, Silvia Tipson, and Blythe. "Oh, social, only. A bit of French, a bit of German, a smidgen of Italian. None of it terribly reliable. Have you travelled much, Madam?"

Madam Amberly began to deal out the cards. "We play

the Jeu - that's the family version preferred here." There was something suddenly rigid there, a tradition that would go unchallenged until the end of time, if she had anything to say about it.

Laura shifted the cards into her hands, as they were dealt, glancing through them. "If I remember rightly, the Fool, the World and one other, those count as fives, along with the kings, yes?" This was the Howard deck, and while not as familiar as the Alpine deck she'd learned to play on, she at least knew the images.

"The Magician, dear." Laura looked up at that, and nodded, though she had a sudden flash of the deck Madam Bertilak had used to read, remembering the card there. She forced herself to take a deep breath, to fight against the memory of the sanitaria.

"The ladies are four, the apprentices three, and the children two. The others are half a point, and the Fool excuses you from following suit."

The briskness, the way they talked, it made it clear these women were skilled players.

"Oh, I'm afraid I can't possibly give you a reasonable game. Are you sure I won't spoil things for you?"

"Nonsense, dear. It's a fine way to get to know someone, to play cards with them." That was Madam Amberly again. "You do your best, and I'm sure that will be quite sufficient."

Sufficient for what, that was the question. Her hand was mediocre, not terribly promising, though with a few cards that suggested her fellows might end up struggling as well.

"Who has the Magician?" That was Madam Amberly again. Laura glanced at her hand just to make sure, and no, it was not there. That was a relief, not to be faced with it up close.

Silvia looked up. "Me." She placed it down. This Magician was the classic Elizabethan era sorceror, all show and flash and inscribed ornate tools. There was real magic there, perhaps, but there was also smoke and mirrors.

The play began, moving as quickly as Laura suspected it might. They played one hand, another, a third, and then finally there was a pause for a round of tea and decorous conversation. "You're unpractised, Laura, but not unpromising as a player with more time."

The proper thing to do was incline her head and accept the portion of that which was a compliment. "Thank you, Madam Amberly. I'm sure I'm not at all up to your standards. That trick, the last hand, very nicely done."

It earned her a smile. "Thank you, dear. You have a good eye. Just the sort of thing I want for Galen."

"Of course, as any caring mother would. He's a lovely young man."

"Oh, he is. So bright, and agreeable, never a poor word to say about anyone. And he's very kind to those less fortunate. Martin Taylor, for example. Comes from quite a different sort of family, though I admit he cleans up well, and we do need more men to make up the dancing tomorrow." The disapproval was quite obvious, for all that she tried to couch it in compliments to her son.

Laura kept her face from twitching. "He's been most polite to me. Galen has beautiful manners, mind. Very attentive. I'm not surprised Martin follows suit with that sort of model."

"You do find him promising then? I really do hope he settles down soon. It's not good for a young man to be drifting."

"Oh, it's a little early to tell, we've only had a few hours to get to know one another. I know that's modern of me, but my parents didn't have an arranged match, and Mother always said she was glad she'd followed her heart."

"She died a few years ago, didn't she, dear? My condolences." The tone was quite kind, but distant. Laura knew her mother hadn't known the Amberlys particularly well, but she appreciated the thought.

"Yes, Madam Amberly. Before my father and uncle disappeared. At least she wasn't missing them like that."

"No, quite. The not knowing must be very hard."

Not having enough to eat was actually more of a challenge, in some ways. Laura did not like remembering that winter before they'd managed to change things, find a new path.

"It is, ma'am." Laura paused. "My sister was a great strength, even though we had spent little time together for quite a while."

"Mmmm." There was a sense, suddenly, that Madam Amberly did not entirely approve of some aspect of Lizzie. Which always made Laura defensive. She could criticise her sister up and down a mountain, but let anyone else try that, and she was having none of it.

"That's a love match, too. I know it's unfashionable, but anyone who sees Lizzie and her husband, well." Laura let her voice trail off.

Madam Amberly sniffed again. "I'd heard a few queer things about Lord Carillon. Didn't he spend simply ages out of the country?"

"Travelling, yes. I think that's part of why he and Lizzie get on so well, they both enjoy it."

"And they're in Italy now, you said? That family does have a tendency to travel, I suppose, but there's no harm in that." That was Silvia, who did not seem to have the same concerns about Carillon. "Attis and I did a Grand Tour, just after we were married, before he started practising properly. But of course, being a Healer doesn't leave one with a lot of time to travel, so hard to leave one's patients."

"He's retired recently, Galen said, ma'am." Laura paused. "Perhaps you could do a little now?"

"Oh, I suppose. It seems like rather a bother, having to pack, not having one's own things handy. Manageable here, for a week, and of course they know all our tastes. But going all over the place, hither and yon..." Silvia waved a hand. "So much fussing, and worrying about the water, and all."

Laura took a deep breath, then said, "I've quite enjoyed the travel I've done, but it wears, yes. So many things different, all the time."

"There, that's a sensible girl." Silvia was very approving. "Not like that Senara, travelling all the time, no particular place to call home."

Madam Amberly had dealt another hand, "Now, I know you had a few tiny health difficulties. I hope you don't mind my inquiring, dear, but I hope nothing that would interfere with having a family."

It was exceedingly impertinent, but it was a form of impertinence that Laura had been expecting. Now was the time for it, when it was just the women and family at that.

"The healers thought I should be fine, Madam Amberly. Of course, it's impossible to be certain without actually - well." She offered a slight blush and a duck of her chin. "But our mother had an easy time of it."

"Only you two girls?"

"By her choice, ma'am. I gather Father declared he thought the two of us were grand, no need to keep trying for a boy. He was rather progressively minded, I think he always thought Lizzie would succeed him. I'm rather more my mother's daughter."

"Your mother was one of the Porters, yes?"

"Yes. Youngest daughter of the Wiltshire branch."

"Are you close to the family on that side?"

Laura paused, using the excuse of picking up her hand. "I'm afraid they rather disagreed with her decision to marry my father. We've heard a little more from them in the past year, but everyone is still being rather cautious." The party she'd been at with the card reading she couldn't get out of her head had been a gesture in that direction. It had been a non-committal test that had gone well enough on all sides that she had an invitation to a solstice party next month.

There was a set of tutting from both Madam Amberly and Silvia Tipson. "Goodness. Well. I suppose that says something about family priorities." Madam Amberly did not approve.

Silvia Tipson tilted her head, as if thinking through the implications, and then said, "Certainly it would have been appropriate for someone to offer to take you two young women in hand after your mother's death, and be a support."

Laura rather thought it said a dozen things about priorities, and she was not at all sure she'd have agreed to help from the Porters, but she would not be so crude as to spell that out. "Do you see Galen going into a particular field?" Perhaps a change of topic would help.

"Oh, well, we're rather expecting he'll be taking on the family duties, the various properties. There's some that with more attentive management could be fairly profitable, I gather. Wood and such. He's worked with our steward for the various estates, and once spring comes around, we hope he'll be doing rather more than that. But of course, we've also greatly enjoyed having him here, rather than off on one of the estates."

It was curious Galen hadn't apprenticed somewhere, actually, and Laura wasn't sure how to ask about that. She considered her hand, played a card, then just asked outright. "Did Galen apprentice anywhere?"

"Oh, no, dear. We've always thought he'd take on obligations for Cassian. And running an estate's quite a lot of work. Like running a large household. Do you have household staff?" That was a deflection, quite clearly, but Laura went along with it.

"We had a maid and housekeeper, growing up, and outside help for the garden, though Mother preferred to make the decisions herself. Ytene has a much larger staff, of course, and Hawk's Breath, the other sizeable estate of Lord Carillon's, up in Cumbria."

"Hmph." Laura could not tell whether Madam Amberly's huff was positive or negative.

"I've helped Lizzie with Ytene, before and since her marriage. The staff there are very well trained, and were quite helpful in explaining the different roles, what Lizzie was responsible for, what she should leave to skilled hands."

"Ah, that would be a large estate, yes. And a fair bit of entertaining?"

"Not as much as some, but quite a bit. Lord Carillon knows a tremendous number of people." Mind, some of the parties were not at all what Madam Amberly would approve of. Some of his friends ran to the notably bohemian.

"Your trick." The comment drew her back to the cards, and Laura realised she must keep her focus firmly on the game or be tremendously embarrassed.

# NINE

## THURSDAY NIGHT

Martin waited until the house had been quiet for a full half hour. No sounds from the hallway outside his door, no sounds from above, where the servants were. Only when he was certain did he ease his door open, then close it silently, before padding down the hallway in his slippers.

He avoided the creaking floorboard just before the stairs, then edged down against the wall, ducking into the servant's stair. From there, it was much simpler.

Galen had asked him how he knew about that. That had been the first trip he'd made here, and he'd shown Galen the trick without thinking anything of it. His mother had been in service, once upon a time, and her stories had left quite an impression. The ways that the servants had hidden spaces so that those they served wouldn't need to see them. How she had been trained to be never seen and never heard, to come and go without causing a ripple in a room.

She had a different life now, and was much better for it, but she kept the stories. His family didn't forget.

He made it down to the kitchen with no problems at all,

as he expected. There was a pot simmering on the back of the stove, stock for the meal tomorrow, and a faint light from the heat. He considered, then eased into the kitchen pantry, where Cook left snacks when they were in residence.

A minute later, while he was looking at the options, he felt a slight breeze behind him, and then heard Galen's whisper. "Dweller at the Forge, how is the fire?"

Martin smiled and made the expected reply for things going well. "Steady and the way is clear." Then he waved a hand. "Cook apparently thought we might need extra feeding." There were ladyfingers left over from the trifle. The keep-fresh box had just enough whipped cream to dip them in. And a basket had cheddar and apples, and a bit of fried sausage.

"It was a grand spread tonight, but I had trouble eating." Galen admitted, beside him. "Not that I was the only one, that Senara barely touched her food. I couldn't tell if she was anxious or picky or one of those women who's obsessed with her figure. She might well be. Laura seemed to appreciate Cook properly." He considered, then moved to hop up to perch on a counter in the pantry, and Martin took the same position on the one next to it. He leaned over, found the bottles of lemonade tucked behind the keep-fresh box, and rummaged for his penknife, opening one, then the other. Galen could never be counted on to have a useful object on his person.

"What did you think?" Galen sounded tired. Overwhelmed. Yes, that was definitely his overwhelmed voice.

Martin handed over the bottle of lemonade. "Where do you want me to start?"

"Oh, first." Galen lifted a hand. "Sorry for that bit earlier. Questioning your skills. You know I don't mean to."

Martin waved a hand. "You apologise when you forget,

which is more than most people." That was the part that made him touchy, people dismissing him and not even noticing they'd done it.

Galen nodded, then returned to the new questions. "What was it you realised about her? That bit about her not caring for jazz?" Galen didn't specify which her.

"Oh, that." He'd known Galen would ask. That was how they worked. Martin noticed things, knew things, remembered things. Galen consulted him as one might consult a reference book and got Martin invited places to hear and learn more. And Galen was generally a charming guest, the kind who could be fit into almost any party and improve it. Young men were rare enough still that getting Martin invited wasn't that hard, especially if Galen said he was presentable and had the right sort of manners.

"Yes. That." Galen was getting less patient.

Martin held up a hand. "Not something I've explained, right? Give me a minute to make it come out in order." He frowned, thinking back. "You know there was all that talk about that drink - parties, for the bright young things. A year ago, May?"

"Not us." Galen's tone was dry. "The kind of thing where they say 'oh, that wouldn't be your kind of fun'." They had a certain reputation for staidness, from people who had not seen them among their closer circle, or with their fellow Dwellers.

"In this case, that's a good thing. Someone came up with a drink, they called it goldwasser. And it had something in it. Gold, I gather. Something about it made people really ill, or made the people making it ill, or something like that. It was shut down thoroughly, by the middle of June, maybe six or eight weeks after I started hearing about it."

"Who told you about it?"

"Graham. You know about him. Dweller who left the year before we started, works at one of the London papers, I forget which one, does pieces for the Trellech Moon sometimes? He's been doing a lot of investigative work."

"Why did he tell you?"

"He was nosing around, seeing if I knew anything. I pointed out it was mostly people who were on the young side of the War, not left out of it entirely. And there's a gaping chasm there, now, isn't there?"

Galen winced, and Martin immediately said, "Sorry. Pax?"

"Pax."

The reliable shorthand, worn smooth and frictionless long ago, apology and forgiveness in three little letters. Galen was quiet for a minute, focusing on eating his apple slices. He was working to asking something, Martin could tell. At such times, one couldn't jostle him, or it would take much longer.

The question that came out wasn't quite what he expected. "How was Laura mixed up in it? Was she making the stuff?"

"I don't think so? I mean, she talked about a job that went, I think it went quite badly, but - there were a lot of people who disappeared, right around then. I don't know if it was trials or house arrest or, you know, what they call gardening leave, when it's a job? Not around. But she was around more, it seemed like? All the flurry of her sister and Lord Carillon, and then their engagement."

Galen frowned. "They got married, what, three months ago?"

"Dated for a year, engaged in May, married in September, now off on their honeymoon. Not sure why the delay, but possibly to establish her better in society. He was considered quite a catch - younger son, inherited Ytene and the Lordship and rather a lot of other land. Aunt Silvia went on about all the disappointed girls from the First Families, who had expected one of them would catch him. Apparently, he was charming, but never escorted any of them anywhere more than two or three times." Martin recited it off from memory.

"That suggests the sister, Lizzie, Laura called her, is more than simply charming or beautiful. There would have been that in spades. Aunt Silvia said she thought it suggested interesting things for the next generation. Stronger magic, she hoped. The Carillon line isn't bad, but that's no need to get careless." He mimicked her tone rather precisely, then sobered. "I gather Laura and her sister were struggling, more than a bit."

"Mother asked around about that. A lot of people blame them, for that expedition going wrong, but Mother thought that was unfair, they weren't the ones arranging it." Galen did have a keen sense of fairness. It was what made Martin like him so much. And forgive him as needed.

"When you mentioned Laura was going to be here, I looked at the records. I gather her older sister, Elspeth, Lizzie, managed most of the business records for them. But I don't think she was making decisions, no. And they didn't go with." He frowned. "Must be hard, not knowing what happened."

Galen looked up, toward the back wing of the house, as if he could look through the floors and ceiling and walls, and see his brother's room. "At least with Julius, we know where he is."

Martin frowned. "I didn't say."

Galen waved a hand. "It's a thing that is." And then he said "You didn't like Senara at all, did you?"

"Entirely too obvious. The sort of obvious that makes me sure she's hiding a dozen things. She may have got here offering your father a business deal but I'm sure there's something else."

"It wasn't just..." Galen stalled, not sure how to continue.

"It wasn't just that she was all over you. Which was horribly rude, with Laura there, mind you, you should apologise when we're in private again tomorrow."

"I just - she sort of swept in, and I didn't know what to do, and women like that, they're intimidating."

"You don't let men like that intimidate you."

"What, like her brother? He's easy to deal with. Well, relatively. Practically fades into the woodwork, aside from that conversation that made Uncle Attis cross."

"No, men like Senara is. Bold and brash and wanting to be the centre of everything, no matter what. When it's a man, you're fine with him, you just stand there. You're ruggedly handsome and you fill up the room, and you don't let that nonsense linger. It's one of your better talents, actually."

Martin was rewarded by Galen blinking, open-mouthed. "What?"

"When it's a man, you just don't let that kind of thing happen. When it's a woman, you do. That doesn't seem fair, somehow. And don't tell me you don't do it with Basil, he's an entirely different sort of person. Mind, he fades into the background like he's working on it, I don't know what he's usually like."

Galen looked remarkably like a fish, gaping. Then he closed his mouth with a click and sniffed, before getting off the counter. He poured two glasses of the medicinal brandy and handed one over to Martin, with a "Cheers."

Martin raised his glass and braced for the question he knew was coming.

"So what's wrong with Laura? I mean, why isn't she five years married? Besides the thing with her father."

"Pretty sure it was tuberculosis, and she's doing much better now. Did you notice where she talked about? The Austrian Tyrol, the Swiss Alps. Seaside places, up north in England."

Galen frowned, and Martin went on. "That's the kind of place people build sanitaria. Fresh air. Lots of fresh air, it's supposed to help."

"How do you know so much about it?"

Martin winced. "My sister. And my aunt. And a lot of other people Mum knows. Or knew. A lot of, well, knew."

Galen immediately sobered. "Oh. You - it's not something you mention."

"People talk about it as elegant. And I suppose it is for a while, people being all pale and fainting onto settees and all that rot. But later there's blood and coughing and people hurting, and it just goes on."

"Doesn't, I mean. Isn't there a cure?"

"Healers can do a bit, sometimes, but not always. And the non-magical cures are awful. Making someone's lung stop working for months, so it can heal. All that fresh air. Bedrest for months or years."

Galen tilted his head, chewing on his lip as he thought. "That explains some of how Laura is, perhaps? How she's - less jaded than some people her age? More aware of the wonder of the world?"

"You like that part, don't you?"

"Yeah. I mean, I could see - I could see hosting parties with her." Galen was trying the idea out, and Martin frowned. It seemed a very mild sort of liking to build a marriage on.

"Not like, who was it, Desiderata?"

"Desdemona. Ugh, no. She will have a fine time with a partner who is up for her kind of fierceness. I am not that man, ta."

Martin raised his glass. "To a better pairing than that," before they settled in to finish their drinks and their midnight snack.

# TEN

## FRIDAY MORNING

"Yes, Mother. We have warm clothes, Cook made a lovely picnic. We're going to walk along down to the north beach, there's the cottage there. One of us can run back if we need anything."

Laura had to smile at how Galen dealt with the fussing. She'd already had her share. Would she be warm enough? Was her cloak sufficient? Could they loan her something else? It was a bit stifling, overall, and he clearly felt somewhat the same.

She said, gently, "I do want to see the seals, and Galen said he knows all the best spots. Didn't you say we should be down there sooner than later?"

"Quite, Laura, or a lot of them will be in the ocean, and much harder to see." She liked how Galen spotted an exit line promptly.

They were heading out the door when she heard the Wilsons begin to come down, noisily, in a burst of chaos. They had breakfasted upstairs, apparently, and only just descended.

"Come on. We don't want to get caught up in that."

Galen set off briskly down the path they'd used last night, Martin bringing up the rear and carrying the picnic basket. The walk down to the beach was tricky footing, rough stairs, and a railing only on the cliff side. She went carefully, even though she was wearing practical boots.

When they were finally down, Galen bowed. "Congratulations on descending to the edge of Llyr's realm, my fair Lorelai. Do you sing like your namesakes do?"

Laura snorted. "I am afraid I cannot claim that gift, but I do appreciate the ocean, a great deal." The water today was showing signs of a coming storm, white tips on the waves well before they struck the beach. She didn't know the way this beach sounded in all seasons, but it seemed fiercer and rougher than it might be.

"Come this way, along the beach. There's a little cottage at the base, around the bend, like I said. A small spot for a fire, we keep it stocked with driftwood. From there you can see the seals and the birds."

"And the flowers?"

"Those are for the climb back," Martin said, cheerfully. "Lunch and seals first."

Laura spread her hands. "Do lead on."

They settled by the cottage, the two men working quickly together to build up a modest fire that kept the November chill away. Laura loosened her cloak and then helped to serve out the packages of sandwiches and apples and pastries. "Your cook seems to think you are still growing boys?" she offered.

"Generally, yes. She also leaves things in the kitchen for a late-night snack." That was Martin.

Galen considered for a moment, then said, "You have a good appetite. Not like some women." It was a rather personal statement, considering.

There was a long pause, while Laura considered how to answer that. In the pause, Martin said "You needn't answer if you'd rather not. But from what you said last night, we guessed you spent quite a bit of time in sanitaria."

Laura frowned, then nodded. "That obvious?"

"The places you mentioned, so many of them." Martin waved a hand. "But also your - desire for things that are not like that."

She flushed. "It - it was a very regimented life." She turned to Galen. "I'd understand if you weren't willing to consider me on that count."

Galen blinked at her. "Is that really a consideration?"

"Rather a lot of people think so. They declared me cured a few years ago, though, and the healers have been most encouraging since. As much as anyone can be."

"I don't know what Mother would say, so I'd rather not tell her. Though she thinks entirely better of you than Senara. I'm sorry supper was so horrid. And that she was like she was, before that." He was very earnest about it.

Laura frowned for a moment. "You're not the one who needs to apologise. Unless, of course, Senara was that awful because you asked her to be. I mean, I can see there being a sort of person who'd undermine his mother's unwanted plans. I don't think you're like that, but I could be wrong."

The horrified look on his face was deeply rewarding, and it made Martin chortle. "Oh, you've got him. Nicely done."

Galen spluttered a moment longer, then said, "Of course I'm not like that. Goodness," with a wonderful air of bafflement.

Laura leaned in to kiss his cheek. "I apologise. It is a queer situation though, isn't it?"

Galen nodded. "Mother arranging things. I know

parents do, I mean, some parents, but it makes me feel queer." He paused, and glanced at Martin, who nodded minutely. "Look, can I be honest with you?"

Laura nodded. "Honesty seems the best way to go forward, don't you think?"

"I've always felt I had to do whatever I could to make my parents happy. Secure." He looked away from her, out toward the ocean. "I was fifteen, when we heard Julius had been injured. At school, thankfully, it would have been horrid at home. And Martin and I were fast friends by then, so I had someone to talk to."

"There's a fair bit of age between you, right?"

"I was - an unexpected child." Galen said, flushing. "They had an heir, Mother was not, I mean, this is indelicate. Mother found pregnancy did not agree with her, and Julius was strong and fine and growing up well, so they thought, well." He shrugged.

"But here you are." Laura considered for just a moment, then decided the moment needed a little more care, and reached to take Galen's hand.

"Yes." He squeezed her hand once. "But when Julius was hurt..." His voice trailed off. "For a couple of months, they weren't sure if he'd live. And he was horribly injured. His jaw was badly damaged."

There were so many things Laura might say or not say here, they swirled in her head. "Not knowing is terrifying," she said finally.

Galen's eyes lit up. "You understand that. I don't have to try and explain that. Oh, thank Merlin."

Laura had to smile at that. "I'm also very good at understanding about long boring painful medical treatments, and all the things they don't bother to tell you in advance."

Galen frowned at that. "Was it very horrible, in the sanitaria?"

"The ones I was at were run well. Kind people. Clever doctors. A lot better than some places." she said. "But - a lot of people die from it. You'd talk to someone, and the next day they weren't speaking, and the day after, their bed was empty. And we all knew, but they didn't let us talk about it at all, it was supposed to be bad for us. I thought it was worse never to talk about it."

Galen nodded, quiet for a long pause. "And it was a very structured place?"

Laura nodded. "A very strict schedule, made all the more queer by the fact a lot of it was resting. There's a lot of time we weren't permitted to talk or do anything but rest on lounges in the fresh air, wrapped up against the cold. Sometimes we were allowed to read, or listen to music."

Martin murmured, "That must have been terribly boring."

"Goodness, yes. One learned to get used to it. How to be," She paused, trying to decide if this was too much to reveal. "To be a good patient."

Galen offered, after a moment, "Maybe Julius felt the same way? He took up alchemy again, when he came home. Potions and things. Father gets materials for him, orders what he needs or goes and brings it back."

Martin tilted his head, as if a thought had occurred to him, but Laura couldn't figure out how to ask, and Galen didn't spot it, apparently. After a moment, she continued. "I feel a lot better when I have something to do that..." She stopped. "I need the routine, but I need to be able to do things inside it?"

Martin frowned, then said, "That must have made coming home difficult. Better than not, but still."

Laura nodded. "Being at home was all right, helping Mother. But then she died, and Father and Uncle Kenver went off a bit after that, and things got more complicated." She waited a moment, then smiled. "Much better now, except that I would like to find something useful to do. It doesn't have to be paid work, not anymore, Carillon made that clear, he's been very kind."

"You said you'd done a little secretarial work?"

"Well, it was a company with some quite shady dealings. And it wasn't very busy. I'd prefer actually doing something useful rather than just looking pretty." Then she shook her head and changed the subject. "Enough about me, I'm sure. I admit, I'm very curious about how you two got to be such good friends."

Galen glanced at Martin, and Martin did something. A gesture, a little movement of his face, then he said, as if it were entirely logical, "The goldwasser."

Laura nodded silently.

Galen then shifted, his movements a little more nervous, quick and darting. "You were at Schola for a few years. You heard about the societies, I'm sure?"

Laura nodded. "I was ..." She blushed. "I always sort of hoped that the Waters would invite me. You know, find the seashell on my pillow one night, have to find the right place on the beach to meet them."

Martin smiled at that. "There is something enchanting about it, isn't there? The mystery of it all, not knowing who's part of it, hoping you measure up."

Laura nodded. "So you - that's how you met?"

Galen said, quietly, "Dwellers at the Forge. I get invited to a lot of parties, am charming and pleasant, and make connections. It's exceptionally useful in a very particular way to the different causes the Dwellers are interested in."

"And I am a firebrand radical, who stirs up feeling and shares information about injustices in a way others can connect with, come to support." Martin came in smoothly, the two of them in beautiful sync again.

"The Dwellers? I didn't - I mean, I didn't know any of my year, I left before that. But I heard a few stories, people doing really odd things in some of the outbuildings."

"Oh, we run to tinkering, on a physical level. Transformative tinkering, one of our elders put it." Martin sounded downright cheerful. "But it's not just making things. I can help things change, that need to be changed, if people read what I write. Or Galen, connecting two people who have a common cause. Supporting the general strike, or pressing for reforms to the examinations for Schola. They depend entirely too much on things one picks up from being," he gestured towards Galen, "one of his sort of people."

Laura looked from Galen to Martin and back to Galen again. "It's all right that you told me?"

He laughed. "Quite all right. We're permitted. After all, the Dwellers can't do everything we'd like by ourselves. Just, don't mention it near Mother, all right? It makes her fuss."

Martin broke in to add, "I think she doesn't approve of the corruption of young landholders to progressive goals when there are staid and established ways of doing things."

Galen picked up again, as if this was no interruption at all, with "Whatever else, if you'd like, we'd be glad of your help in different ways. Nothing you'd be uncomfortable with."

"Even with Lizzie married to one of the Great Lords?"

"Goodness, we don't have an objection to the land magics," Martin said. "Even I don't. Lord Carillon's got quite the pleasant reputation as a progressive himself, and we need more of that, not less. The exam reforms, he's written several letters to the papers about that. Now, I might agitate for getting invited to some of his parties, the interesting ones. Something like that."

Laura let out a breath she hadn't known she was holding. "Right. Tell me more, then, before we go look at the seals."

## ELEVEN

### FRIDAY EVENING

Galen waited for the knock at the door. "Come." It would be Martin, they weren't expecting the footman, Oswald, for another half hour.

Martin pushed the door open. They'd been back from their walk for two hours, to allow time for Laura to have a bath and rest. Galen was very clear that women getting ready for a formal event took rather longer than men, even if he was a bit uncertain of the details.

It had been a pleasant afternoon, at least. Laura was an easy companion. She listened well and asked thoughtful questions. Her experience of the world was somewhat narrow, outside of the travel she'd done, and she did not seem overly inclined to pry into private matters. The conversation had stuttered a few times, until they found new topics.

He and Martin had come upstairs almost immediately, not wanting to be caught between the Scylla of his mother and the chaotic Charybdis of Senara. The little he'd heard coming through on the way upstairs had been more than enough. His mother had that tightlipped look that meant she was desperately unhappy, and magic help anyone who got in the way. Perhaps especially at the moment his father.

"Any news?"

"You know you hear more gossip than I do. And Oswald's not been up yet. Do you need help with your cuffs?"

Martin waved a wrist. "Eventually." They were flapping at the end of his sleeves. It was, as usual, one of Galen's cast-offs, a colour that hadn't quite suited Galen when it was made up, and suited Martin rather less. Ironically, given their conversations with Laura, it made him look pale to the point of consumption. Martin insisted he liked that, it gave him a proper literary flair.

"I think she's quite agreeable, Galen, don't you?" Trust him to cut to the heart of it.

"It seems rather unfair on her though, isn't it?" His mother was herding him, and he did not at all like the idea Martin was too.

"To marry you? Or someone like you?"

Galen nodded. "I mean, why shouldn't she have her own life? I can't tell if she even likes the social things she's helped her sister with."

"I suspect you would be glad to encourage that. Other than the familial obligations, of course."

"There's her health to consider."

"That would be true for anyone." Martin settled in one of the easy chairs looking out the window, toward the ocean. "I like that she was honest about it. With us, at least."

"You think some people wouldn't be?"

"I think rather a lot of people wouldn't be." Martin said. "It's a terrifying thing. Haven't you known anyone who had it?"

"Oh, a few, but not - close. Not close enough to see how bad it was."

Martin nodded, going quiet.

Galen let him think for a few minutes, as he continued to fuss around with papers on his table. Eventually he said, "She seems a nice woman. But I'm not sure if that's enough."

"Go on?" Martin at least sounded encouraging.

"It is more than most people get," Galen admitted. "Arranged marriages. Or semi-arranged, or whatever you call your mother inviting suitable people to stay."

"I'm surprised Xanthippe didn't put her off the idea entirely."

Galen shuddered. Xanthippe had been a fortune hunter, which had become abundantly clear as soon as she saw the house, the silver, and his mother's jewels. "Xanthippe would have done better to put her talents into jewellery appraisal. Or one of the auction houses."

Martin laughed. "I am quite sure she considers honest work beneath her. That does not answer about Laura, though."

Galen frowned. "I don't know that she knows what she wants. I'm not sure I know what I want. I'm fairly sure that's not a good combination. And oughtn't I know? I'm supposed to by now, long since." It was an old uncertainty, that he had not earned his place among the Dwellers through passion, that he was seen as a dilettante.

Martin spread his hands, one of their little gestures of acknowledgement to something that had no answer. Answers were not his role, anyway, in their partnership.

"I know what I'm supposed to want - marry, have an heir at least. Take over more of the management of the mainland estates. Father would be very pleased if I would. I just - I feel pressured into it. And could I have even helped, with everything you were doing in the spring, if I was stuck doing that?"

"How's the reconstruction doing?" The slight shift in subject let him get his feet back under him, even if he knew Martin was asking mostly to put him at ease before prodding some more at the complexities.

"There are problems. There are always problems." One of their estates had been claimed for war work, details classified, and restoring it had been rather a challenge.

Of course the family had agreed, it would be disloyal to do anything else. But there were holes and damage to the gardens all over the place, and the interior of the house had been badly managed. Chips off plaster and breakage of furniture, beyond the disruption of the agricultural and protection magics.

His mother had fussed and fretted about the difficulty in getting proper supplies in, and the cost, during the strikes. He had had to keep his mouth shut rather than set her off on one of her prim little diatribes about how he needed to set aside childish things like the Dwellers and learn to take on proper responsibilities.

Galen's family had money, but not so much as all that, especially on top of the care for Julius. It made him frown, and withdraw, not wanting to talk, just look out the window. The angle caught the back corner of Julius's rooms, not enough to let him see anything that mattered, but enough he couldn't ever escape the implications.

Martin at least understood the importance of a companionable silence, and it was about ten minutes before he spoke again. "How do you want to play it tonight? Who else is coming?"

Galen shrugged. "Mother said mostly the usual. Sarah

and Andromachus Fortescue. Melitta and Lysander Scott. That lot."

"So, the married couples, around our age. Singles?"

"I'm not sure she had your dancing in mind when she was planning. Ugh." The thought hit him. "I suppose we'll both have to dance with Senara. To be polite."

"You, at least, can get away with a single dance there. With your other obligations. At least two with Laura, and make sure one of them's a waltz. One with your mother, another with your aunt."

"I don't think Senara understands the rules." He was frowning now.

Martin leaned back. "I can do my best to be a distraction to her? Or perhaps she'll set herself at another guest."

"Don't. That's worse. Then I'd have to do something, or deal with Mother being upset. Neither of those is actually palatable."

"Needs must." Martin was rather looking forward to the challenge, Galen could tell. That would be a problem if he went charging off.

"Look," Galen tried to put all his seriousness into his voice. "Please, don't make things worse for Laura? Or preferably, for my mother?"

"You're really worried." Martin sounded surprised. "You really think I'd go off half-cocked?"

Galen shrugged. "You have your moods, brother." He was quiet. "Just."

"Promise. By the forge." That was a thing Galen especially appreciated about Martin. He was absolutely reliable once he'd made a promise. "May I make things difficult for Senara, though?"

"Merlin and Nimue, yes, please. I mean, I wish I knew

why Father..." He stopped upon hearing the knock at the door.

"Who is it?"

"Oswald, sir." The voice was muffled.

"Come in." Oswald was a bit older, in his late twenties, as befit the first footman. His father had encouraged him to see what he thought of the man as an eventual valet, when Galen set up his own establishment. Galen wasn't sure, honestly. Oswald wasn't at all like Belford, his father's long-time man. There was always a hint of disapproval in Oswald. Of Galen, of the household, of other details. Galen found it rather uncomfortable to live with.

He worked quietly for a moment, standing to let Oswald dress him, shrugging off the dressing gown. They continued in silence for a few minutes, just the little gestures for one hand, then the other. Oswald was definitely in a mood tonight, he could tell by the little sniffs and sharp jerks of his hand on the buttons on the shirtfront.

That mood could sometimes be useful. "Oswald. Is there talk about the Wilsons in the servants' hall?"

Might as well be blunt with it. Nothing else for it.

"Sir," A tiny sniff. "They are American. We suppose that they may not know the proper manners for a country home, sir."

"Being demanding, then?" That was Martin.

Oswald did not approve of Martin, but in this case, the prompt was well-timed. "I presume you would prefer I speak freely, sir?" They both knew there were limits to that freedom, but Galen nodded, then shifted, to let Oswald work on the cuffs.

"They persist, sir, in asking for things at most inconvenient times. Drinks and sandwiches - no fish, Miss Wilson was very clear on that - long after supper last night, when

Cook had already gone to bed. Breakfast at eleven, when we were about to sit down to luncheon. A late tea this evening, when the whole staff was preparing for the party."

"Extremely untimely," Galen agreed. "I gather they had some business with Father, but he's not explained what, even to me. Materia, I'm guessing?"

"They are not his usual sort." Oswald said, not confirming the guess at all. He might not know. "I heard a few things from Millicent, who is acting as maid to Miss Wilson."

"Please, do go on."

"Miss Wilson's clothing is very fine but several pieces have been remade in recent years. There are several German dresses, remade since the War with additional trim or flounces. I gather." Women's clothing was below Oswald's direct attention. "The American pieces are not as high quality as her party dresses would suggest. Some have been taken in or let out inexpertly. Though I suppose the Americans do not have the high standard of service that we in this household care to provide."

Galen smiled at that, letting Oswald do up the small fastenings on his shirt, nimbly. "You provide excellent service, Oswald, thank you." Stand and wait and let him do everything. He knew it was the proper thing, but it always made him feel like he was a toddler in leading strings again, not trusted to do anything at all on his own. It wasn't Oswald's fault, but Oswald didn't make him feel any less awkward about it.

Martin had made him realise it was ridiculous, and also that pulling the entire aristocratic apparatus down would lead to other problems. Martin was a radical, not a revolutionary. He wanted better opportunities for everyone, whether it was education or profession. Better places to live.

Better care for those who were ill or infirm. More options for veterans and others badly hurt in the War, rather than exiling them like his brother.

He realised with a start that Oswald had continued with something, but now here he was moving to settle the jacket on Galen's shoulders. "There, sir. Do you need anything further?"

"How long until the gong?"

Oswald pulled out his pocket watch, peering at it. "Your mother would like you downstairs in five minutes, sir."

"Well, then, shall we, Martin? Give me your cuffs, you still haven't done them up." Oswald would disapprove, either way, and at least if he did it himself he wouldn't feel like he was being treated as too helpless to do his brother's buttons.

Martin nodded, straightening his jacket as he stood. "Of course. Can't keep your mother waiting."

# TWELVE

## FRIDAY EVENING

The party was quite chaotic, and Laura wasn't at all sure what to make of the guests. There were a good thirty or forty people there. They had spread out between the large ballroom at the back of the great staircase, the conservatory at one end, and then through the public rooms of the ground floor. The servants seemed like they were struggling to keep up, and she'd seen Blythe pass through several times, wearing a sepia-coloured dress, making sure things were in order, as if the entire evening would fall apart without her.

It was a little queer to have a large party on the Friday, but she had finally gathered from overheard gossip that there was some other party, near Penzance, that most of these people were going to on Saturday. Not one that Galen or his parents were invited to, she thought.

Laura had been asked to dance so many times already her feet were aching, and not just because the last two partners had trod on her toes. Though that certainly didn't help. She had been abandoned in the last bars of the most recent dance, when Senara Wilson had aimed a perfectly arched eyebrow at her partner and he had rushed to her side.

Laura did not believe that bare shoulders were quite as scandalous as some argued, but they were certainly not hurting Senara's numbers of admirers tonight.

"Here, you look like you need some refreshment. May I offer you an arm? A glass? A seat somewhere no one will notice you for a few minutes?" It was Galen, looking as dashing as when she'd come downstairs.

"Oh, please." It came out in a rush. She knew she wasn't supposed to be quite so blatant, but the offer of all three was overwhelming. "The last one, particularly?"

"Mother is quite pleased with the party. I hope people have been kind?"

"Kind enough." Cornish society was complicated. She was sure Madam Amberly had not known that the Fortescue family had heavily backed her father and uncle's failed expedition. Or that there was a generations-old feud with Lysander Scott's grandfather. He, at least, had been kind enough to look embarrassed when he ducked conversation with her.

Galen leaned in, looking at her more closely. "Here, come this way. Let's find a quiet spot." He whisked her off into the conservatory, and toward the left, the quiet end that looked out on the back of the house, and settled her into a wicker chair. "Let me go raid for refreshments. And tell Martin where we are."

He was off before she could say anything, and she watched him go, entirely bemused. Blythe passed him, coming out of the dining room with a tray, and looking thoughtful, but she smiled at Galen as if seeing him were something of a relief. Rather like Laura felt at the moment.

He was young, yes, but he was attentive. And by all her experience of him so far, good-hearted and kind.

He didn't seem to have one face in front of his mother, and another with her. Or if he did, the one she was getting was kinder and gentler, if anything. She knew she could do a great deal worse than someone like Galen. He knew about the things she was afraid of people knowing. The large fears, anyway.

She heard people walking through, between the dancing and the buffet set up in the dining room, laughing and teasing, sounding entirely at home with each other. She wondered what that felt like, being somewhere where being included wasn't such work, and if she'd feel that comfortable with it ever in the future.

Laura supposed that was part of the benefit of a husband willing to be a partner. She'd seen how Lizzie had learned to manage the large social affairs her husband's inheritance required of them both. But more to the point, she'd seen how Carillon had taken care to include her, to ease her way. And Laura's own, for that matter. If other people's grudges had meant it hadn't worked as well as he had hoped, it was not for lack of their effort.

Maybe being married had benefits. She supposed she could deal with the more physical parts, even. Her experience so far had been unpromising, even though some of it was fogged by the goldwasser and half-memories, and a few scarce experiences before that.

Galen came back, just as her thoughts were tangling, bringing with him a whiff of orange and citrus, and set a tray down on one of the little tables in front of them. "Punch, and a pot of tea, if you want something less alcoholic. Savoury tarts, here, and some petit fours. Is that all right?" There was something terribly earnest about him, like a dog wanting to please. She found it endearing, largely, but she was not at all sure what to do with that earnestness, whether to comment on it or ignore it.

In the end, she smiled and said, "This looks grand, thank you. Do your parents throw this kind of party often?"

"A few times a year. Not monthly, but - oh, four or five times? Mother gets lonely, I think, and she thinks I ought to expand my social circles. They've known the Fortescues and the Scotts for ages."

Laura nodded, not sure what to say to that, then offered, "There's some - family history, between my family and both of theirs."

"Oh, goodness. I'm sorry. That must have been entirely awkward, I wish Mother had known."

"It's not the kind of thing I think either of them would mention, honestly?" Laura leaned forward for the glass of punch.

"I didn't know how you felt about magical potions in your drinks - I promise, that's the unadulterated version. Just a little alcohol. But there's Sunrise Cordial, if you care for that. Or that berry one, Heart's Ease, Blythe was just bringing it out."

She looked at the cup, then shook her head, trying not to shiver at the memory of the goldwasser. "No, this is exactly right."

Of course he noticed. That was a decided downside to someone being observant, she was beginning to realise. "A problem?"

Laura nodded. "The - matter with the goldwasser. It left a bad taste, I suppose, is the best way to put it. Figuratively speaking. For magical drinks."

"You don't need to speak of it if you'd rather not."

Again, there was the earnestness, he was leaning forward, not too close to her, but very focused.

Laura shook her head. "I don't even know what most people heard about it."

"We weren't the sorts to get invited to that kind of party. It really annoyed Martin. He tried to get into a couple of them, had no luck at all, and someone else broke the story open." He snapped his mouth shut. "Sorry. It must have been rather awful, to be in the midst."

"I made, well. Quite a few choices I regret."

He was quiet for almost a minute, occupying himself in the small tasks of pouring tea, adding cream and sugar, taking a petit four, eating it. "I won't make you talk about that. Look, is there anything I can do to make the party better for you? Mother won't mind too much if we go outside, if I'm with you. She really quite likes you, she's made that very clear."

Laura frowned, then risked asking. "What do you think about that?"

"Well." He smiled suddenly. "I think it's rather early to make wedding plans. But I like you, and I think maybe you enjoy my company, and I'd be glad to keep seeing you. Mother's putting a lot of pressure on me, but that doesn't mean I need to pressure you." He waved a hand. "Just, if there's no hope, tell me when you realise that, so I can figure something else out."

She liked that attitude, really, given the fact he was being pushed into marriage with someone. "What does courting look like to you then? Or being married?"

"Goodness. You're the first person who's asked that. Though I assume Martin has it right without asking, he's like that. Courting, well, taking a girl out, supper or performances or walks in the Trellech parks, or a museum or garden party, or what have you. Charitable galas, when things got a bit more public."

"The usual sort of social events for your people."

"Yes. And some of them are actually enjoyable." Galen waved his hand. "This is not the best example, really. Senara, the Wilsons, they're making whirlpools. And it's agitating Mother, she's been even more pushy about me picking up the associations she approves than usual. People she went to school with. People from my own house. Not Martin, certainly."

Laura considered that. "That's quite a metaphor, but you're right. It makes everything about responding to what they're doing, whatever else you want." She sipped her punch, then said "And marriage?"

"Father would like me to take over at least one of the mainland properties, fully. Oversee the place, steward the resources, supervise repairs. There's quite a lot for a lady of the manor to do."

"Mixed tenants?"

"Two of our three houses, yes. A few magical, each place, but the villages are non-magical. So, passing out the permitted salves, blankets with warming runes, that kind of thing. That can go unnoticed, it's actually quite a help for the lady of the manor to do."

Laura considered that. "I've never had a lot of experience with people without magic. The sanitaria I was at were all people like us."

"Oh, they're very pleasant. And really, very skilled. There's a stone carver near the place in Cumbria, he's been doing some amazing restorations." Galen fairly lit up, talking about it. "I got to watch him work for a bit. Mother and Father always rather ignore people who don't have magic, but watching him, it's a different kind, he's doing something you can't do with magic anyway."

"That's - " she paused. "There's a dressmaker Lizzie uses, she's magical, but I liked how much of what she does isn't about that, it's about choices, human choices, about what works and what doesn't. What suits the moment. Or with your stonecarver, the building." His enthusiasm was a bit contagious, but then she remembered she had important questions. "We shouldn't get too distracted. What are your mother's expectations? Or your father's?"

"Oh, yes, the usual social whirl, expectations. A child eventually, preferably two, but I hope that part wouldn't be too difficult for you?" He suddenly made a connection in his head, she could see it in his expression. "That's not a problem for you?"

"Physically? Not that I'm aware of. But my experiences with men, um, that way, have not been brilliant. I mentioned some bad choices."

Galen frowned. "If someone took advantage, I'll, I mean, that's not on."

Laura shook her head. "Fussing like that isn't helpful, please." He subsided, almost immediately, looking at her with wide uncertain eyes.

"I just. If that's a thing you're looking for in a wife, I'm not sure it's a thing I'll ever especially enjoy. Maybe it would be different. I mean, you're very kind, and thoughtful, and that's loads better than they were already. But." She let the words trail off. And she continued to wonder if maybe Galen and Martin were close for reasons most men wouldn't dream of mentioning. That might not be so bad, in a marriage, really. Martin was easy to be around, he paid attention to the little things.

Galen was quiet again for a rather long stretch, letting

them both listen to the bustle and music from the other spaces near them. Finally, he reached to cover her hand in his, cautiously, like he thought she might jerk it away. "Anything I say, anything I promise about doing differently, that would just be words. I can only prove by my actions what kind of man I am, and how I would treat you. I do hope you'll continue to give me the chance at that."

It made her smile, and she turned her hand to twine her fingers between his. "I am very glad to give you the opportunity to convince me." Even if what he said only deferred her questions, and didn't answer them.

# THIRTEEN

## FRIDAY EVENING

Martin did not like the fact Galen had abandoned him to the social duties. Taking care of Laura was all well and good, and expected. Twice Madam Amberly had swept him away to introduce him to someone, and he couldn't argue with his mother. But it left Martin as prey for Senara and the small gaggle of women around her. There was a cluster of four, younger daughters of families the Amberlys knew or younger sisters of some of the wives. They found it amusing to make Martin dance attendance.

He couldn't say no. He was entirely clear that his role in this party was to help make up the numbers of men for dancing and that Madam Amberly had no patience for his presence if he did not fulfil that function. He even enjoyed dancing, in the right circumstances. Laura had been a pleasant partner, but Glanna and Ida had both trod on his feet and elbowed him in the ribs.

He made his excuses, claiming a need for a breath of fresh air, and escaped to make a circuit of the dining room and the terrace. It was on the terrace he heard something a bit curious and stopped to listen.

"They're saying that it's a business deal, but you know there was a history there, don't you?"

"Goodness, Orion. You can't just mention a thing like that and drop it. What history, go on, do."

It was a little knot of people. Four people, maybe five, and Merlin knew every posh family seemed to have an Orion, that was no help at all. The light was behind them, and he couldn't see faces, or even a rough sense of the shape of the bodies, with how the shadows fell. Martin pressed himself into the corner of the terrace and listened.

"Well, I heard from Perry Lawton - you know, he was a major in the Army, and he had quite a lot of stories about the Wilsons. I gather they were much seen in Berlin, before the War, and then they pop up in Paris, of all places, in 19... oh it must have been 1915, early in the year. Because I remember saying it was not long after the Christmas Truce. We weren't all going home for Christmas, but maybe soon."

"Senara?"

"And her brother. Throwing around money, flashy - rather like now. No expenses spared, champagne dinners and furs. Mind, she does look right nice done up in furs. Very smart. And well before most Americans were anywhere near the War."

One woman in the conversation coughed sharply.

"Anywho, I started hearing gossip about them. He'd flirt with anything that moved, and she was worse."

Martin was not at all sure how to reconcile the Basil he had met with that description.

"Like now? She seems to only require they be male."

"There was a story, about her and - actually, that was Julius Amberly, I'm sure of it."

"The son of the house?"

"He was posted to Paris, some staff position, I never knew the details. But he was seen squiring her around town, on the regular, for months. Then poof, he was off to the front, and she was gone, and no one knew where she ended up."

"Such a pity. I remember him!" The woman seemed pleased to. "Cheerful, make the best of anything, wasn't he?"

"Rather like the younger brother, that way. A bit over-earnest, sometimes, but meant well. Improved things around him, more often than not."

Martin hated how they talked like he was dead. Galen would never say a word about it, of course, if he heard it, but that didn't mean he couldn't see how he hurt over it. Martin had never met Julius, but he could see the shadows on the wall as clearly as anything, how they'd shaped everything Galen was.

"His house, Fox, I assume?"

"Fox, though I heard from Master Fowler that they had a grand wrangle about it. If it hadn't been for the family connections, he'd likely have ended up in Bear. The protective instinct, you see. And that sense of justice, too. The sort who'd throw himself between someone and trouble. Not a surprise he wound up like he did, really."

"Huh. Julius volunteered, you know. Long before he'd have been called up, I heard. But anyway, the Wilsons, you don't know why they turned up here, then?"

"What could they be trading?"

"Not the foggiest, old man."

"That's no real help at all." It was a different voice, a man's.

The speaker shrugged, Martin could see the shift in the

light. "I heard they turned up again a few times. Like a bad penny. London. Trellech. I heard a story or two about Russia, and another about Egypt. I'd believe Egypt, she'd cut through the archaeologists there like butter."

"And now they're here." The woman who said that sounded quite thoughtful, and she leaned to peer into the ballroom.

"Do you think she wonders about Julius? I would. But she's not the sort of girl you could bring home to mother now, is she?"

"An American? It would have given Nell fits!" That was one of the women again. "And a woman like that, twice over."

"Oh, I'm sure Nell never knew."

"Some sort of ghastly injury, wasn't it?"

"Later in the War. June 1917, I think. To his face, and that was, well, that's not for ladies."

Martin thought he heard one of the ladies snort.

"So you think Cassian didn't know either?"

"Oh, he might have softened if she mentioned knowing Julius in his prime. Especially if there was a bit of profit in it for him. Not the done thing to be seen doing business. But have someone to a country estate for a Friday to Monday, spend an hour or so meeting, both go away better off."

Martin had wondered while he was talking with Galen and Laura if the Wilsons were trading materia that Julius might use in his experimentation, and that was the source of their invitation. He hadn't figured out how to ask Galen about it, but maybe he needed to. This connection only deepened his suspicion that their presence was tangled up in things the Amberlys would rather sweep under the rug.

One of the women laughed. "And they could use the

money, I'm sure. They spent chests full, I'm sure, fixing this place up."

"What are they up to, then, do you think? What sort of business?"

Another shrug from the man who knew more. "Oh, I don't know. The clothes are very brash, but they're good quality. They must do well for themselves. I heard Basil mention they'd come over on one of the better liners, I can't place the name right now. But a good ship, the right sort of people in first class."

"You always think about that, Orion." That was teasing. And then someone asked something he couldn't hear, and the group seemed to migrate back into the dining room, toward the drinks.

Martin stayed out on the terrace for a few minutes longer, committing the details to memory. Finally, he decided that meeting brashness with a bit of boldness might pay off, and went back, looking for the dance floor. They were coming to the tail end of a faster dance, and as the music ended, the band struck up a waltz.

He stepped right up to Senara's left side, and said, "Senara, may I have this dance?" The red of her dress caught the light, a shimmer on the fabric that brought out a deep orange, like a flame.

She blinked at him and waved off her brother. "Go find that delightful Gemma or whatever her name is, darling. I'm sure Mark won't step on my feet. And I'm sure this young man can be quite useful, one way and another." She sounded smug, if anything, but there was a sense of a serpent coiling around prey. Perhaps she was plotting some sort of vengeance for the young men not paying her the kind of court she had obviously expected so far. There was nothing to be done about that now.

Names were not her particular gift, Martin realised. She'd done that other times. "I think I saw Glanna there, Basil." he said, gesturing at the far corner. "Yes, there she is, in the bright blue. I'm sure she'd be delighted." Basil nodded at him, and turned his back on his sister, something sharp suddenly in the set of his shoulders.

"Shall we?" Martin did his best to pretend to be as charming as Galen was naturally. It was an effort for him, but at least the start of the dance gave them an excuse to avoid talking for a few moments. He swung her into the music, and she let out a delighted squeal.

"Oh, aren't you strong, sweetheart. What do you do with yourself?"

"A lot of walking. A fair bit of carrying books and papers around." True enough, he helped haul newspaper bundles to their destinations when he was skint.

"My. And you know how to dance. Why hasn't some lucky girl snapped you up yet, what secrets are you hiding?"

"Oh, not that secret at all, Senara, love." He let his accent broaden, deliberately. "I'm not from the right sort of people as these folks have it. Fine to have round to make up the numbers, but not the sort their daughters marry."

She laughed, and he knew the sound was carrying. "Tell you a secret, darling. I'm not from the right sort of people at all."

"Well, you're American, aren't you? That's one part fashionable, and one part far too colonial for most folks."

"I don't have nearly enough money to be sought after that way, honey. I'm not an Astor or a Vanderbilt or a Duxbury." The Duxburys had made a great deal of money mining the Americas for materia, as it were. Mines, plants, woods, furs. Anything that could be swept up by their hired hands.

"There must be something else. Cassian Amberly - oh, you're quite charming, in your way, Senara, but that sort of thing doesn't usually turn his head."

"Oh, I've something he might like, we're talking about it. Connections. Resources. A bit of shared history." She let her voice trail off.

"And I'm not going to get it out of you, of course." He put on all the charm.

"Clever boy. No, braver men than you have tried and failed. And the consequences of prying are... not at all pleasant. Not like some things I might offer." She paused, considered him. "But if you came by my room tonight, after everyone's in bed, I might whisper a few things in your ear that could help a clever boy improve his life."

"Tonight? Rather late, no?" He tried to play it calmly.

"You've stayed here before, I'm sure you know some way past that stodgy Laura. Besides, I'm sure she'll be fast asleep as soon as she's upstairs. Not a late-night girl."

Martin wasn't sure how to answer that, so went with the simplest option. "When?"

"Half an hour after everyone else has gone to bed. I do need my beauty sleep, darling. You come in, you knock, like this." She tapped a pattern on his shoulder with his fingers, a rhythm from the music. Da-dah-da-da.

"Your brother?"

"Oh, he's in the next room, and he sleeps through anything. He's slept through earthquakes, even. But he won't mind, he knows me." Martin rather thought her brother was a tad peeved, being sent away, there was something in the set of the man's shoulders. He couldn't tell whether Basil didn't want her talking to Martin, or didn't want her talking to anyone else. That was an unpleasant thought any way he drew the implications, and drew him back to the conversation.

"All right." It came out a bit grudging.

She brushed against him. "Oh, I'll make it worth your time, honey. Don't you be worrying about that. More than just secrets."

Martin sucked in a breath and plastered a cheerful smile on his face. "Oh, I'm sure. A woman of experience, like you." He'd need the prophylactic charms, and the reagent for the one he actually trusted was up in his luggage. Well, he'd need to change, anyway. He'd need something he could skulk through the hallways in believably.

The dance ended, and he handed her off to another partner, leaving her to wiggle her fingers, with a "Later, darling." and a half-blown kiss.

# FOURTEEN

## SATURDAY MORNING

That was a scream. Laura shot upright in bed, trying to figure out what was going on, her hair tumbling over her face. Another scream, definitely, not just the howling of the wind. She couldn't tell where it was from. Downstairs. It was only logical.

She shot out of bed, overbalancing and almost toppling, before she caught hold of the bedpost and steadied herself. She couldn't go down in a dressing gown, she had to slip something on, but there was no time to wait for a maid. It was grey out, but what little light there was suggested it couldn't much into the morning. She spared a look at the clock. Eight. No wonder she felt exhausted, she'd had only about six hours sleep.

She rummaged in her trunk, coming up with a day dress she could shrug on with as little fuss as possible. She brushed her hair and pulled it back with a couple of hair pins jammed in to make a bun hold. Finally, it felt like ages later, but was only about ten minutes, she was fit to go downstairs.

Laura made her way down the main stairs, and came

into the dining room, where people were clustered at the door to the conservatory. The sound of rain battering against the glass drowned out the low, agitated burr of conversation.

Galen turned and spotted her. "Come away, Laura, it's not a fit sight." Martin was standing beside him, chewing his lip in thought.

"What happened?"

"Come away, do, let's get out of here. Drawing room." He offered his arm, with a kind of insistent gesture.

Laura let herself be steered, a bit unwillingly. Galen settled her on a chair in the drawing room. "I'm afraid..." He paused, stopped, and looked up at Martin, who had predictably followed behind them.

Martin said, "The second housemaid, Millicent, found Senara's body in the conservatory. Healer Tipson says she's been dead some time. Hours."

Laura put her hand to her mouth. "Oh. Goodness." She was not at all sure what to say. Finally, she asked, "What - her brother, oh dear."

"No one knows where he is. Not in his room, and who knows if he fell down dead drunk in some pantry somewhere and won't be seen before noon. Blythe said the last she saw him he was drinking like he was trying to store it up to go back to America."

Laura frowned. She must be missing something.

Martin caught her expression and spread his hands. "We're not sure of all of it ourselves."

"How horrid. Do they - does Healer Tipson know how she died?"

"It could be natural, but it ... I'm afraid it could be murder."

Laura blinked, mind racing, then looked hard at Martin.

Both the young men were silent, but Martin became more and more uneasy, shifting on his seat. "You," she said, after a moment. "You went down the hall last night. After everyone had gone to bed."

"I swear, she wasn't in her bedroom." It came out of him in a rush, and Laura had heard enough people lie - and lie to her face - to trust that was truth.

Galen said quietly, "You won't let it rest, will you?" He sounded disappointed in her.

Laura shook her head. "Wait. Is the Guard coming?"

Galen looked embarrassed. "I'm afraid something's gone wrong with the portal. Willet went down to receive the papers and post this morning and it wouldn't open at all. Made a sort of distressed noise."

"In this weather? How dreadful for him. But, does your father have a journal? Oh, he must. But I need mine." She paused, then stood, abruptly. "Both of you stay here. Don't move."

It came out as a deliberate order, and she was entirely startled to see how well it worked on them both. They sat there, open-mouthed. But stayed. She didn't linger to enjoy that moment, so rare in her life so far. Instead, she turned on her heel, and went back to her room. She rummaged in her day bag, drawing out the large leather book that was a present from her brother-in-law, and then took it back downstairs with her.

When she came into the drawing room, it was still just the two young men. Waiting.

She sat. "Tell me what you know."

Galen blinked, not saying anything, and Martin said cautiously, "What are you going to do?"

"Write to Carillon."

"Father wrote to the Guard." Galen sounded uncertain. "That's the proper thing to do."

Laura snorted. "There's Guard and there's Guard. You probably have a local, one of the bigger islands? Older, half-retired. Experienced, but not - not the sharpest tack in the box?"

Galen's eyes got wider and wider as she continued and Martin snorted. "That's Guard Trevallen in a nutshell, yes. Good man, but not very energetic these days."

"First, if it's a murder, I know they've got specialists. I don't know much about it, I just remember Carillon, there was a thing last summer, he explained it afterwards. And second, if the portal's out, that's particularly complicated. I don't have an earthly idea how to fix it, but they need to bring someone who does. Have you had trouble with it before? Goodness knows it got a great deal of use last night, people coming and going."

"No, not at all. It's been perfectly reliable as far as I'm aware." He sucked in a breath. "And what is Lord Carillon going to do? He's abroad, isn't he?"

"Oh, probably write something to exactly the right person saying, 'Sorry, my sister-in-law's staying with the Amberlys, out on the isles of Scilly, you know the place, and she seems to have run into a spot of bother, someone turned up dead. Could you send so and so round? Or if they're not handy, this other person?' And then half a dozen pleasantries, inquiries after children, horses, or hounds. Possibly all three."

"That is terrifying."

"You think that's terrifying, he and my sister together are far worse. Here, let me write."

She spent a minute or two setting up the letter properly.

*Dear Carillon and Lizzie,*

*Sorry to bother you, but there's something urgent. You remember I said I was going to stay with the Amberlys? They had an American guest, two actually, a brother and sister, and the sister has turned up dead, and the brother can't be found. Senara Wilson is the dead sister, and Basil Wilson is the brother. Mid-thirties, she was the kind of brash that makes enemies in sentences.*

She paused, considered, and then added a note saying more details would follow shortly and pressed her thumb to the leather tag that sent the message. She waited for it to finish, then began a new note, listing the guests at the house overnight, and as many of the others as she could remember. That basic list done, she looked up. "Right. So. What do we know about last night?"

"Senara propositioned me. I wasn't sure I wanted to take her up on it, but she'd promised some information I might find useful." His voice got softer, like he didn't want to admit he'd willingly gone to her.

Galen said, trying to sound more like normal, "Martin's easier to seduce with secrets than skin." Then he looked shocked he'd said it.

"Galen, go get someone to make a pot of tea, and bring it back with you, please. You clearly need a cup." Her voice was crisp. She'd seen this enough times now to know the best remedy. Tea was a suitable remedy for so many things, and firm direction a palliative for a fair fraction of the rest. He obediently stood and went off.

Martin watched, and once the door had closed behind him, he murmured, "Nicely managed. He likes to know what he's supposed to be doing." Then he said, "You - this is more practical than I expected."

"I spent rather a lot of years watching people disappear

in death," she pointed out. "And the last few, learning how to - make better choices."

Martin frowned, as if to say something, then he said, "Should I continue, or do you want me to wait for Galen?"

"Have you told him this already?"

He considered, then shook his head. "Not all the details."

"If you tell me and I write it down, and you don't tell him, at least not yet, it's probably more - more formal."

"But I'm telling you?" Martin sounded confused.

"I am not your best friend of more than a decade. I met you two days ago."

"Point." Martin frowned. "Right then." He settled in to explain. "Some of it is indelicate."

"Murder is indelicate enough, thank you. Stop stalling. It only takes so long to get tea."

"You are relentless, Laura." He looked at her, blinking, as if she'd introduced some new puzzle, even more intriguing than Senara's secrets. "All right. Briefly, then. During the dancing, Senara propositioned me, and said that if I came to her room, I'd find her willing. And if I was pleasing, she'd tell me a useful thing or two."

"On what topic?"

Martin winced. "The precise wording was something that might help a clever boy improve his life. It's no secret I don't come from the right kind of family. And I'm not ashamed to use what tips I can to get a bit ahead. I'd been trying to figure out what the two of them were up to anyway, they're - there's obviously a story, right?"

Laura wondered, for a moment, just how far that might go. But now was not the time for that question, and she was not the person to be asking it.

"And then?"

"A few more dances. I saw you come back with Galen for the last waltz. People departed for the portal, and the guests here went upstairs. I went with Galen to our rooms, we could hear other people moving in the building. I don't think the Wilsons had come up yet when we did. She wanted a last drink or something."

"Right." Laura did not offer what she'd heard or not heard. She made a few notes on the next message for Carillon, then said, "Next?"

"Senara had told me to wait half an hour after I heard people moving and make my way to her room. That's what I did. I knocked, the way she'd instructed me, a particular pattern." He knocked on the table, lightly. Short-long-short-short, like a measure of music.

"But she wasn't there?"

"No, there was no noise inside. She seemed the sort not to go to bed as early as we were, on average. I mean, we know they were up until two or so the first night here, they came downstairs at nearly noon. So I eased the door open, and there was no sign she'd been back in her room since getting dressed. Her cosmetics were out on the table, there were papers across the bed, that sort of thing."

"Did you touch anything?"

"No. Not other than the door handle. Maybe the edge of her dressing table."

Laura frowned. That could be bad, if they tested for fingerprints or magical signatures.

"What happened next?"

"I looked around - took a step or two inside, enough to see the dressing table and the bed. And then I went back out and back to my own bed."

"You didn't leave a note or anything?"

"Nothing to write on that wasn't hers, and I didn't fancy

leaving her something of mine to use against me down the road."

Laura looked up, then nodded slightly, "Right. Let me finish the notes here."

She settled into adding a few parenthetical details and added below her own details.

*I heard someone move quietly down the hallway at quarter to two in the morning. I was still awake. I eased my door open and saw Martin Taylor go down the hallway. I can confirm he opened the door to Senara Wilson's room, went inside, and came back out in a minute or two. He was wearing a dressing gown, but had nothing obviously in his hands or pockets, either when he went in or came out. Though the light was poor - only a few dim hall charmlights.*

There. Maybe that would be a help to someone.

# FIFTEEN

## SATURDAY MORNING

"Galen, darling." That was his mother, just as he was hoping to get through the dining room to the kitchen to ask for tea. She was standing in the dining room, talking rather fiercely at Aunt Silvia.

"Mother? Can I help with anything?" Aunt Silvia pulled away, leaving the room.

"This is all rather horrid, isn't it, and I'm sure it can't be making the best impression on dear Laura."

"I was," He paused, then said, "She asked if I'd fetch some tea." Perhaps that would let him make an amicable escape.

"Oh, it must be too, too, upsetting for her. Goodness. What will she think of us? Entirely unsuitable, I'm sure. And I don't know what we were thinking, letting such people on the island, people not from the right sort of background."

Whatever Laura thought, he was sure that it was not whatever it was his mother was worrying about, which he did not understand.

"I'm sure the tea will be a help, Mother. Is Father all right? Can I ask what's happening?"

"There seems to be some sort of tedious problem with the portals. Your father has written to the Guard, of course, but did you see? A storm's blown up, so they're not likely to get here today. They've instructed us to close off the conservatory. How horrid, we'll have to redo the entire place, as much as we can, all the furniture and tiling at least. And all my poor plants, they must be in shock." Oh, dear, his mother was in full fluttery ramble mode. That was a terrible sign.

"Mother, why don't you sit. Can I ask Aunt Silvia to come sit? Or Blythe, here, Mother could use a hand." Blythe was pale, as if she'd had a particular shock, and there was no way he could ask. "Can I fetch you something, please?"

Blythe waved him away, rather insistently, and instead turned to his mother, with a "Come sit, Nell, please. You'll worry Galen, and we can't be having that. I've asked Agnes for tea, she'll have it in just a minute or two, I'm sure. She's a good girl, Agnes."

Galen was not at all sure what he thought of being that particular kind of excuse, mind you. He waited a moment longer, but no, Blythe was clearly angling to leave him out. He asked, without a lot of hope of an answer, "Where's Father?"

His mother gestured through into the ballroom, and Galen went that way.

His father had his feet planted. "We need to sort things out, and promptly, and come on, logic, man." He was clearly lecturing Uncle Attis about something. Uncle Attis looked less than patient.

"You can't just assume that's what happened. You're

letting - " He cut off, as he saw Galen in the door. Very abruptly.

"Father?"

"There you are, boy. Look, your mother needs someone looking after her."

Galen waited the bare minimum for politeness. "Blythe is with her now. Is there, could I be a help here?"

"Oh, no. We've done what the Guard asked, for the moment, they'll be along as soon as they can. You should focus on your guest. Guests." His father often forgot Martin existed.

Galen paused, trying to think of what might be useful to say. "It seems rather awful, Father, just to go on. And it's Saturday, should she let her people know she won't be leaving tomorrow?"

"Oh, I suppose, and until the portal's fixed or the weather settles enough for a boat, she can't leave as it is. We're glad to put her up as long as needed. More the merrier. A bit more time to court the girl surely won't hurt anything."

The longer this conversation went on, the odder it felt, like his parents were doing their best to pretend that nothing at all was wrong.

His father cleared his throat, and Uncle Attis was looking pointedly at him. "I should go - upstairs and check on things there. Can you see that your mother is settled somewhere? Blythe will know what to do, Blythe always does."

Galen sighed, and said, "I'll fetch the tea for Laura, then." He lingered a moment after closing the door, to try to hear if the argument started right up again. Martin would approve of the attempt, at least. Whatever they said was quieter, though the murmurs had an intensity Galen didn't expect to hear from his father.

He went off to the kitchen, because at least the kitchen made some sort of sense. Coming down the hall, he heard voices. Cook and Agnes, he thought.

"No end of difficulty, rearranging the meals, and how long is that to go on for? Probably half of them wanting trays."

Galen coughed and said. "Pardon, Cook. I'm sure you've so many things to be arranging. I'm very sorry. Could we get a tea tray, when you've a moment?"

"Oh, hot water I've got. Where, sir?"

"I'm glad to take it up. For me and Martin and Miss Penhallow."

"Is she having vapours, then? Pardon, sorry, sir, I shouldn't have said that."

Galen smiled, amused. "Actually, no, she's fine. She thought I needed a cup."

Cook looked him up and down, and there was a little snorted "Huh." Then she turned to bustle around, putting together a pot, cups, and a small cake stand full of biscuits and scones. "If you want, sir, Agnes can take it up after she takes the tray for your mother."

It was a peace offering, and he shook his head. "No, I'm fine. I've carried things up to my room often enough." He picked it up.

There was a pause, then a "Sir, none of us liked that woman, and she wasn't at all kind to Millicent. But there was something - odd. We're not sure what."

Galen set the tray down again.

"What do you mean?"

Cook spread her hands. "We know what it's like when the house is - in order, sir. Running as it usually does, even with the various considerations." Someone else might have meant the isolation and location, but they both knew she meant how everything changed because of Julius. "And there's something wrong here. New."

Agnes dried her hands on a cloth, where she was putting together another tray. "It feels like something's watching. Lurking, sir. Like she's haunting us, sir, for her vengeance on - on whoever. Or that brother of hers, skulking about like a weasel, he's going to pop out at any moment, I swear it."

Galen paused, then said, "I don't know what to do with that information." Particularly in proximity to the reference to Julius, her anxiousness left him feeling prickly and uncertain. "But, um. Thank you for telling me. It helps to know what you're - you know the house differently."

She changed the subject immediately. "Miss Penhallow's been quite welcome, sir. You can tell she's quality."

"Can I ask what Senara was like, then? I feel like I know nothing about her."

"Bearing in mind this is second hand, sir. We thought it best for Millicent to go lie down, the shock." Agnes was being rather forceful about that.

Galen said, "If anyone gives you trouble about it, tell them I said it was all right."

"Thank you, sir." Agnes had a clear idea of how things worked, but she knew how to use that permission to get what she felt was needed. "Miss Wilson was..." She paused, as if trying not to be as insulting as she wanted to be. "Some ladies are careful with their things, go out of their way not to make more work for staff than is needed. Miss Penhallow is like that. Lays her things out neat and tidy. Doesn't fuss. Has sensible expectations for what a maid can do with the time available."

"And Miss Wilson?"

"Expected Millicent to do wonders. Tore two stockings and then threw a fit because they weren't mended that same afternoon. Mending stockings is terrible complicated, sir, takes fine stitches, and you remember, it was cloudy, makes it hard to get enough good light."

"When was that?" Galen wasn't sure it mattered, but Martin always said having information you didn't need was much better than not asking.

"Saturday, sir. When they came down for lunch, they'd got torn somehow."

Galen frowned. "On Friday?"

"Must have been, sir. They weren't downstairs before that. Just in their rooms."

Galen considered. "And the other things?"

"She was very demanding, sir, when Millicent was doing her hair for the party. Not like she'd enough of it left to be worth being demanding about, sir. Very particular, and Millicent's a good girl, sir, and a decent lady's maid, but she's not trained like they are at some of the noble houses."

"So Senara was unreasonable. Did she - hurt Millicent? Threaten her?"

"No, sir, but thank you for thinking to ask, but she made her uncomfortable. She said the brother, Mr Wilson, he was in the room when she was dressing. Didn't think it was proper, sir. Thought they were maybe fighting about something. Disagreeing? But they spoke pleasantly when she was there, just not the right tone, sir. People making nice in front of the staff so we wouldn't carry tales."

"Except of course you're clever and notice that too."

Agnes bobbed. "As you say, sir." She paused and added, "The way he said 'business', sir, over and over, like he was worried she didn't have her mind on it. Might get distracted and take up with someone instead of making their deal, Millicent thought."

Galen nodded and tried not to think about Martin. "And this morning?"

"I was getting the tray for Miss Penhallow ready, sir, and the footmen had taken up the trays for you and Master Martin and your parents. Millicent had gone to start tidying after the party, bring in all the cups and glasses, so we could clean up properly without worrying about breakages."

"And she went into the conservatory?"

"Yes, sir."

"May I ask - what did she see? Precisely? They've closed it off now. If that's not too upsetting?"

"I'm not the one that saw it, sir, but since it's you asking. There she was, on the wicker settee in the corner. Her face was all white, and her lips were blue, and her eyes were open, and she was really very truly dead, couldn't mistake it for the world, sir. But Millicent said it was - peaceful. Didn't look like there'd been a struggle or anything like. Just like she sat down and died."

Galen wanted to ask more, but he wasn't sure what Agnes would know. "Thank you, Agnes. And Cook, for your time. And I'm glad Miss Penhallow knows how to treat staff well. You let me know if there's anything else you think of, or if you need someone to make a decision and Mother and Father aren't available."

"Thank you, sir." The reply came from both of them. Galen knew his cue and picked up the tray to bring it upstairs.

# SIXTEEN

## SATURDAY MORNING

Galen was gone rather longer than was required to fetch tea. It gave Laura plenty of time to write a note of further details to Carillon, but also plenty of time to fuss. Her brother-in-law's note back was prompt but not much help, simply saying to keep sharing details as they became available. No one was going to tell her much.

Martin had settled into a chair, chin on his hand, watching her. She looked up, and he said, "Do you think that will help?"

"Don't you do that? Write things out?"

"Usually not to someone else. And besides, I can't afford one of the journals."

"I couldn't either, but Carillon wanted to make sure I could stay in touch with Lizzie. And he has a really excellent staff, but he wanted someone he could write to if there was some more private matter to deal with, about the estate or whatever."

"Or at least that is the comfortable excuse to allow him to give you something like that?" Clearly she had given him the correct impression about Carillon's oblique schemes.

She would have to decide whether or not she wanted to apologise to her brother-in-law later.

"Rather, yes. And this has all the bells and whistles."

Martin got a queer look on his face and frowned. Laura wondered if it was envy or the expense of the thing, money that could be put to better use.

Before he could say anything further, the door opened, with Galen bracing his back against it as he brought the tray in. He stood there, saying, "We could go up the upstairs sitting room, I thought? We'll be out of the way there. If you don't feel it's inappropriate, Laura?"

"I probably ought, but I'd rather somewhere quiet," Laura agreed. "Where is it?"

"By our bedrooms, up on the first floor. Not..." Galen flushed. "Not our rooms. That wouldn't be proper."

Laura waved a hand. "Lead on."

They got upstairs without anyone stopping them, though Laura could hear voices in the room at the end of the hall as they filed into the sitting room. Galen's mother's voice was shrill, Laura couldn't make out the words, but there was a hiss of sound that might be Cassian's name. Or possibly Julius. Then there was Cassian Amberly, sounding gruff, frustrated, talking over her.

"My parents." Galen said, "Their rooms are down at the end."

Laura blinked and paused. "Rooms?"

"Rather the done thing to have separate rooms." Galen sounded tired. "They're not unhappy together. But they've always had separate rooms."

Laura blinked at Martin, who spread his hands. "The ways of Galen's kind are just as mysterious to me. Except that yes, I have observed they have different bedrooms. An adjoining door. The custom among the tribe is that from time to time the lady of the house invites the gentleman to join her. At all other times, she is not bothered by his demands. Not familiar?"

"Mama and Papa spent a lot of time apart - Mama was with me, when I was ill. And Papa travelled a lot. But no, if they were both home at the same time, they'd actually - I mean, they never came out and said it? But we knew they spent a lot of time in bed."

"That's sensible people for you, who love each other. And your brother-in-law? Or no, that's indelicate. Even if, having asked, I am now tremendously curious."

She laughed. "If you promise to keep a confidence."

Martin clearly had to think about that, and Galen chortled. "Oh, he doesn't like that, does he?"

"Come on, you weren't going to write a tell-all about the Lords of the Great Families. That's not the sort of thing you count as journalism."

Galen roared. "A point! A point! A very palpable point!"

Martin tried to look stern, and then gave up, laughing. "My fair Laura, I do solemnly promise that I will not take information you give me about your sister, your brother-in-law, or other immediate family and make it public without your explicit permission. Barring the necessity to save someone from death or serious harm."

Laura considered that and said, "That's fair. And considerate, even."

"So, tell. And do have a seat." Martin settled in one of the easy chairs, designed to be comfortable, and perhaps a bit worn around the edges.

Galen took another, letting her have a small sofa. She considered, then tucked her feet up beside her. "Ytene has rooms for the lord of the estate, and his lady, but there is a joining door. And in practice, they share her room. He sometimes naps in his, or if she's away for some reason."

"Huh. Your sister sounds fascinating," Martin said finally. "Pity she's married." That was clearly meant to tease.

Laura snorted. "Before you start, she'd be the first to tell you she and I are quite different, always have been."

"Which house, at school?"

Laura shrugged. "She's Salmon, I'm Seal. Two water houses, but rather different in implementation. And Carillon is Owl, not Fox, despite his birth."

"Suggests he's a bit more clever than he puts on." Martin was relaxing now, but sounded intrigued again.

That, Laura would not comment to. He had already got enough of an admission from her about the journal, and it wasn't her secret to tell. She just smiled and said, "Shall I pour?"

Galen raised an eyebrow at her. "Do pour, of course. And try the scones. There's cream here. Are you sure they'll send someone competent?"

"Carillon said he was on it, so I assume so. When someone can get here. Did you learn anything more?"

"Nothing that makes sense. I was hoping Martin would help me sort it out. And you too." The last bit was hurried.

Martin waved a hand, amiably. "What did you learn, then?"

"Mother and Father were doing their utmost to brush over things. Each in their own way. No major problem here. And I can't figure out why."

Martin frowned, then said, "Wait. First thing to establish. That none of the three of us could have done it."

"Senara propositioned you. Did anyone else know about it?" Laura felt they should probably start there.

"She might have mentioned it to her brother, but I'd suppose not anyone else. And you saw me go down the hall. Which is not where she was found."

"Is there a back staircase from her room, or anything?"

"Not down to the conservatory. Unless you have a rope harness, as for rock climbing, and a way to open the glass." Galen frowned.

"A rope harness certainly doesn't seem sensible, and as a sensible person I'd have to change clothes and take off my stockings for that sort of nonsense. It's not like one does that in a fashionable frock, either."

Martin hooted, then took a long drink of his tea, before managing an amused, "Do you mean, then, you go without stockings? I'm almost afraid to ask about rope harnesses."

"Goodness, yes. At home. Other times when they'd catch. We had rather a lot of years we couldn't afford to spoil them, even after the War." Laura paused, remembering walking away from the last of the goldwasser parties, stopping to slip her stockings off, ball them up in her pocket, with the one bag she could manage to carry, and get back to a portal.

They both noticed. They were annoyingly observant at times. Martin immediately sobered and murmured. "Sorry. We overstepped."

She waved a hand. "Bad memory. About getting out of somewhere - the goldwasser parties. The last one. Lizzie told me not to drink it, that it was dangerous. And I hadn't wanted her to be right. Not the thing to talk about right now." She took a deep breath, then focused on pouring for Galen, offering the cup. "Tea?"

He took the cup. "Oswald - that's the first footman, he valets for me for big parties. He helped me get out of the formal clothes, the buttons, and then I went to bed. I heard

Martin leave, and I turned my light on and off twice, when I heard him. It's one of our signals."

"Signals?"

"Depends. That we're aware something's up, mostly. Usually it's just for sneaking down to the kitchen and bringing things back, but sometimes..." Galen shrugged minutely.

"Martin told me he saw that when we were talking earlier. And I saw Martin. He did not see me. So I suppose that makes me a suspect. Technically." Laura figured more than one person could talk about who was where.

"Doesn't it make a lot of people suspects?" Laura could see the thought dawn on Galen's face. "Basically everyone here? Except maybe Martin."

"Unfortunately, yes."

Martin was following a bit better. "You, because no one saw where you were. What did you do?"

"I came up while the last outside guests were leaving - I could see the portal flare, the light, from my windows. That stopped when Agnes was finishing with my dress, hanging it up, and she turned down the lights, and I went to bed with a book." Laura paused. "Books are terrible alibis, I gather."

"Do you promise you did not do it?"

"Yes." Of course, she could make a promise on her magic. That made her realise something. "Wait, how does the Silence work for Americans? Do we even know?"

Galen didn't make the jump with her, but Martin did. "You were thinking about the formal oaths, right? That if you swore on your magic, and someone was there to ask the proper questions, we'd know for certain? Well, in that case, we just have to wait for the Guard to get here in proper force."

"Or it was Basil. Do they even make the same promises to the Silence we do?" If they did, then one of the Guard could presumably sort this out in short order, get them all to swear on their magic that they were telling the truth, and then see what came out or who refused to answer questions.

Galen frowned, like he was half-remembering something. Martin shook his head. "Not quite the same, I think. Though the oaths got brought over to the colonies, of course. But I think they changed things. A different age? A different commitment? I'm not sure."

"And none of us can enforce an oath, or make someone take one. Unless healers can?"

"I don't think so at all." Galen paused, then shook his head. "No, I remember Uncle Attis complaining about it. That a lot of treating patients would be a lot easier if you could be sure they were telling the truth. Different line of magic, I think. If it's tied to the land magics somehow then who knows what would work on Americans."

"Right, then," she said. "I'm afraid for the moment, that means everyone's a suspect unless we can rule them out with actual evidence."

"Does it matter? If the Guard will be here?"

"Well, it does potentially mean - sorry, Galen, since most of them are your family or staff - that there might be someone here who is a murderer."

# SEVENTEEN

## SATURDAY MORNING

Galen made a series of faces, overwhelmed, upset, settling into a grand roiling displeasure.

Martin watched, and then it hit him. What they could do. What he knew how to do, in fact, and Galen knew how to help with. "We can investigate ourselves. Gather evidence for the Guard, when they get here? Since Galen's mother and father clearly aren't going to do that kind of thing."

Laura was right there with him. "That would be sensible."

Galen frowned, then said, "I'm not sure I like the idea."

Martin settled in to wait. It took Galen a few minutes to think through things. He leaned forward, prepared a scone with clotted cream and jam. Laura picked up his cue and poured more tea around.

After five minutes, Galen said, "You won't make things worse? Promise?"

"We'll consult all the way. If you feel something is wrong, we can sort it out. Come on, you know me. And if they tidy something up they oughtn't have because they don't want the fuss, we can testify to how it was so they get in less trouble for it. Or if it actually matters, then we'll be able to share that, too."

Laura sensibly stayed quiet, but Galen turned to her. "Why do you want to do this?"

"You're a good sort, Galen. And this is a horrible thing. And I'd like to - understand it. There's lots of ... pettiness, in a sanitarium. Or one of the spa hotels, for that matter. Little squabbles seem much bigger. I'm used to figuring that out, it's, that's a thing that keeps you safer. But murder's a whole different sort of thing."

Galen took a deep breath, then another. He opened his mouth as if to ask something, but made a tiny shake of his head before he said, "All right. How do we do this?"

Martin leaned back again, feeling more secure. "We figure out who to talk to. There are some people who will talk more to one of us than others. I think most times it can be conversational. Let's start by you telling us what you found out when you got the tea."

"Cook and Agnes had some comments. I think Agnes would talk more to you, Laura. She said you knew how to treat staff properly."

"That's a particularly interesting sort of thing to say?" Martin caught the flicker of Laura's expression, shifting from discomfort to the more settled expression she normally maintained.

"I gather Senara was rather unpleasant to the second housemaid, Millicent. She'd put huge holes in her stockings, and Millicent didn't fix them quickly enough, or something." He sounded baffled.

Laura made a rather incredible face, as if she was being reminded of something rather sizeable. "Men. Goodness."

"Do explain the mystery of the stockings, please. As you

no doubt noticed the last time we talked about them, we do not understand these things." Martin was broadly amused. And perhaps her explanation would be helpful.

"Silk stockings are tedious to repair. You understand, of course, it is improper to be seen in public with bare legs. Stockings come in many weights, the weights of the threads used. Silk or cotton or there are other materials now. Rather a lot of women add charms or runes for different purposes to the cuff at the top."

"That's a thing?" Galen was leaning forward.

Laura waved a hand. "The heavier weight stockings hold up well, but the finer ones - like anything I've seen Senara in - ladder fairly easily. You brush against a splinter on a door or a rough bit on a table, your shoe catches when dancing." She held out her ankle. "These are middle weight, and fairly sturdy. Heavyweight would be - oh, I had that on when we went out yesterday. I have a pair with warming charms on them."

Martin blinked, considering the implications. Women were utterly mysterious. "So you're saying she was doing something that caused them to ladder."

Laura nodded. "It could be all kinds of things. It doesn't tell us where she was, or anything useful."

"Why did she fuss about repairing them?" Besides the obvious, which was money.

"Well, they're expensive. So if you have a nice pair, you repair them, rather than getting new. But it's very difficult to repair fine stockings without it being obvious." Laura frowned. "Some people are just frugal, but she didn't seem the type. More the type to make a show of having money, when she wasn't so well off." That meant the whole murder might in fact be about money somehow. Martin mentally filed the possibility next to his earlier suspicion that materia trading was involved.

"Why do you say that?" Galen shifted in his chair, then took another biscuit, apparently needing something to do with his hands.

"Her dresses were like that. A showy sort of expensive. But they were..." Laura was searching for words, her eyes half closed, focusing on her thoughts, and Martin found that utterly absorbing. Distractingly so. Then she opened her eyes, and said more clearly, "Her dresses were designed to be showy, but not up to the minute fashionable. I suspect most of them were several years old. Minor details redone."

"Are you sure?" Oswald had said as much, but confirmation would be a help.

"I'd have to look more closely, but Agnes would know for certain. Or your mother's lady's maid, she must have one."

"Haley." Galen said, automatically. "Margaret Haley." He rarely saw her outside his mother's rooms, or at least in the family spaces. "How?"

"Up close, there are signs of things being taken in or let out or modified to be a la mode. Hemlines, the decolletage, that sort of thing. Now I'm rather curious about her lingerie." Then she put her hand to her mouth and blushed.

Martin tilted his head. "Why?" It was a practical question.

"It would say a lot about where her financial priorities were. And her physical ones."

"Nice underthings, either she had money, or having those be her most recent additions was important somehow?"

Laura nodded. "Exactly. I've known several women, their

dresses were classic, you know? And their underthings were all darned, but they pretended they still had pots of money. The stockings are," She waved a hand. "More ambiguous."

"That still doesn't explain what she was doing to tear them. If she was doing anything in particular, since you say they're so fragile." Martin tapped his fingers on the arm of his chair. "Let's try a different direction. Did Cook and Agnes say anything else, Galen?"

"That Senara and her brother had some sort of disagreement, before the party."

Martin tilted his head. "All right. Let's go about this systematically." He was becoming sure they were missing something. "We're fairly sure that everyone not staying here last night had left before Senara was killed, correct?"

"Someone could have hidden, but that seems unlikely?" Galen agreed, uncertain again. "Or a poison that takes time? Only they'd have to have been confident it wouldn't work before they left."

"And, pardon, it does not look like Senara took her own life." The more Martin thought about it, the more sure it was.

"How do you tell?" That was Laura, but then she started thinking out loud. "I suppose if you were going to, it would be your bedroom or something. Not a public room like that? Possibly?"

Martin tapped his glass. "She did set up the assignation with me. It rather implied she expected to be alive through the night." He looked at Galen. "What did you hear?"

Galen closed his eyes. "Cook told me what Millicent saw. That Senara was very pale, her lips were blue, but it looked like it was peaceful, no signs of a struggle or anything like that. Just like she'd sat down and died."

Martin frowned. "That means not enough air, I think."

"I could ask Uncle Attis?" Galen offered. "If he'll talk. He was abrupt, earlier. Or Aunt Silvia."

"Why your aunt?" Laura leaned forward, visibly curious.

"She's made rather a study of particular plant properties, and alchemical aspects. Healing plants, but what can cure can harm and all that rot."

"Huh." Laura considered. "Do we know where they were?"

"They came up to bed when we did, went to their rooms - they have adjoining rooms. And I heard Healer Tipson snoring when I went down the hall," Martin said.

"And your parents?"

"Made sure that Senara and her brother had everything they needed. Mother stopped by my room briefly to say goodnight."

"Not your father?"

"No, but I could hear him and his valet, talking, past Mother."

"And then they went to bed?"

He nodded. "Twenty minutes or so after I heard everything quiet down, I heard Martin's door open, and watched him go down the hall. I flicked my lights so he'd know I'd seen."

Laura nodded. "And you didn't hear any noises from downstairs, Martin? Or anywhere else?"

Martin shook his head, trying to figure out how to explain it. "But I wasn't expecting to, I was going straight across the top of the main staircase to your wing, and the end of the hall."

"Where do the servants sleep?"

"So, the house is sort of a square with some bits extending, right? An odd shape, but growing a little over the years.

Like coral." Galen moved things to one side of the tray to clear space. "Right. This long dish here is the front of the house. This glass is the conservatory." He placed it adjacent, to one side.

Martin picked up the theme. "Day rooms on the ground floor, here, the plate with my scone. Ballroom across the back, dining room and such here, under the guest rooms." He moved a tea cup to the other side of the square, opposite the conservatory. "Family rooms on the first floor. Nursery rooms and Julius on the second floor - his half is the back half."

Laura nodded. "And the servants are over the guest wing, here?" It made a C shape open toward the back and a small garden once Galen obligingly laid out the guest wing in teacups.

Galen nodded.

"Do you have - I don't know? Hidden passages or rooms or things like that?"

"There are the servant stairs. Here, here, here, and here." Tucked into the corners of the building and marked with sugarcubes. "And there's an outdoor walkway here, from the room across from you, no one's in that one right now, all the way across on this level, above the rooms." He laid it out with precariously balanced cutlery, all around the arc of the house.

Laura frowned. "Why?"

"Something to do with weather readings. Father's never explained it. It goes most of the way to Julius, I suppose, but I don't know if it connects."

Martin frowned. "Where does Blythe sleep?"

"A little suite here, made out of part of the nursery. There's a wall, and Julius has the rest of that floor."

Laura frowned. "He must be lonely. All the way there. Not even hearing people around. Except Blythe maybe."

Martin glanced up at this, to watch Galen's face. Galen had gone paler, tight-lipped. "It's what our parents thought best."

Laura said, "I'm sure there's a good reason. Just..." She let her voice trail off.

Martin coughed, and gestured at the table. "So. We have the Tipsons here. About where this currant is. Your parents here, Galen. You here. And you here, Laura." He moved a few bits of fruit from the scones around to make it easier to see. "Blythe up here. The servants presumably where they were expected to be."

"What if it was one of them?"

Martin had been considering this. "First, if it was one of them, I don't think we'll be able to find it out. And the Guard can question people in ways we can't. But more to the point, why would they? Senara was rather awful, and unpleasant to them, but I don't think they'd have had time to work up to murder. They just have to wait out her leaving. Or are we assuming it was a poison?"

Galen shook his head. "We need more information. Laura, you talk to Agnes. And if you get the chance with Mother or Aunt Silvia, and can figure out how to ask, well, you'd be much cleverer than I."

Laura laughed, and said, "You?"

"I'll tackle Aunt Silvia, Uncle Attis, and my parents. Martin, can you see who else you can talk to?"

They parted ways there, with Martin trying to figure out where to start.

## EIGHTEEN

### SATURDAY AFTERNOON

Laura went back to her room, thinking about how to approach things with Agnes. It had to be something that would keep her close for a period of time, and give them time to talk. Mending a frock wouldn't do, Agnes could take that away.

She was not used to having a maid. Ytene had quite a few people attached to it these days. Carillon's man, Benton, though Laura gathered he was about to shift into some new role. A housekeeper and cook. Lizzie's lady's maid, Mally, who was fiercely loyal to Lizzie in a way Laura could not get in the way of if she wanted to. A handful of housemaids and footmen, who disappeared into the woodwork, and would never talk to her like she needed Agnes to. A small army of gardeners and stable hands.

Once she was settled in her room, though, she had a brilliant thought. She rang the bell, and when Agnes appeared a few minutes later, she asked, "Would it be a terrible bother to set up a facial steam? I'm afraid I've started a cough again, the weather's different here."

Agnes blinked, and then said, cautious and polite. "May

I ask what is needed, miss? If we have it, I'm sure it can be arranged."

"Oh, nothing too challenging. A bowl of water, a cloth - cotton or linen - to drape over my head. And some lemon, or a suitable herb. Thyme or rosemary or peppermint all work well for me. Or lavender, if you've some of that. Dried is fine, even, so I'm sure Cook has something."

"And would you need me to stay, miss?"

"Please, yes. If you could bring up a jug more of boiling water, so I could do two rounds, that would be lovely. Would that take you away from your duties for too long? And perhaps you could tell me a little more about the house, to keep me from getting bored?"

Agnes nodded and bobbed. "It would be a help if I could be ready to help with supper, miss, but I could make time now, if that's convenient? Unless the young master is expecting you?"

"No, no. He was going to go see if his parents needed anything, I think. I'll see him soon."

Agnes almost said something, then bobbed again. "Let me go fetch water and the other things, miss. I'll be a few minutes."

Laura nodded, and said, "Of course." She settled back in the chair in the little sitting area to wait.

Twenty minutes later, there was a knock on her door. "Miss?"

"Come in." Laura set the book aside. Agnes entered, bearing a large tray with quite a nice sized basin, several small glass bowls with herbs, a large linen cloth, and a few small bottles.

"Pardon, Miss, but Mrs Tipson saw what I was doing, and she offered some of these oils, extracts, if you would find them helpful?"

"Oh, essential oils, yes. I'm quite familiar. I didn't know if anyone would have any here." That did rather support what Galen had said about his aunt's interests. "It's very kind of her. What did she offer?"

"Here, miss? You can look? She said if you were asking for the steam, she suspect you'd know what you like. But if you have questions, she's glad to come and suggest something."

"Oh, I'd not want to bother her at the moment. Ah, here, that's good. And this one. Oh, and you have a lemon, fantastic. I feel it's so brightening, somehow."

It took a minute to prepare things and mix the herbs. "You don't mind talking a little, while I do this? It's so terribly boring, with your head under a cloth."

"No, Miss. Mr Jacobs, the butler, he made it clear I was to offer my help."

"Well, good, then. Can you pour the water in here? To about two-thirds full, yes, like that." Laura took a deep breath, inhaling the sharpness of the herbs, then dropping a few drops of each oil in. "Oh, that's excellent."

She lifted the linen cloth, draping it over her head. She'd done this so many times. It was no problem to make sure the linen didn't go in the water or that there was just enough drape to bring the steam where she could breathe it easily. And, most importantly, she knew how to position herself so she didn't end up with a crick in her neck after.

Once everything was settled, she said, "I've been so grateful, Agnes. You seem to know just how to manage everything. May I ask, have you been with the family long?"

"Three years, miss. Before that, I was a maid with the Scotts, Miss. The brother of Mr Leander Scott, who was here."

"That must have been interesting, then. Aren't they

based in Trellech? Did you like that, or do you prefer country living? Or I suppose this is island living."

"Oh, the island, Miss. I found Trellech ever so noisy and complicated. So many people and doing things so fast! I'd much rather be here, doing things steady. The master and mistress entertain regularly, but not too often."

Laura smiled, not that Agnes could see it. Or perhaps because she knew Agnes could not. "And now you're first housemaid, right? That's quite a thing."

"You're familiar with big households, Miss?"

"I've been living with my sister and her husband a fair bit of the time. He holds Ytene, and they've been doing more entertaining. His man, housekeeper, butler, cook now. Maids, footmen. A lot of stable hands, he breeds horses."

"That must be interesting, miss. Do you ride much?"

"I'm not very good at it, not compared to him. Galen rides, he said. I do enjoy looking at the horses, though. And the foals are lovely. Learning how to do things."

"Oh, yes, miss. Cook told me stories about when he was younger. She's been with the family a long time."

Ah, that brought them to a delicate bit. Asking someone like Agnes what they thought about the family they worked for, you couldn't do that straight up.

"Agnes, it must be - scary, to have someone die here. If you need help, or you ... if someone else does, I'm glad to do what I can. Help find another position if you need that, that kind of thing."

"Thank you, Miss, that's very kind, but no. I like it here. And they're a good family, not like some. There's special considerations of course, but nothing that would put us to any risk."

'Special considerations' likely meant whatever was

going on with Julius. "Oh?" The response to an unspecific query might well be interesting.

"There's some, miss, who do charms on their servants, means we can't do things, choose things."

That was startling enough to make Laura lift her head and pull the linen back. "That's illegal."

"Doesn't mean people don't do it, miss. Not that many of them, but more than none. But they're kind, the master and mistress. Reasonable. Keep enough staff even though we don't always have that much to do, so there's not too few when there are guests. It's a bit of a rush for big parties, like last night, but the rest of the time, it's comfortable. There are places that would understaff all the time, and bring in strangers for a big party, and they never know how to do things."

Laura settled the linen again, and after a moment, said, "Is there a lot of gossip? About Miss Wilson?"

"Well, no one likes to speak ill of the dead, miss, it's bad luck. But for all the shock, miss, the Wilsons were not familiar with how things are done. And that makes our work more difficult, miss. By rather a lot sometimes."

"You're very diplomatic, Agnes."

"I felt sorry for Millicent, miss. She's the second housemaid. And I think she thought she should get preference. Being older, miss, and invited by the master."

"But Mrs Amberly thought otherwise?"

"Oh, yes, miss. She was ever so careful to make sure you'd enjoy your visit. This is the best guest bedroom, the newest bed, more comfortable furnishings."

"It is a very pleasant room, and I appreciate all the attention to detail." She paused, trying to figure out how to turn the conversation the way she wanted. "Do the Tipsons visit often?"

"Oh, yes, miss. They're quite close, Mrs Tipson and Mr Amberly, as brother and sister. They visit most months for several days, unless they're visiting others."

"And she knows a lot about oils?"

"Yes, miss. I believe she's had papers published with her husband, about what they discovered. He was highly respected in the Healing Temple."

Laura waved a hand in the direction of the tray, feeling she'd run out of things she might reasonably ask at this point. "More hot water, if you don't mind?"

## NINETEEN

### SATURDAY AFTERNOON

Galen turned in the hallway, heading for the small family sitting room on this level. He could hear voices from there. His mother, for certain, her voice was very distinctive, the rise and fall of the pitches, even behind a wooden door.

He knocked, and said "Mother, it's me." Inane, but there things were.

There was a muffled noise, and then a "Galen, darling." He opened the door, and came in to find his mother, Blythe, and Aunt Silvia, in chairs, all looking like he had caught them out at something. If he hadn't had serious matters on his mind, he'd have been delighted.

"Mother, Aunt, Blythe."

"Galen, darling. Shouldn't you be making sure Laura is all right? It must be a frightful thing for her."

"She went to rest for a little, Mother, I'm not neglecting her, of course. Can I do anything to help?"

Aunt Silvia coughed once. "Why don't you go check on things, Nell? Galen, do come sit."

His mother blinked. "I should go check with Cook

about the next few meals, yes. I won't be long, Silvia." She bustled out, Blythe trailing after her silently.

Once they were gone, and the door was closed again, Aunt Silvia said, "You're here with a purpose, aren't you?"

"You always see through me, Aunt Silvia." Galen was amused. She always did, whether it was snagging apples from a special tree, or exploring her laboratory when he was supposed to be studying.

She waved a hand. "Sit. Tell me. Your mother won't take that long over the menus."

How to put this? Specifically, how to put it so it was not a horrific accusation of his aunt, who he did in fact love. "We were talking, Aunt Silvia. The three of us, me and Martin and Laura."

"That was the goal of the weekend, yes. You and Laura talking, that is. We can take Martin as read." Her tone was even, in the way that made him sure she'd been talking to his parents, and was thinking about how to handle something.

He smiled. "Quite. I wondered, while we were talking, if you might know anything about what caused that kind of death."

There was a moment where his aunt went completely still. It was as if she were suddenly evaluating a dozen different considerations and had nothing to spare for a facial expression or two. "Why do you ask, Galen?"

"I know you've studied different materials. Oils and salves and potions and such. And their effects."

She nodded. "I have." She said nothing else.

"And I, we, thought you might tell us a little more." Perhaps offering something in return would entice her. "Laura said something about the risks of exposing bare shoulders, and of course she was - well."

"Decidedly not a conversation for your mother. It would distress her. Your ears are better. It is your job to let me know if someone is coming."

"Yes, Aunt Silvia." He leaned forward. "Please?"

"You know, I know Nell has explained, that there are various substances that can be applied to skin, or to food or drink. Some are harmless, bar a very unusual reaction."

"Like shellfish." Galen shivered. "I knew someone at school. It was a problem, given we were at Schola, on an island."

"Quite." His aunt continued, after a moment. "Some, of course, are designed to do specific things. Make one feel good, like Sunrise Cordial. Prolong the pleasant effects of alcohol. Other substances." Her tone got more prim. "I hope you have not tried those. Dangerous things, and people have no sense of proper laboratory technique."

Galen ducked his head, a little amused. "I have paid attention, Aunt Silvia." He paused, then mentioned, "Laura was a little caught up in the edges of the goldwasser mess."

"Oh, indeed? Would she be willing to talk about it, do you think? There's a paper about it that made no earthly sense, and I can't figure out why." His aunt in full intellectual mode was rather a stampede. Galen let her realise for herself that she'd got on a tangent. "Pardon. Do you think she'd mind?"

"I think she'd consider talking if you let her know why. That it wasn't just curiosity. It's a delicate subject and I haven't wanted to pry too much."

Aunt Silvia nodded. "So, there are in fact substances that can kill on contact. Or combinations of substances. I don't know what it was in this case, your father shut the conservatory up before I could see a thing."

"I heard a few things from Cook and Agnes?" Galen offered, as another token.

She leaned back. "Tell me, then." It was not quite an order, but it was so very close.

"They said - it was Millicent, the second housemaid, who found her. That she was very pale, her lips were blue, but it looked like there hadn't been a struggle or argument. That she was sitting peacefully in the chair."

"Thank you, dear boy." His aunt closed her eyes, steepling her hands for a moment, thinking. "There are quite a few things. Some developed during the War."

Galen caught a flicker of something in her eyes, and asked, "Something you know about specifically?"

She looked at him for a long moment, then said, "Not as mild as everyone thinks you are. Good. I always thought you ran deeper than that." She peered at him for a long moment. "I think the Dwellers might be good for you. Or at least having an interest in the larger world. A fondness for alchemy does run in the family, you could do more with that."

Galen wasn't sure what to make of that. Insult? Compliment. Definitely a break with his mother, at least, who disapproved of all those things. In the end, he leaned forward, and said, "Please?"

"Why do you want to know?"

"I'm worried Mother and Father are hiding something. And if they are, well, I want to know why they're hiding it from me."

Aunt Silvia nodded, considered matters for a moment, then said, "We're not the only people in the house. I suspect your parents are worried about Julius. You know why as well as I do. But I've caught a few glances, a word here or there."

Galen frowned. "That makes little sense. He never even met the woman. Did he?"

She shrugged. "Fears aren't sensible." Then she visibly decided something. "I did some work on various substances during the War. How to prevent their use, more than the other way around, but, oh, you can't do one without knowing something of the other. I was working on the Healer side, but of course we talked rather a lot to the alchemists, especially those coming up with newer methods." Her voice hitched for a moment.

"And this?"

"That she was peaceful, or as peaceful as I suspect that woman ever was. That suggests something like a two part application, or something with a very rapid paralytic effect."

"Pardon?" Galen was baffled by the terminology.

"That means it would have prevented her moving, even breathing. I don't suppose you know if her eyes were open or closed?"

Galen thought back. "Agnes said Millicent said they were open, but I think someone might have mentioned if she were visibly scared? And wouldn't you be scared if you couldn't move all of a sudden?"

It earned him a broad smile from his aunt. "Quite so, yes. Good point."

Galen frowned, then said. "Are there things that would make you - feel good? Or tired? Something that wouldn't make you struggle? And then slowly paralyse you? Take your breath."

Aunt Silvia nodded. "There are alchemic compounds,"

Galen heard steps and had to interrupt, though he entirely regretted it. "They're coming back."

"We have been talking about what you think of Laura," his aunt said. Her voice was crisp and even.

Galen took a breath, trying to figure out about where that conversation would be now. "I told her a bit about the house in Cumbria. And how I miss riding. And she seemed to like that. Her brother-in-law breeds horses now, he's restoring some of the stables after the War."

"Oh, that seems quite suitable, yes. Pity you can't take her out here, but there's no space. I'm sure we'd be glad to have her visit, and you, if you wanted to try that for an outing. Some other young people in the area, that sort of thing."

His mother opened the door before he could figure out what to say to that. Asking Laura to stay on was rather a specific escalation. He could only assume both Aunt Silvia and his mother approved of her, then. It was confirmed a moment later.

"We were talking, before you came in, about how charming Laura is, Galen. And I do hope you and she are getting along?"

Galen nodded, now decidedly off balance. "Don't - um. We're still getting to know each other, Mother, please don't rush things? But I do enjoy her company. And she seems very sensible, really. Realistic about what's involved."

"And not inclined to do away with the silverware." His aunt had not approved of Xanthippe. At all. Or for that matter Desdemona or Chryseis, both of whom his mother had suggested and introduced at various gatherings elsewhere.

Galen smiled. "No, certainly. Is Cook settled, Mother? It must be a challenge, not knowing how long it will be before we can leave? I mean, even once the Guard gets here, they'll want to talk to people. Or figure out where Basil Wilson is."

His mother made a very sour face. “Do stop that, Galen, dear. It’s not becoming.”

“It’s necessary, Mother, isn’t it? To figure something out?”

“Oh, I’m sure not. We just need to be patient. Some sort of medical fit, or something entirely innocent, I’m quite certain.”

Galen frowned. “But.”

His aunt cut him off. “Nell, darling, you know that they have to investigate. It’s standard procedure. Especially with so many different substances floating around, and people who don’t know what they’re doing experimenting. I know you don’t hold with it but there’s nothing to say one of those young people might have brought something in, and broken the portal taking it out again besides.”

His mother sat, with much less than her usual grace. “It’s entirely inconsiderate, is what I think. Dying in someone’s conservatory. We’re the ones with all the bother.”

It gave Aunt Silvia a chance to tut helpfully. “It will be better once the Guard gets here. Do you have any more news about when?”

“Not until at least this evening, possibly tomorrow. The storm’s quite bad, and apparently they want to send someone specific out, and whoever that is isn’t free until tomorrow morning at the earliest. So very tedious.”

Galen supposed that might well mean Lord Carillon had managed to intervene.

# TWENTY

## SATURDAY AFTERNOON

"Well. That doesn't make much sense."

Galen and Martin had met Laura at her room to escort her to lunch. The Amberlys were insistent that everything was normal, but the meal was awkward, the food a mix of party food that might spoil and things easy to prepare in the kitchen. Afterwards, it seemed like everyone went their own ways. The three had begun in the parlour, then as the sounds around them faded, eased their way to the doors between the ballroom and conservatory. Martin set out some small pebbles with warning charms, in case anyone came that way.

"Ready." Martin dusted his hands off and came over.

"Do you think she's..." Laura couldn't quite finish that sentence.

"Oswald said they moved her - the whole chair - out to the shed outside. Cool enough for preservation charms to take easily. I gather we aren't getting our Guard today. Tomorrow if we're lucky."

Laura frowned. "That will, well. It was rather an awkward lunch."

"Oh, I'm sure Mother will find some sort of distracting topic by supper time. Look, before lunch I got Aunt Silvia alone for a bit. She explained there are many different substances. She did some work on them during the War. And she mentioned alchemists kept coming up with more. But Mother came back before she say much."

"Well, that's no good." At times like this, Laura wished she had a better range of swears that suited both her and the situation.

Galen looked away for a moment. "If you're willing to talk about the goldwasser, I think she'd be very interested. I said if she wanted to learn about it, not just gossip, you might be willing."

Laura frowned, tapping her toe slightly on the floor as she thought. "Do you think she'd tell me more if I told her things?"

"That's, that's..."

Martin swooped in, grinning. "That's a brill idea." He then moved to ease the conservatory door open. "Here. We can at least look around."

Laura followed him, leaving Galen open-mouthed behind them.

"That's where the chair was." Martin indicated the spot, with a chalk line drawn around it. "Don't get too close. I don't know what kind of testing they'll want to do."

"What kind of testing can they do?" Laura frowned. "I don't know much about it."

"Oh, there're charms and devices that can tell you what things were newly added. I don't know all the details, but I've covered a few crime cases for the paper. Plants or oils or whatever. Not so much people, though if someone's wearing something very distinctive, it helps. I did an interview with someone who loved that women wear very distinctive perfumes. If you can isolate the fragrance notes, you can tell who was there. But all three of us were here that night at different times, so that won't matter here."

"Huh." Laura considered that, beginning to look around carefully at the raised beds and pots. "Also, I wear rather little scent."

Martin laughed at that. "You look there, see if you see anything unusual."

"Shouldn't Galen? It's his house, he'd notice something out of place."

"Galen, go look at the perimeter. You'll notice things there, the subtle parts."

Galen sketched a wave with his hand and went off.

"You do take charge, Martin." Laura said it quietly, not entirely sure what she thought of it.

"Sorry. Did I order you around? Galen knows to tell me if I'm too much."

She wasn't sure if it was too much or the right amount. She was finding his approach distracting, honestly, and she couldn't figure out why. It was pleasant to have something other than Galen's indecisiveness, though. "You did, but it's all right." That sounded weak, even to her. "What am I looking for?"

"Any subtle signs of a struggle, or anything dropped, or anything out of place."

Laura nodded, and began opposite of Martin, working clockwise around the small central area where the chair had been, careful to avoid that immediate space. "There's something here," she said, after a couple of minutes. "This leaf seems very shiny."

Martin came over, skirting the chalk lines. "You're right. That's much more than the one here, or here. Galen, do you know this plant?"

Galen looked up from where he was inspecting some small smudges by the outside door. "Hmmm?"

"Do you know this plant? Or why it's shiny? It looks almost like drops of oil spread out on it."

"That would imply some sort of - liquid?" Laura tried to think through the options.

"Aunt Silvia said some poisons have two parts. So there could be something in her drink, and something dropped on the skin."

"She wasn't at all careful about covering her shoulders."

"Why is that? I mean, it's only posh women who do that."

"It's only posh men who have access to the potions and such that can cause a woman problems." It came out sharply and Laura immediately wanted to hide.

"Hey," Martin turned. "Sorry. Sore spot?"

His kindness was more than she could bear, and she could only nod and turn away. He gave her the space, murmuring something to Galen, and the two of them went back to at least part of what they were doing. Two minutes later, she said "I had someone use something of the kind on me. Related to the goldwasser. One of that set."

Galen frowned, but she was startled to see Martin bristle. "You mean, you mean someone tried to take a thing should be gifted?"

She shook her head, something in the reaction unnerving her, how he rose so quickly to her defence. She wasn't at all sure how to answer him, because things were more complicated than that. If she were to marry Galen, that was a conversation he deserved to have in private.

Finally, she said outright, "I'd rather talk about it in private." Then, trying to recover her wits, she added, "I'm not at all sure how to have that conversation with both of you at the same time."

Galen reached for her hand, letting her place her fingers in his. "We shan't press, Laura. It would be quite rude."

She squeezed back, then said, briskly. "So what are our plans? If the Guard can't get here until tomorrow?"

"We hope tomorrow." Galen agreed.

"We have a few hints. Maybe we can ask your Aunt Silvia, whoever gets a chance, Galen, about the oiliness? That's got to be unusual."

Laura nodded. "If she wants to talk to me, I can try it. Though not with your mother around, Galen."

"I think they may go up and see Julius tonight. Aunt Silvia thought they were being more - worried than usual."

Martin raised his chin, then, a signal that meant something to Galen, but not to her.

Galen just continued on. "No formal withdrawing room, or anything. Especially if you look like you'll be fine with us. Aunt Silvia won't go with them, so that might be an excellent time."

She took a breath. "Oh, I think I can manage that. What about your uncle?"

"Oh, he'll go off and have a cigar, but Aunt Silvia hates the things, and we don't smoke. Well, much."

Martin snorted at Galen's comment. "Rarely. I don't have the budget for it."

Laura looked Martin up and down. "And you spend it other places?" she suggested.

"That too. Books, mostly. Typewriter paper. Ink."

She nodded. "And you, Galen?"

He looked up, startled. "Oh. Books, too. Different books. Various projects. I get an allowance from my parents, plus anything that I can justify as learning about the estates and their possible issues."

They seemed to have come to a dead end, and Laura closed her eyes, then said. "What else do we do now?"

"Keep looking around that corner, would you? Over near the ballroom entry, we haven't done that yet."

Laura nodded, then stopped, peering into a pot. "There seems to be something here. A small jar?"

Martin came over, careful to avoid touching it. "That looks like some sort of powder. Huh. I hope there's a way to point that out to the Guard."

"Do you - what will it be like?"

"You're the one that wrote asking for specific help from them. Haven't you met some?"

"A few. Captain Lefton and her husband - he consults for the Guard? But I don't think she does murders, I didn't recognise the names he mentioned, so it's not people he knows socially? Or at least would invite socially?" There were distinct classes and groups at play, and she wasn't quite sure how to explain it to Martin, or to Galen. They seemed, if anything, rather naive about details like that, the nuances of the invitations.

"Will you be all right? It has to be rather awful for you. We're all strangers. And who knows who did this."

Laura paused, then retreated to a bench well away from the scene of the crime. "I've had plenty of experience being in difficult situations."

"When you were abroad?"

She nodded, trying to figure out how to explain. "It involved a lot of being at someone else's mercy. Having to hope they'd be decent. A nurse for a glass of water, or to fix a problem, or sometimes even bring a book or change the music. Doctors for all sorts of things, and sometimes they'd sweep in, look at you for a minute, and sweep out, declaring some, some, some terrifying new treatment." She hated how she stammered at that.

"That sounds..." Galen frowned. "That sounds like nothing I know about. Not really. So I won't pretend I do."

She offered him a weak smile.

"So this is like that? You don't have too much choice?" Martin's comment was sharper, more precise.

Laura nodded. "Make do and mend." Neither of them had much to say to that.

# TWENTY-ONE

## SATURDAY TEATIME

After their investigation of the conservatory, they had retreated back to the parlour. Martin was trying to figure out how to get Galen on his own for a little, when Agnes came to ask Laura what she'd like laid out to wear for supper. It had given Martin a chance to share the gossip about Julius and Senara from the party, at least.

Galen had grimaced, but Martin knew not to push him, not just yet. Galen would chew on it, privately. Rather than try and find some other topic of conversation, Galen had gone to take Laura off for a quiet tea. He could be pleasant and charming and harmless for hours on end, after all, so long as Martin hadn't mucked that up for him.

Martin had other work. He made his way down to the kitchen and knocked on the edge of the door.

"Sir?"

Martin waved a hand. "Cook, pardon. But I realised you might be a bit short, today, after the party. Could I lend a bit of strength to any devices down here?" He smiled, the most charming smile he'd learned from his mother and from

Galen. "And maybe get a bit more sturdy tea than I'd get upstairs?"

He watched her think it through. His magic, his energy, instead of one of the footmen. Which would leave them less tired tomorrow, spread the load out.

"Oh, aren't you thoughtful, sir. We are running low on the stoves, with all the cooking for last night. And people staying on here and expecting to stay longer and who knows how many Guard and they do eat. If it's not a bother, sir. That stove, and perhaps the keep-cool? The footmen are getting a nice meat pie for tea today, nice and filling, and I made spare from the last of the party roast meats."

Martin nodded, at Cook and then the two footmen who were working on cleaning shoes at a table in the hall. He settled his hands on the burnished metal plates of the stove. Taking a breath, he opened a door to his magic, letting it flow out. His mother described it as water flowing downstream, his sister as a breath of air, blowing leaves away.

He had never talked about it with Galen. Galen had never needed to fuel a stove with bits of himself and never would. Martin took a deep breath, then another, feeling the stove begin to fill. There was the little purr under his fingers until everything smoothed out and went quiet. "Definitely enough for the keep-cool, Cook, if you're feeding me up."

She nodded, indicating a long wooden box, one with several cabinet doors that opened up. Quite large for a household this size, though with their regular parties, that would be needed for everything from fruit to sherbets.

It was easier, this time, cooling was less work in this season, more efficient, and he rather thought someone had renewed this within the past few days. Only when it too had fallen still under his hands did he remove them, rubbing his palms together automatically to seal the edges of his magic.

"Come along, Oswald, Willet." The two footmen had finished their tasks, and had been leaning on the wall in the hallway, but they straightened and came upright. The housemaids came in from the other side. This was obviously the sort of household where the butler and housekeeper dined in separate splendour with the valet and lady's maid.

"Master Martin's been most generous with his energy. Sparing you, Willet." That was to the younger footman.

Oswald sniffed slightly. Martin knew it was not his place to be down here, as a guest of the house. On the other hand, he felt much more comfortable away from Galen's people, among the sort he had known as a child. Everything was more substantial, below stairs, not just the food. Below stairs had its own rules and decorum, but there were so many fewer tight little smiles that tried to brush away all unpleasantness, or the sniffs that marked him as entirely out of place and not worth anyone's time. "A pleasure." he said, "Cook, the pie smells fantastic."

There were little ones, for each of them. Nothing complicated, just crust and scraps of beef from last night's carved roast and vegetables, and a thick gravy, but it was well made. Sandwiches, for the maids, which suggested the division of labour in the household. Not that cleaning and laundry wasn't quite a lot of work.

As he expected, it was Oswald who asked, after the food was served, "Master Martin, you have some familiarity below stairs?"

"My mother was a nursemaid, before she married." It sounded simple, but he knew and they knew it wasn't as simple as that. "I was fortunate to do well on the exams, go to the same school as Galen, or I'd likely have ended up in service too. My father's an accountant, but I've no head for that kind of thing."

No one was quite sure what to say to that for a minute, then Cook said, "So you know what it's like, to make everything run smoothly?"

Martin did his best impression of Galen's charm. "Oh, I know I only have the barest glimpse, but I do know about renewing the magics. I do it for the newspaper presses, sometimes, when they need a bit extra. Or my mother's kitchen, of course. It's a kindness."

"Do you see her often?" It was a polite question, if a somewhat daring one.

Martin nodded. "My parents have a small house in Trellech, my father works there. I'm more often based in London at the moment." His father had worked his way up, which Martin respected no end.

There was a little quiet chatter, then Martin ventured, "It's rather odd to be here as things are. I hope it hasn't made it too difficult for you?"

Oswald looked at him, a moment of piercing attention, enough to make Martin wonder about the cause. Then he said, his voice rather clipped, "Did the family ask you to inquire?"

"Galen and I were talking about it. The challenges. The party and then having to sort everything out." He nodded at Agnes. "He said he was glad to hear that Miss Penhallow wasn't an added challenge."

Agnes ducked her head. "Most considerate, she is." There was a tiny pause, then Agnes said "Not wanting to speak out of turn, sir, but do you know Master Galen's thoughts on her?"

Martin smiled broadly. "They're still getting to know each other, but she's been clear she likes it here, and finds him agreeable. It's early for that kind of talk yet, but she's quite ..."

He paused, trying to find an appropriate word. Not fierce. Not passionate. Not decisive. Though those were the things that popped into his head. There was something about her focus, where her attention went, that he found compelling. "Quite interested in the place, and his family, and what he cares about. We took her down along the beach, yesterday. And I think Madam Amberly finds her quite agreeable."

"Sir." Agnes subsided into a pleased silence.

Martin nodded and let the conversation ebb and flow around him. As the various servants finished and took their roles cleaning up, he asked, "Willet, could I have a word before I go back upstairs?"

Willet glanced at Cook for approval, and she waved a hand. "We've time, and the supper isn't complicated upstairs tonight. You've twenty minutes without causing a bother."

Martin stood. "Thank you for a lovely meal, Cook. And for your hospitality."

As he withdrew to find the bench in the hallway, he heard the murmur of "There's a lovely sense of manners for you."

Willet followed him out. "I know Galen's checked with Oswald, but - is there anything you saw last night that the family should know about, Willet? Or that you're not sure about telling?" He might as well be blunt. He'd seen Willet in action long enough to know that where Oswald tended to be sly, Willet was solid and unyielding.

There was a long pause as Willet visibly weighed the options in his head. "I didn't like moving her, sir, but the Master insisted. Said leaving her in the conservatory wouldn't be good. But aren't you supposed to leave a person where they die, for the Guard to look at?"

"I'd heard that too, but the moving was done before we had time to say anything." Martin paused for a moment, then said, "Did you notice anything particular?"

"You know about Master Julius." It wasn't at all a question. "I bring his trays up, and Millicent sees to his rooms while Master Julius is in his study. The master asked if I'd seen anything out of place. And I hadn't, but then I worried why they were asking. But he's always been very kind, Master Julius has, the few times he's spoken to me."

Martin frowned, then nodded. "I can see why you'd wonder. I'll see if there's anything to it." He considered, then said, "Were you seeing to Basil Wilson before the party?"

"Yes, sir. Now, that was a man I'm glad to be rid of, if you don't mind me saying so."

"You're sure he's gone, then?"

"If he's hidden about the house he's done a right good job of it, sir. I went about with a stick, earlier, to poke in the storerooms to see if I could scare him up, but not hide nor hair to be found. If he took a walk after the party, drunk as he was he probably fell off the cliff." He paused, then offered, "I thought to go have a look when the storm lets up, sir."

"If you don't mind, and they can spare you. It would help the Guard, I'm sure." He could not shake the oddness of the gossip about the man, could not imagine him as a rake about town at all. "I didn't get that much sense of him, honestly. His sister rather drowned him out, sun to his moon." A rather more literal drowning also seemed plausible, he did admit.

"As you say, sir. But he ..." Willet paused again,

searching for words. "The way he looked wasn't like how he was. His bags were very tidy and there were things he wouldn't let me see. Which isn't how things are done, sir, I'm sure you know." There was something earnest about him now.

"All of his things, or just some of them?"

"He had a smaller case, sir, he wouldn't let me see. And he unpacked his clothing, sir, himself. Not just the usual sort of locked compartment in the trunk, like you have, for the personal things."

"Can I ask - I heard some gossip that suggested he used to be quite the centre of things socially. Did he, were his clothes like that?"

"I didn't get a good look at most of it, sir, but I did see waistcoats and cravats and such that were - not what he was wearing here. Bright, some of them."

"But not here." Martin shook his head and rather thought Basil was playing up being a sober man of business. "But not letting you see to his clothing, that's definitely not how things are done, no." Also rather definitely a sign of someone with something to hide. "How did he treat you? Abruptly? Well? Poorly?"

Willet frowned, thinking. "He's the sort of man I would have thought would want a bit of information, sir. Many people do, asking how the household runs, where things are, what the usual routine is. But he didn't want any of that, and when I tried to offer, he dismissed me. He went to talk to his sister, I think, in the sitting room they shared."

Martin nodded. Then, there was a call of "Willet, they need more wood upstairs."

Willet ducked his head. "Sir. Perhaps later, sir?"

"Of course. You have duties. Thank you." There was nothing else for it but retreat.

## TWENTY-TWO

### SATURDAY TEATIME

Galen had come by, after Agnes had gone off to her other duties. The knock on her door had startled her, but when she had opened the door, there was Galen, earnest. "Would you care to have tea with me? Down in the library?"

She had nothing better to do and sitting alone with her book did not appeal. Besides, she was here to get to know Galen better. "Won't someone expect us?"

"Everyone else is elsewhere." He made a vague gesture. "I can get someone to bring a tray up."

"Of course. Please." Laura then smiled. "I've not seen the library yet."

"It's grand! Not one of the big public rooms. You like books? I mean, some books?" He almost fell over himself explaining.

She bent to retrieve her shawl from the chair, before joining him at the door again. "I like rather a lot of kinds of books, actually. I had all those years when reading was the most exciting thing they permitted me in a day, remember?"

He held out his arm, inviting her to tuck her hand into

his, then led her off and back downstairs. This time, it was to a room facing the courtyard, lined with bookshelves, with a comfortable sofa and chairs. Once she was settled on the sofa, he rang the bell will the great hanging bellpull by the door, and then came to sit down beside her.

"You didn't mind being pulled away?"

She nodded. "Agnes was very thoughtful. Figuring out what to wear that would suit a more - somber evening."

Before he could say anything, there was a prompt knock at the door, and Agnes brought in the tray, setting it on the long low table. "Is there anything else, sir?"

"No, thank you, Agnes." he said. "If anyone asks, we're in here, but I'd rather not be disturbed for a bit?"

"Of course, sir. Your parents and the Tipsons are upstairs, and we'll make certain Master Martin is seen to."

"Thank you." She withdrew, closing the door behind her.

"Will there be gossip in the servant's quarters?" Laura asked.

"Oh, perhaps." he said, amused. "They seem to like you, though. And I - well. I think everyone would feel better if I married."

Laura was quiet for a long moment, then she said. "Everything changed for you, and yet..." She frowned. "I knew someone, up north, Yorkshire, I think. His older brother died, and he said he at least he knew what he was supposed to do, if he could. Step up, become the eldest son. Take on all those roles. But with you, it's not quite the same, is it?"

Galen let out a little sigh. "I'm glad you understand." He reached for her hand, uncertainly, and she moved to offer it to him.

"People don't?"

His hand was still around hers for a long moment, then he squeezed. "No, they don't. They assume they know. That it's like other deaths or illnesses or whatever. And it isn't, not at all."

"The distance, between. Do you - do you talk with him much?"

Galen shook his head. "He - his injuries make talking tiring for him. Difficult. And our parents," He frowned. "Our parents discourage it." He turned away from her, like he wasn't sure what to let her see. A very delicate point, then.

Laura tilted her head. "Were you close, before?"

He moved a little, instinctively closer to her. She squeezed his hand again, unsure what else to offer. "There's quite a few years between us. I can't say - I can't say close, but he was always..." He could not finish the sentence, but she could fill in the gaps.

Laura considered, then said, "Sit closer, if you like?" Then, she risked. "Like looking at the pole star. You looked to him."

There was a long pause, in which no one moved, and then he shifted, offering an arm, and she leaned against him. Only when they'd moved did he say "I'm used to being on my own. So much younger. I mean, I studied alchemy because of him? To be like him? I'm not very good at it, but it's fascinating. And then, when I was in school, he came home from the War, and he was hurt and he..." His voice trailed off.

"Oh." She wasn't sure what to say to that. At all.

They sat in silence for a good minute before he asked, "Your sister. How is it with her? For you?"

"It was hard for a long time. I was ill, and she got to go and do things. I had Mama with me, and Mama was wonderful. She never said a word about being away from Papa, or Lizzie."

"And Lizzie?"

"Oh, she wrote. She'd travel with Papa and Uncle Kenver sometimes, when they were doing trips somewhere safe enough. A lot of docks, a lot of ports, they're not very appropriate places, for young women. And expeditions are, well." Her voice trailed off.

Galen shifted his arm, holding her a little closer. "They're not safe, expeditions. Plenty of things aren't safe."

Laura nodded. "I think Mama had rules about it. What things Lizzie could go on. I don't know if Lizzie realised."

"And now?"

"Oh, there's more there." Laura paused, thinking back. The distance. "Mama died, and then Papa and Uncle Kenver didn't come home, didn't end up anywhere we know of. And we had less and less money. So Lizzie decided she had to find work. A decent position, enough to keep the house from falling down."

"And you?"

"Oh, I couldn't let her do it alone. Even though I don't have much in the way of skills. But I insisted, and someone offered me a position, the office girl. A new business, a small one. Simple correspondence, welcoming visitors to the office." She paused, and her voice turned dry. "Being pretty."

"Did..." Galen hesitated for a moment. "Did someone take advantage?"

Laura shook her head. "Not - there. That was Tiberius Morland. Tibbie. He's in gaol now. For a long time."

"The goldwasser?" Galen's voice had got softer.

"That. And he'd introduced me to the younger set of the people involved. The people who were supposed to get it shared around. Get people addicted to it. And oh, it is addictive." She couldn't help but shiver, remembering what it was like, and then what it was like not to have it, to know she'd never get it again.

"Complicated?" He was more measured now, careful, as if he were holding something very fragile. She realised, all of a sudden, that he must worry she were the fragile thing in need of protection.

"Better now," she said firmly. "Without getting stuck in a bog about that, Lizzie was talking to me more. Because she was worried and fussing, partly, but we sorted a lot out, eventually. And then she invited me to things, with Carillon."

"You call him that, his family name?"

Laura smiled. "She calls him Geoffrey. I still can't manage it. But she needed help organising, and figuring out seating charts at parties, and who was who. And that sort of thing I turn out to be quite good at once I have the information I need."

Galen nodded, then returned the favour. "I remember Julius spending a lot of time in his laboratory. When I was really good, and promised to stay right where he put me, he let me watch. All the glass jars and tubes and the crucible and the heat and the smells." He inhaled more deeply. He was brooding about something, but the memories seemed pleasant ones.

"You liked that?"

"Oh, yes." It was immediate and warm. "I felt included. Not too young. Unexpected son. Spare. Unneeded. A little brother tagging along."

"It was like that with me, too. I thought Lizzie didn't need me. Didn't want me. Why should she, she had her own life, it had wonderful things in it."

Galen frowned, chewing on his lip for a moment, an utterly undignified expression. "What was it like, changing?"

"Terrifying." The word came out before she could stop it. "And I was - I was drunk on the goldwasser, giddy with it. It made you dream of exotic things. Far-off places. Things I'd never had, and she had. So I hated that she was telling me not to. Hated she'd had that chance, some of them. And she wasn't letting me. So I was all - angry and small and shouty in my head."

He shifted to look at her. "You don't seem the type."

"It wasn't good for me." It came out dry and a bit sharp.

He ducked his head, then leaned forward. "May I?" he asked. She realised all of a sudden that he would like to kiss her, and she inhaled, then said "Yes."

He pressed his lips to hers, a chaste kiss, something gentle and soothing rather than fierce and passionate. She wasn't at all sure what to do with this. It wasn't like Tourney had been, all charm turning to roaming hands and possessive kisses. This gave her space. She returned it, gently, then drew back slightly, to watch him.

Galen's eyes were closed, but then he smiled, relaxing. "You're lovely." It came out quietly. "And you've - had a hard time of it. Ways I don't understand at all. But you're willing to tell me."

"You seem surprised." Her voice had got just as soft, like they both needed to whisper.

"People don't let me in. Martin. The Dwellers. They do. Not other people. Mother - Mother thinks I'm flighty and childish. Aunt Silvia doesn't, but Mother doesn't always listen to her."

There was a moment when she could see things, how a

door pivots on a hinge, two paths in a maze. "Give your brother a chance. For my sake. And Lizzie's. Please?"

He drew back at that, though he didn't drop her hand. "What if, what if it doesn't work?" It came out half-stammered.

"Then you'll know you tried." She tried to sound as confident as she could. "Otherwise, I think you'll keep wondering."

# TWENTY-THREE

## SATURDAY EVENING

Later that evening, after supper, Galen made his way to the back wing. Martin and Laura had conspired between them to get his aunt whisking Laura away to discuss her experience with the goldwasser. Martin was occupying his parents and uncle with something else.

He wasn't sure what to expect, it had been so long. Faced with the door, Galen took a deep breath, and knocked.

"Not tonight, mother. Not again." The voice inside was a bit muffled, uneven, but that was what his brother sounded like now. Even that was something of a relief to hear. He was certain with the utter conviction of a younger brother that his brother was not mad, but again and again he had come back to wondering if that was childishness. Surely he was kept away for a reason, after all. That voice did not sound like a man out of his mind, he was certain of it.

"It's Galen, Julius." He stopped. He should have thought of what to say before he got here. "I - I wanted to talk to you. With you." It sounded utterly feeble.

There was a long pause, a terribly long pause. Galen had almost decided to retreat downstairs, no matter what Martin might say about his courage. Or Laura, which would probably be worse.

Finally, he heard the voice again. "It's open."

Galen turned the handle, feeling it give under his fingers. When he opened the door, he saw the small sitting room, a glimpse of the laboratory in the next room through the open door. Julius was standing by the door, leaning against the frame. He had the ceramic mask on, the white unmoving surface stark against the darker wood behind him.

He cleared his throat and again cursed a lack of preparation. Finally, he said. "Are you all right? Just. I didn't know if anyone had told you." It came out in a tumble, earnest, and making him sound like a puppy.

The mask hid so much of Julius's expression, but something in his eyes was tremendously complex. "Told me." And then more quickly, "Thought they wouldn't?" that was feeling out something new and unexpected. "Sit."

It came out like an order, but this was Julius, and he was glad to obey. Galen glanced around, found one of the chairs. Faded, they'd been in the parlour in Cumbria before they moved here, he remembered the print. He perched on the edge of one and then nodded again. "I wasn't sure." Then it slipped out of him before he could stop himself. "They don't tell me much."

"Huh." It was a rough sound, echoing oddly. Julius came over, walking with the slight limp he'd picked up with his greater injuries. He settled in the chair he'd clearly claimed as his own, half facing the window. "What did they say?" Like all his words, they were carefully spaced, parcelled out as if each movement were precious.

"I don't think Mother liked Senara at all. Father invited her, but he wouldn't explain why. And I'm confused." Oh, he wanted to be less confused. To feel less like the baby of the family, never told anything.

"So you came here?" It was almost disbelieving, as much as that careful spaced and muffled voice could be.

"Laura said I should."

"Laura?" That was harder for him to say, there was a burr there, an odd sound.

Galen took a breath and said "Laura is one of the people Mother has invited, to see if we might marry. Um. Continue the family, that kind of thing."

There was a long pause, then a rougher "Mother has ideas," that was decidedly disapproving.

"Some of her guests have been pretty horrid. One tried to steal the silver plate. And another was just awful. Rude and small-minded and unpleasant."

"Laura?" The name was not easier the second time, but Galen could see his brother was determined.

Mind, the question made him shy. Very shy. "I like her. She's kind. Thoughtful. She listens. She shares what she's thinking. I think she likes me? She let me kiss her." He was aware then how painfully young he sounded, like a schoolboy with his first infatuation, not a grown man considering marriage.

His brother just nodded, and there was a long silence. Finally, he said. "Senara?" The R caused him the same problem, but there was more sharpness to his tone.

"She was very brash. Very sharp and showy. She was rude to Mother, and trying to be nice to me in a sort of, um..." He was still not sure how to describe how she had made him feel, the way he loved the attention and didn't want it from her. "And she was sort of smarmy to Father, and rather awful to Laura at supper, and taking up, Martin says it's taking up all the space."

"Martin?"

"My friend. My best friend. We were Dwellers together."

"Tall. Dark." A pause, then a "Not well off."

Galen nodded. "His parents are - his father does accounts. His mum was a nursemaid, before she met his father. Lots of her family in service. Not the sort of people Mother thought I should associate with. Several ways around, for all he doesn't talk politics where she can hear him. But he's a great friend. He - he makes me better. Braver. Smarter. More thoughtful. I don't deserve him, but I try to."

"Huh." Again, that small grunt of a noise. "He - what did he think of Senara."

Galen considered how to phrase this, how much to say, and then decided to share all. "She propositioned him, asked him to meet her in her bedroom. For, I presume, the kind of things people get up to in bedrooms."

"She was like that." It was a bit grudging. "Good at it. But dangerous." He seemed to be weighing something, but Galen couldn't figure out how to ask what it was.

"He got that sense. But he thought he might learn something more. And he's got experience enough to -" He paused. "More than me."

"Mother trying to marry you off. Not bachelor?"

"I like women. I just get very ... confused by them." Galen said after a minute. "And I - I don't want to go to bed with people I don't know. It doesn't make sense to me."

It earned him another grunt. "Huh." Then he added "Sorry. Obligations fell on you." He gestured at himself, a sweep of his hand.

There was silence for a long stretch, and Galen felt more and more uncertain. "It's all right I came up to talk to you?"

"Kind." There was another pause, but this time he could see Julius was trying to decide about something. Work up to something. "I knew Senara. In the War."

That was not at all what Galen expected, even with Martin warning him about the gossip. "Do you think that's what she told Father?"

"Expect so. He didn't say."

"What," No, that was a bad sentence. What was she like. And did you sleep with her, that was worse. "Will they want to ask you questions?"

Julius snorted. "Likely. Father was afraid. That. That I did it."

"Did you?" It came out before Galen could stop himself. Aunt Silvia had been talking about alchemical poisons, and the lab was right there in all of its suddenly menacing potential.

There was a laugh. It was odd sounding, resonance in the wrong spaces, but it ended in a broad chuckle. "No. Might have, years ago."

Galen swallowed, trying to reassure himself that a laugh like that wasn't a sign of questionable sanity, then he said, "What do I need to know, Julius? So I, so I don't make things worse for someone."

Julius gave him a long look, as if measuring him. Galen was sure he wasn't measuring up, but he sat still, took a deep breath, willed himself to be patient. A minute passed, he thought. Maybe two. Finally, there was a gesture. "Lab."

This was another surprise, but he stood, watching Julius for guidance. His brother went to the door, then opened it. "Follow." In the next room were broad tables, topped with marble, with all sorts of alchemical bottles and jars and appliances. A crucible here, a small cauldron over a low flame there.

"Table."

At the back, away from the devices and glass, was a large desk, with a chair on one side, a stool on the other. "Should I sit?" He hadn't been in a lab other than Thomasina's, with the Dwellers, in years, not since school, and he missed it every time, the tang of the chemicals, the coolness of the glass. Mother had disapproved, both silently and at times volubly, at the idea he would spend time that way, and eventually he'd given up on trying.

"Stool." Julius went to a bookshelf behind the stool, bending, and Galen could hear his laboured breathing now they were close. Close enough to touch, not that he would, not without being told it was all right. That was the thing his parents had impressed on him, how badly Julius had been hurt, and how he would never mend.

What Julius set in front of him was a scrapbook, full of photos and clippings. He set it on the table, then thumbed through several pages, before stopping. "There." It was a photography of Julius as he had been, and Senara. Galen thought it might be Paris, from the buildings behind her.

"You knew her well?" She had her arm around Julius, she was laughing. And she looked much less hard and sharp and awful than she had when Galen met her, though the way she leaned, that was very much like how she had been at the window.

"Six months. Dancing. Bed. Breakfast. All of it." The words came out short and spaced.

"What happened?" It was like watching something awful about to happen and knowing you couldn't turn away.

"Accused her. Spying. Had good reason." It sounded so improbable Galen could only blink, looking from the photograph to his brother. Nothing helped him sort through it, neither the stillness of the mask nor the oddly calm eyes behind it.

"Was she?"

"Never tried." He sounded terribly tired, now. His brother took the scrapbook, running a finger down the photograph for just a moment before snapping it shut. "Wonder if she wanted..." His voice trailed off.

"Wanted?"

"Confession. Absolution. She - religious, once. As a child."

"Why would she come to you?"

"Not many left."

There was a gaping chasm there, now, somehow Galen had asked a completely wrong thing, he could see it, hear it in the abyss of a silence. He shuddered, then said "I didn't mean to, I'll go."

"No." There was a hand, all of a sudden, on his shoulder. "Don't."

It was the second word that did it, that brought Galen's eyes up, like the strongest compulsion charm. His brother was right there, in front of him. Hand on his shoulder, something sturdy. This was the brother who had given him rides on his back, who had played with him, who had taught him to ride, once upon a time. This was his brother, still there, and he felt himself settle into a clear, pure faith that Julius was still in his right mind, and, therefore, innocent.

"Will you tell them?" Their parents, Galen assumed.

"That I saw you? No. That you told me? No." Galen squared his shoulders, feeling the weight of the hand shift against him.

"Anyone else?" Julius was leaning in slightly, meeting his eyes, searching them.

"They're sending a Guard. A serious one, not Trevallen. Laura's brother-in-law knows someone. Or was going to make sure they sent the right sort of someone."

"Who?"

"Ca...." He paused. "Lord Carillon. Married her sister a few months ago. Did you know him?"

"Reputation." It came out more quietly. "Tell the Guard. Private. Don't let Mother fuss about it. She'll," There was a long pause. "Better not."

Galen let out a long breath. "Thank you. I'd lie for you."

"Lie badly. Safer to tell the truth. In the right ear."

He nodded, then said "I will."

His brother looked at him then patted his shoulder, before releasing it. "Go now. But - come visit. Again?" It seemed to offer something Julius hadn't said yet. That he was working up to.

Galen looked up, startled, then he nodded in turn. "I will. Promise. Show me some of your work, maybe?" It was that, the memory of his brother's eyes, before he left, that he'd treasure for a long time, the surprise and pleasure and agreement.

# TWENTY-FOUR

## SUNDAY MORNING

The butler appeared at the parlour doorway. "Captain FitzRanulf is here, madam, with two Guards. They say, pardon, they say the sailboats are gone in the storm, there's wreckage on the rocks near the dock." They had finished breakfast and most of the household were awkwardly gathered. Laura had a book she was barely reading, and Galen and Martin were playing cards in a very desultory manner. His mother was doing some sort of puzzle with his aunt, and his uncle and father had disappeared into the library. The news about the boats got barely a ripple of reaction, as if it were one more blow on people already entirely numb.

"Captain FitzRanulf. I'm Parnell Amberly. Jacobs, would you let Cassian and Attis know, please?" He nodded and moved out of the way, letting everyone get a clear look at the captain.

Laura had met a couple of captains in the Guard through Lizzie and her husband, but Captain FitzRanulf was not like them. She had hair that was already going silver, pulled back severely from her face into a tight bun, and a sharply tailored uniform. Good wool, Laura realised, but not the fine privately woven stuff that some of the more well-off captains wore. Her posture was entirely in control of herself, sharp, even a bit defensive.

A moment later, the butler brought the men in from the library.

"Good morning. I am Captain Hippolyta FitzRanulf, assigned to this case. I have Guard Margh Trevallen, the local Guardsman, with me, and Guard Ulric Ames, a specialist in these cases. Kindly introduce me to your household and guests, Madam Amberly?" It was all said with a crisp politeness that had no yield to it at all.

"My husband, Cassian. This is our home. Silvia, his sister, and her husband, Attis Tipson. Retired Healer. Our son, Galen. His friend, Martin Taylor. Laura - pardon, Lorelai Penhallow, a guest."

"And you also had Senara and Basil Wilson as guests?"

"Yes, Captain." Madam Amberly's voice was smooth, almost easy. "We do not know what happened to Basil. No one here has seen him since his sister's body was discovered. We had two boats that could do a crossing to the mainland or larger islands, but I gather they are missing? And of course the portal is not available." She paused, and added. "I believe the footmen had a look around the cliff paths, one of them can show where they've looked already."

That earned her a nod, then a "I will need a private space to speak to each person here, including every member of your staff. Guard Ames will need to see the place where the body was discovered, and the body. I assume you have not moved anything."

The Amberlys had the grace to look embarrassed. "I'm afraid we did, but with levitation charms that Attis said would leave the least trace. The conservatory gets quite warm during the day, even in November, and it's quite close to the kitchens. The smell, you understand, the nature."

There was a long pause, and Laura rather thought the captain was repressing an entirely unprofessional set of swears. "Trevallen, assist Ames for the moment, please. Ames, I'd appreciate an initial report as soon as possible."

She then tapped her foot on the floor, just once, allowing the frustration to break through for an instant. "Who else is in the household?" She said it like someone who knew a large household in and out.

"At the moment? Besides our guests, there is Blythe, my companion. Our butler, housekeeper, and cook. A valet and lady's maid. Two housemaids, two footmen, a kitchenmaid, two gardeners who live in cottages nearer the docks."

Mr Amberly coughed. "And our eldest son, Julius. He was badly injured in the War and keeps to his rooms at the top of the house."

"I will need to speak to him as well." It came out just as firm.

Laura could see the Amberlys wanting to argue, wanting to deny it, but after a moment Madam Amberly nodded. "As you wish. We'd ask you to go up to him, if you don't mind. But for the rest, we are glad to turn over the library to your use, or any other suitable room."

"The library will do. Miss Penhallow, I'd like to speak to you first, please. Someone will fetch you when I am settled, but it may be a few minutes."

Laura nodded, and said, "Of course, Captain. I'm glad to help."

There was a long pause, then a slight click of heels together, as the captain strode out of the room, the two Guards following.

"Goodness. Not the sort of person I thought we'd get at all."

"There was some story about her, her family." Silvia tapped her fingernails on the table, the slight clicking sounding loud. "A good family, but she must be a byblow connection somehow, given the name," Galen and Martin left their cards and came over to join Laura on the couch.

"Will you be all right? Did your brother-in-law say anything about her?"

"No, just wrote that they were sending someone competent, and to do my best to help her with information. That might be why she's starting with me? I don't know."

Martin frowned. "You give a yell if there's a problem, all right?"

"Do you know something I don't?"

Martin shook his head. "No, just that there are Captains and Captains, and I don't know which sort she is." He was about to say more, but at that point, there was a sharp cough at the door.

Jacobs was waiting. "Captain FitzRanulf is ready for you, miss."

Laura stood, leaving her book on the table, and said, "Thank you, Jacobs," before following him along to the library. He left her at the door with a "Miss Penhallow, Captain, and I will have the supplies brought up."

Captain FitzRanulf had claimed a large table at the back, sitting on one side of it with a chair on the other. The lamps were angled to light the space rather starkly. "Please sit." It was cordial enough. "I understand you're related to Geoffrey Carillon?" Fascinating, there was no title there.

"Yes, Captain. He is my brother-in-law, he married my sister in September. I've spent quite some time at Ytene over the past year."

"And you wrote to him, asking for help here." It wasn't a question. "Why?"

Laura settled herself, folding her hands in her lap. "It seemed a very queer sort of situation, captain." Which was true. "The Wilsons were out of place here, rather noticeably so. I thought there was something more complex about it. Beyond the scope of Guard Trevallen, though I understand he's well-respected in the region."

"How well do you know the family?"

"Not terribly well. I'd seen Galen in passing at a party or two, and his mother liked me. She invited me here to see if we became," Laura stopped and blushed. "She would like Galen to marry, and she thought he and I might find each other suitable."

"So you have no particular loyalty, no strong one, at least, yet? But you have the benefit of being outside eyes."

"Yes, ma'am. I mean Captain."

There was a slight nod at the correction. "And of knowing what is usual in a house like this. Which not everyone does."

"That too, Captain." Laura let out a breath, then said, "How many I be of help?"

It earned her a small smile. "Carillon commends your observation skills. I would like a precis of the people in the house, as fairly as you can manage."

"Madam Amberly has been very kind to me. She is clearly attentive to how the household runs. She did not invite the Wilsons and has been confused at best by their behaviour. Her husband is more a patriarch, a bit distant from the day-to-day affairs. He has spent most of his time with his brother-in-law."

"That is Attis Tipson, yes?"

"Yes, I didn't speak much with him. More with Madam

Tipson, of course, withdrawing after supper. They were both kind to include me, but it was the usual sort of social chatter with people you don't know well. All of us avoiding topics that might be sensitive or complicated. Though I did talk to Madam Tipson privately about something that isn't related, later."

"Avoiding topics. Like the eldest son?"

Laura grimaced. "Yes, rather. They don't talk about him. I gathered from Galen and Martin that Galen's parents visit Julius daily, or nearly so, but that they discouraged Galen from doing so." She paused, and then said "I should tell you, captain, that Galen went to speak to his brother last night. At my urging."

"Why did you do that?"

"I spent a number of years resenting my sister." If she were going to be honest, there should be honesty. "I found my life better, in several ways, when we figured out a new way to interact, to be together."

She looked up to catch a flicker of expressions across the captain's face, unreadable, but visible. In a woman with such rigid self-control, that was baffling.

"And Martin Taylor?"

"A longtime friend of Galen's. They were in one of the societies at Schola together, and have been close since. Martin is a journalist." She considered, and ventured, "I am not sure Madam Amberly likes him much, from things they've said and, well. Not said."

Captain FitzRanulf wrote a series of notes with quick strokes of her pen. "Blythe? Do you have a last name?"

"I'm ... I'm not sure anyone said. She's a cousin of Madam Amberly's, I believe."

"And the household staff?"

"I've only seen much of Agnes, who's served as lady's

maid to me - mostly for the party on Saturday. Blythe was helping out there, too, seeing to drinks mostly from what I saw. And Jacobs, of course. The household seems to run smoothly, though there are fewer people to help with the heavy work than I expected. Madam Amberly had the footmen helping with something for the party when I arrived, and it was Galen and Martin who brought my trunk up."

She wasn't sure why she said it, but she saw the captain raise an eyebrow and make several notes. "The young men. You have spent a great deal of time with them, then?"

"Well, yes. That's why the Amberlys invited me."

The captain gave her a hard look. "I would expect they invited you to spend time with the son."

"Galen and Martin rather come as a set," Laura said, with a nervous laugh. This line of questioning did not seem to have much to do with the murder.

"How have they behaved?"

She developed a strong suspicion that this bit was Carillon's meddling, and quietly resolved to have words with him about it later. "Quite gentlemanly, thank you," she said, unable to keep the sharpness out of her voice. "They warned me about Madam Amberly's scheme to marry Galen off immediately and he has been entirely decorous going about it."

Captain FitzRanulf made a noncommittal noise. "All the proper things, then. Bringing you drinks, a shawl against the chill." She seemed to be fishing for something, almost.

"Yes, exactly. They've been very thoughtful about my comfort."

That seemed sufficient to win her a change of subject. "What did you think of Senara and Basil Wilson?"

"Basil was polite and blended right back into the woodwork. Though he was always around somewhere, close by. He danced well, but he seemed a tad distracted by something." That was immediate, she'd had several glimpses of him almost hovering. "I had the impression he was someone who had difficulties with large gatherings when he felt at loose ends, and filled the gaps with drink."

Figuring out how to explain his sister was a bit more challenging. "Senara was altogether and deliberately rude. She paid attention to the men, and she quite ignored Madam Amberly. She dismissed me at supper on Friday. At the party on Saturday, she tried to make herself the centre of attention, she had a small knot of young women around her. Some unmarried, some younger wives." Laura tried to keep her opinion of it out of her voice and largely failed.

"You didn't like her, did you?"

"No, Captain. I learned a long time ago that people being that showy were hiding other things, and often unpleasant ones."

It was not what the Captain expected, but she just nodded, and continued. "Those other things, did either of them do anything that might suggest what they might be?"

Laura tilted her head back, trying to recall. "Looking back on it, I can't tell if it's what happened later making me think it," she began.

"Granted," Captain FitzRanulf said, rather curtly, and gestured for her to continue.

"All right. I think she was nervous about something? Something about Galen, maybe? She gave him the oddest look before she swooped in on him. I don't think it was their business arrangements with the Amberlys, she didn't actually seem all that interested in talking to Mister Amberly at all, her brother was handling all of that. That conversation was the other end of the table, though, at dinner, I hardly caught any of it. Healer Tipson was not impressed."

She wondered suddenly if that odd, frenetic air that Senara had had might have been related to whatever she did to damage her stockings.

Before she could figure out how to mention that, though, the Captain said, "When is the last time you saw her?"

"I went up to bed at about half-past one. I'm afraid I don't have the stamina some people do. She was still downstairs with the last of the guests. There was enough noise from below that I was up reading until the last people went down to the portal. I saw the footmen coming back up with the lanterns, and then the house went quiet."

"Did you see or hear anything else?"

Oh, goodness. If she did not say what she'd seen, and it was needed later, that would be a problem. "I heard footsteps in the hallway, Captain, half an hour later. It was Martin, making his way quietly to Senara's room. I am sure he will explain the situation if you ask him. He was there for a few minutes, not very long."

It earned her an "Oh, indeed" and more notes. "Anything else?"

Laura shook her head. "Not that's relevant, I think. We spent a little time trying to make sense of things but didn't have much luck."

"I may have more questions for you later, when I've talked to the others, particularly about your, shall we call them investigations? Please ask Mr Taylor to be ready, I'll want to speak to him shortly."

"Of course, Captain."

"And don't tell him anything we talked about until I've interviewed him. Or anyone else."

"Of course not, Captain." She stood, then asked, "I assume the portal isn't working yet?"

"No." The response was clipped. "Or we'd be doing this entirely differently. We'll be needing you to stay until we conclude the initial investigation, but we can take you back to the mainland with us then if you prefer."

"Thank you, Captain."

# TWENTY-FIVE

## SUNDAY MORNING

"Martin Taylor?"

"Captain."

Captain FitzRanulf gestured sharply with the end of her pen. "Sit."

Not a cordial interview, then. Laura had come back, very quiet, She only had said she'd been told not to talk about it with anyone. "If you don't mind, Madam Amberly, I'd like to go lie down for a little while? If anyone needs me, I'll be glad to come back down."

That had got an immediate bit of fuss made, that carried them all through until Martin was summoned. No one was worrying about him, clearly.

A sharp cough reminded him exactly where he was. "I gather you are a regular guest here? Well known to the family?"

Lying would do no good. "Galen and I are close friends. Members of the same society at Schola, Captain."

"Expand, as far as your oaths there permit. Bear in mind that we will likely apply the full weight of the Silence in court once the initial investigation is concluded."

The warning was not strictly required, he knew that, but anyone sensible would see it coming. "Yes, Captain." He cleared his throat, then said "Galen and I are Dwellers at the Forge. Are you familiar, Captain?"

"Assume I am not." It came out clipped and precise. He wondered if she had some particular reason to be cold to the Dwellers, it seemed somehow more than just testing him to see how he would reply. He wondered if she had been involved with the coal miners' strike, but that hadn't been murder. No, it was Ames who was the murder specialist, maybe she could have been. Or some other thing that had people tangled up with the Guard, there were certainly enough of them.

"There are a number of so-called secret societies, not only at Schola, but the other schools. The ones I am familiar with invite new members, depending on their priorities and goals."

He let his voice settle into the slightly clipped educated accent he'd had to learn so quickly once he got into Schola. Protective disguise, his father had called it. "The Dwellers focus on progressive interests, and we are often considered the most eclectic of the societies. As one might guess, given they took both Galen and me in the same year."

"And you have remained friends?"

"Yes, Captain." He pauses, then added, "Our oaths, our particular oaths, require us to provide accurate accountings if questioned by the Guard or other relevant authorities." It was not much of a protection, but that was the intent. Even with those oaths, he was entirely too familiar with the touch of the Silence.

"Do they now." That was not quite a question. "Interesting. So. Tell me about Saturday evening."

"Beginning when, please?"

"From when you came downstairs for the party."

"Galen and I met in his rooms to finish getting ready. Oswald, one of the footmen, assists him, and also assists me occasionally with a few things that need someone else's hands. Galen looked very smart, as he should."

"A clotheshorse?" It was a mild inquiry.

"Galen's quite aware of his role in the family."

"And how does Miss Penhallow fit into that?"

Martin paused, considering how to phrase his answer. "His mother invited Laura to see if they might make a match of it. It's kinder than some forms of matchmaking, but her previous attempts have been unsuccessful."

"And what do you think of Laura?"

Martin stopped, frowning. He thought a lot of things about Laura, actually, many of them confusing. He enjoyed talking to her, her range of interests, her sense of clear boundaries, her disarming honesty at moments.

It must have been longer than he realised, because Captain FitzRanulf cleared her throat. "Mr Taylor?"

"Pardon." He coughed. "Madam Amberly feels a lot of modern women are too modern, I believe. Rather like Miss Wilson, actually. Short hemlines, bare shoulders. She was hoping someone like Miss Penhallow would be more conservative in her manner."

"And is she?"

"She had no objection to the lack of a chaperone, captain, but she has been very proper when in our company. Unlike Miss Wilson."

"Do tell." It was an order, barely couched as a request.

"Miss Wilson flirted outrageously from the moment of her arrival. With Galen, with me, until she realised I was the poor friend." He paused. "At the dance, however, she offered an assignation."

"And?" Captain FitzRanulf looked up, waiting.

"I accepted, because we wanted to know more about her. Why she was here, what she was up to. She suggested that there would be unfortunate consequences if I pried into things she did not want investigated, but implied she might tell me something else instead. She was playing to the presumed commonality of us both being," he paused, trying to sort out words that he could say without wincing, "the wrong sort of people."

"Explain." The tone was quite flat.

"She said she wasn't from one of the particularly well-known American families, to be in demand. A Vanderbilt or a Duxbury, she said. I tried to get her to tell me what her business interest was, how she got Mr Amberly's attention. She said there was some shared history, connections and resources. I would guess materia but I don't know for certain."

Something in there was clearly noteworthy, but Martin could not tell what. "So she refused to satisfy your curiosity." The tone was carefully and precisely neutral.

"Yes, Captain." There was no decorous way to to continue. "She propositioned me instead, implying she might tell me something else of interest. Told her brother I looked likely to be useful, but I don't know if that was a euphemism. He went off to dance with someone else. She told me to come to her room half an hour after the house went quiet. I did so, but she was not inside."

"How long were you in her room?"

"A minute or two. I did not look at personal items, but I looked around the room from the door. Trying to get a sense of her, and whether she might return."

"What did you see?" And then, a pause, before she said,

"Given the circumstances, you will be required to testify under Silence oath."

Martin managed to suppress a shiver, but nodded. "I assumed so, captain, yes."

"So. Kindly confirm what you touched, and what you did."

He thought back. "I touched the door, the door handle. Possibly the edge of the dressing table. Nothing else."

"And what did you see?"

"Several dresses strewn around. I presumed the maids had not had a chance to pick things up, due to the party. The Wilsons came down after other guests were already arriving. Cosmetics, like you'd expect, and some papers on the bed. Most of them were face down, I couldn't see what they were."

"Quite rude, then." It was said so mildly he initially misheard the comment.

"Yes, Captain."

"What was Senara wearing at the party? And her brother?"

"She was quite noticeable. A bright red dress, with an orange undercast. And she had no wrap for her shoulders. She'd been cutting her way through the men." He had to think harder about her brother. "Her brother was in evening dress. Jacket. Waistcoat. Cravat. I believe his was a rather deep blue, possibly blue grey. Very staid, compared to her."

"Why did you approach her?"

Oh, that was a sharp question. "I'd overheard some gossip, and I was concerned about whether she meant something of a problem for the Amberlys. They keep Galen out of the business side, but still. I thought I might get a little more, possibly get wind of whatever trouble was coming in advance."

"What kind of gossip was that?"

"It was five people, three women and two men. I only caught one man's name, Orion. Which is not much help, I'm sure."

There was an instant where her professional mask broke. "No, not at all."

"If you got the guest list from Madam Amberly, I'm sure it would be easy enough to narrow down. He had fought in the War, been posted to Paris, so I'm assuming he is in his thirties, possibly his forties."

His reward was a raised eyebrow, and a softer, "Thank you," as she made a few more notes. "What did you hear?"

Martin swallowed, then said, "A glass of water, if I may?" Captain FitzRanulf looked at him sternly, but then nodded, and pushed a pitcher of water and a clean glass toward him. The fuss of pouring gave him enough time to arrange his thoughts.

"The man spoke about seeing Senara with Julius, Galen's older brother. He thought it was the early part of 1915, and he was quite definite it was in Paris, and that Julius squired her around for some months. Then something changed, and Julius was sent off to the front, and she disappeared. People talked about her being seen other places. Berlin, before the War, Russia and Egypt, as well as London and Trellech. Some of it more believable than others, but all plausible."

"I gather Galen is not close to his brother?"

Martin closed his eyes, knowing it would give him away. "They talked yesterday, but no, they have... it has been difficult. Galen's parents discouraged it, from what I've heard."

"Do you know why?"

"I'm afraid not, Captain." Which was true enough. He had guesses, but he didn't know. "I know they worried a lot about Julius, about - how his experiences affected him. Maybe they worried that he might harm Galen somehow."

"What did Galen tell you about their conversation?"

"Not a lot. He was still thinking about it. He's the sort that needs to think things through, then talk them through, before doing much about it. I was surprised Laura got him to speak to Julius so easily, honestly." That was a bit more forthright than he'd meant to be, but it was all true. "But he said they'd talked, that Julius showed him a photograph of the two of them in Paris."

"Anything else?" It was said very evenly, like she knew there was.

"He didn't come out and say it, but I got the sense that someone worried Julius had done it. I don't know if that was Galen, or his parents, or someone else. Just. Knowing him."

It earned him a nod. "I appreciate the clarity. Where do you think Basil Wilson is?"

The sudden change of direction almost threw him, but he'd been expecting it from an investigator as controlled as she was. "Not on the island. One of the footmen, Willet, was going to see if he'd fallen taking a walk in the storm, I don't know if he had the opportunity. But I gather both the boats suitable for an island crossing are missing, and there was wreckage sighted? One person could manage either of them alone, they do routinely for getting supplies. I don't, however, know if Basil Wilson had any particular skills at sailing."

"Do you?"

"Enough to aim at one of the larger islands. Enough to get to the mainland? Probably not. The currents can be tricky."

"And what do you know about portals?"

"That they're exceedingly complex magic, well beyond

my skills, and I'm certainly not from one of the families known for having a knack for them. I do know the one here is relatively recent, less than a decade. Still growing, I believe is the phrase. It's been quite reliable in the past, they use it a dozen times a week when there are no guests, and more frequently when there are. Someone gets supplies in Trellech, for example. Or they get materials for Julius there."

"For Julius?"

"He has an alchemy lab, he does some sort of research. I have no idea what."

"You seem to know a lot about the household." Again, not a question.

"I've been a guest here dozens of times by now. School vacations, at their other homes, and here, oh, every few months. It's convenient, when I don't have a current story, and Galen prefers having me around."

"And his parents?"

Martin shrugged. "To fill out the dancing. We're young enough not to have fought, but the men a few years older, well. And there's plenty of women. I clean up well enough to meet Madam Amberly's needs. She tolerates me, more or less."

"That doesn't explain your comfort below stairs. You know rather more about what the footmen have been up to than the lady of the house." Captain FitzRanulf had a fine knack for finding the weak point. He'd admire her skill a great deal more if it were aimed anywhere else.

"My mother was in service. Mostly as a nursemaid, but as a housemaid briefly." He paused, then added, "I had tea with the servant's hall yesterday. I'd offered to replenish the stove and cooler. I wanted to ask a few more things, but there wasn't much."

"Who did you speak with?"

"Willet, the second footman, mostly. The rest was pleasantries. And Oswald thinking I should know my place better, but not saying so."

That, surprisingly, earned him an actual laugh. "Oh, you do know where the lines are, Mr Taylor." She tapped the pen on the paper, and then said "I'll want to speak to you again later, I suspect, but you may go for now. Don't discuss the details of this interview with anyone, and avoid conversations with anyone I have not spoken with yet to the best of your ability. You may tell them I so instructed you." She had relaxed more than he expected, given where they started. It made him wonder what he'd let slip.

"Captain. Should I have someone else prepare?"

"Mr Amberly, Galen, if you don't mind. And ask someone to send up some tea and whatever he likes to drink." One more sign of the chasm between himself and others, that the people after him got offered certain comforts. "When you've done that, report to Ames. I expect you would rather willingly open the magical seal on the private compartment in your trunk rather than have us do it." Which meant they were doing a full search, at least.

"Of course, Captain." He stood, made a slight bow, and then retreated, with the shreds of his composure around him.

## TWENTY-SIX

### SUNDAY AFTERNOON

"Laura." It was Martin, in the doorway. He had changed into a different outfit, one more suited for the outdoors. Laura had tried to go upstairs to lie down, and had completely failed at it before coming back down and finding the smaller parlour, not wanting to face the others. It was at least an hour since her interview, possibly rather longer, and there had been an oddly unsettling message from Carillon besides.

"Martin?" He looked rather pale under the layers. "Are you all right?"

He waved a hand. "Think I need a bit of fresh air. I was going out for a walk. Do you want to come?"

She considered for a moment, then shook her head. "I'm not sure I feel quite up to it," she said. "I can let Galen know, when he's done?"

"That would be kind." There was something terribly muted in him, like clouds over sun, or cotton wool in the ears. "I'll be back in an hour. Can't go far, anyway."

"Of course." He turned and went, without another word, and she frowned.

She was still frowning, a minute or so later, looking out the door after him, when there was a sharp knock on the frame. "Miss Penhallow?"

"Yes?"

"Guard Trevallen, miss. I was asked to see how you were doing."

Laura frowned at him now. A different frown. She did not like where this was going. If Martin were here, she'd arrange a bet with him on whether it were her sister or her brother-in-law behind this.

"By whom?" Two could play that game.

He had the grace to look moderately embarrassed. "Um. Both Lord Carillon and Lady Carillon. In separate notes, as it turned out. Five separate notes."

It made her smile for just a moment, and wonder about the precise breakdown, but the smile faded as he went on.

"I was instructed to check and see if you needed anything, to tell you that we could get your preferred Healer in from Trellech, if needed. To see if you had enough of - there's a tonic, Miss?" He pulled a notebook out of his pocket, thumbing through it.

"I am quite sure none of these are in your duties for the guard."

He flushed. "Um, not precisely, miss."

"And they would like me to let them know how things are?"

"Um. Yes, miss. And there was a comment about a scarf? To make sure you wore one. Can I get someone to fetch something for you?"

"No, no." She paused, considering her options. "Thank you for relaying that." There was no point blaming him, they'd put him in a rather dreadful position. "I do have a few questions? Nothing about the case specifically, I do understand you can't talk about the case." Being charming and inquisitive worked against the fussing, sometimes. Often enough to be worth trying.

"Miss?"

Oh, now she'd puzzled him. She gestured at the chair. "It would help me - you do understand fretting isn't good for me?" It wasn't good for anyone, really. "So it would be a help to understand the next steps here. Can you help with that?"

"Oh, um. Yes, miss."

"You've been a Guard a long time?" He was in his sixties, by the look of it. Near retirement.

"Yes, miss. Based near Penzance. You're from Lanyon?"

"Yes, we are. Me and my sister. Beautiful country, but rather different. Not right on the coast."

"Yes, miss."

"And you've been familiar with the Amberlys for a while?"

"Since they moved here, Miss. They'd not spent a lot of time here until..." His eyes glanced up and to the back.

"Oh, you've been out here before?"

"A few times, miss. Checking after bad weather, if anyone needed help, a few charity events. Madam Amberly's very kind, invites the Guard when it's something relevant."

"She seems very attentive to that sort of thing."

He lit up at that. "Oh, yes, miss. And in the summer, it's beautiful here. Quite a lovely garden, too. Her pride, that is."

"And you know the others in the family?" She settled back in the chair. This, at least, was better than being prodded and nagged.

"Yes, miss." He paused, and added. "There's some talk

that you and Master Galen are getting on well?" He sounded so hopeful.

"We're still getting to know each other, and this has been," She paused the right amount, it would not do to overstate things. "Rather difficult. It would be such a help to have some resolution. Do you have an idea what the Captain needs to do?"

"Well, miss, first she needs to talk to everyone. That's standard, that is."

"Of course. And she seems very attentive to detail."

"Rather, miss, yes." She got the sense he wasn't sure how to deal with that. "And Guard Ames has to make a report. And then if there's enough to charge someone, we'll do that. If there isn't, everyone will have to be questioned. None of the magistrates were available to come out here. Not and be gone for a good two or three days without much contact, so we have to wait on that."

"Any idea how long?"

"A day or two, miss."

"Goodness. So we all have to stay here?"

"Yes, miss. Some other people are checking to see if there's a place Mr Wilson might have gone down, if he took a boat that is. The Guard pays fisherfolk for that kind of thing, a bonus."

"Very efficient, that part. And I suppose they know the local waters much better."

"Yes, miss. Exactly."

"And you and the Captain and Guard Ames all stay here?"

"Yes, miss. With one of us on duty at all times."

"That must be quite a challenge."

"Oh, yes, miss. But we are here to serve, Miss. That's

what the Guard is for. Even personal requests like Lord and Lady Carillon's."

She frowned again. Blast. Back to that. There was a slight knock on the door. "Laura?"

That was Galen, and she offered him a smile. "Is there a problem?" Galen looked from Laura to the guard.

Trevallen stood, immediately. "Pardon, sir. Miss Penhallow's sister and Lord Carillon had some requests for her."

"Well, I'm sure that's kind of you. Did you reassure them, Laura? I'm sure they must be worrying."

She paused, and oh, she didn't want to hurt Galen, even if he was making this rather more difficult. "I've not yet gone to get my journal, no. I will when I go upstairs again."

"Are you sure? It must be very hard for them, not to know how you are." She thought, with perhaps a little less charity than he deserved, that fussing and dithering like his mother was not one of Galen's more attractive qualities.

Laura frowned, trying to figure out how to get him onto a different tack. "Thank you for passing the message on, Guard Trevallen. I'm fine now, thank you, and I'm sure you have other duties to attend to?"

He, at least, got the hint, and nodded, then stood and bowed. "Sir. Miss."

Galen looked after him as he departed, almost hurt. "You didn't have to send him out."

"I do not need two people fussing over me here, and two more people fussing over me from Italy. That is entirely too much fussing, even without the part where my brother-in-law is actually being slightly useful but only in the worst possible way."

"But you said you didn't feel well....." Galen's voice trailed off.

"There was a very large party, including some people who did not like me much at all. I am on an island with no way off for the moment, with people I barely know, even if a number of them have been kind to me. There has been a murder and a disappearance, and the murder method involved one of my worst fears, not being able to breathe. If that weren't bad enough, the people in question have influential friends somewhere and for all I know influential enemies as well. Carillon is not terribly specific. Though I suppose he gets some allowance for being in Italy, and not actually knowing everyone involved."

She took as deep a breath as she could. "There is an abundance of fish in my diet, which I don't precisely mind, but is more than I have been used to in the past few months. I am sleeping in a strange bed that no matter how comfortable is not mine. The taps in the bathroom are quite odd. And I have a very insistent housemaid and every passing adult wondering how I am several times an hour." It came out of her in a rush. "A woman might want to have a lie down to get a bit of peace and quiet."

Galen shrunk back at the torrent, then said, very carefully, "So I did something wrong." He looked like a scolded puppy, and she wasn't at all sure what to do with that.

"Martin went out for a walk. He said he'd be back in an hour."

"Oh. I - um. And you?"

"I'm in a foul mood." she agreed. "Sorry. Just. The fussing is utterly the wrong thing. Any reasonable person would feel tired and out of sorts with everything that's happened. People fussing more over me because of being ill years ago, that just makes things worse."

That at least got Galen more engaged again. Not just reacting. "Oh." He stood after a moment. "Later, maybe?"

She nodded, rather weakly. "Later. I think I will try and lie down again." And then as a concession, she added, "And I'll write to my sister, at least."

"I think I'll go see if I can find Martin." She wasn't sure if he meant it as an admission of weakness, or letting her off the hook, or both.

"Probably do you both good. I think the questioning went a bit hard for him."

That got a completely different expression, with all that worry that had been about her turned sharply around to a new target. "I'll see you later." He didn't even bother to offer to walk her out, just took off for the front door.

She stood, relieved he was no longer fussing, pleased by his loyalty to his friend, and mildly peeved that he hadn't at least seen her to the stairs. The last was unfair.

# TWENTY-SEVEN

## SUNDAY AFTERNOON

Galen knew just where to find Martin. Jacobs, at the front door, almost stopped him as he stopped only long enough to grab a cloak from the front closet. That was a sign of how unsettled everyone was, normally the staff would never dare. "I'm going to find Martin. Be back in half an hour or so. Maybe a bit longer."

He didn't stop to hear a reply, just kept going. This time, he went left, to the top of the cliff. If you knew where to go, you could scramble down to a ledge in the rock, not really big enough to be a cave, enough to sit in if you were young and limber enough.

Galen paused at the top of the ledge. "Dweller at the Forge, how is the fire?"

There was a worrisome long pause, then the voice that floated up sounded tired and faded. "The foundry door is open." That was not at all encouraging, though not as bad as it might be.

"Coming down." Galen scrambled down, carefully, placing each foot before putting weight on it. When he got down to the ledge, he turned, and Martin was in his usual spot, leaning against the wall on the left.

"You're not all right." It wasn't a question.

There was a long pause, then Martin shook his head, silently.

Galen frowned. "The interview? Something else?"

Martin let out a long sigh. "Several things."

Galen reached out a hand, resting it on Martin's arm, and at least Martin didn't pull away, just quivered under the touch for a moment. "Laura said you didn't look well."

"So you rushed off to see to me? Instead of her?" Martin's voice was suddenly sharp.

Galen took a deep breath. And another one. And then he got a sudden blast of chill air as the wind changed, and started coughing. It took all his dignity with it, and when he finally managed to breathe evenly again, he said, quietly. "She went up to lie down, she made it very clear she didn't want me fussing."

"So you came to fuss at me, instead." Also not at all a question.

"You are in a foul mood." Galen let his hand drop, then tucked it in under the cloak.

They sat without talking for several minutes. Not silence, there were the sounds of the seabirds, and the crash of the waves, and a few sounds Galen couldn't place. It started to get darker as the twilight deepened.

As the light dimmed, Martin finally said, "I am in a foul mood, and it's not your fault. I'm sorry."

"If you want to talk about it, we've got about fifteen minutes before people start wondering when we'll be back."

"So precise." It was amused, a little teasing.

"You keep me for charm and precision. I keep you for courage and observation."

It made Martin smile, just for a moment, and Galen counted that as a significant victory. "Observation. Courage." He fumbled on the ledge for a small pebble, then snapped his wrist sending it to fly out and bounce down the hillside toward the water.

"Not feeling too courageous at the moment? Was the interview awful?"

"Rather. Feeling on the outside. And needing to - tell her things. And wondering if she's looking for wedge to disrupt the Dwellers."

"Senara?" Galen didn't like thinking about something driving a wedge into the Dwellers.

"Oh, I'd expected that. There'll be Silence oaths for me, no matter what else they do. Because I was in her room." His voice sounded hollow.

Galen frowned, then felt a small pebble under his fingers and offered it to Martin, his palm up. "The family, then."

Martin's fingers brushed his palm as he took the pebble, then there was the same sharp movement of hand and fingers, the same skittering sound on the rocks. "She didn't come out and ask, but she nearly did. Why you put up with me. Why I'm invited."

"Because you are my friend, and my chosen brother, and we work much better together than separately." Some things were very clear to Galen. Then he considered how Martin would respond to that line of questioning. "You went all defensive at her, laying out everything she could criticise."

"It's easier to bear than someone dragging it out, word by word. Glance by glance. Mercury's sandals, she's terrifying."

Galen snorted. "She was very polite to me. But we'd

expect that, wouldn't we." The we, very deliberate here. His brother, his chosen brother, had to know where he stood. Martin was brave and fearless and confident. Most of the time. When he wasn't, he needed to know there were people who had his back.

"So you told the truth. That's what we're supposed to do." He paused. "I had to, too. Only now," He let his voice trail off.

"What did she ask you about? Can you talk about it?" The second question chased the first, like Martin was suddenly scared he'd asked something wrong.

"A lot about the family. How I felt being out here, being married off." He paused, picked up another stone, and experimented with tossing his. It did not go nearly so far as Martin managed.

"There was something else?"

He never could fool Martin. Most of the time that was a good thing, but right now he wished his friend were a bit less observant. "She asked a lot about Julius. Did I think he had reason to hurt Senara. What kind of injuries he had. If it had affected his head. And then suddenly sideways, what does he do with his alchemy. What materia does he use. As if Father would ever tell me anything about that. As if they even let me talk to Julius, or do anything with alchemy."

Martin frowned. "I - I had to tell her about some of the gossip I heard. I told you about that."

"After talking to him last night, I want to think he didn't have anything to do with it. And she asked about that."

Martin tossed another stone down toward the water. "You didn't say much about it after."

"It's the first time I've really talked to my brother in years. About anything important. Or for more than a minute or two. And I had to," Galen stopped. "I couldn't keep it private. Even for a day."

"Oh. Oh, Galen." Galen felt Martin's hand rest on his arm, the echo of earlier. "That must feel awful. Grubby."

"Grubby's a good word. The kind of oily muck that takes forever to clean."

"What... " Martin clearly thought better of that sentence, because he stopped. "What would help?"

"We're going to have to go back, and go in to supper, as if everything were all right. She was going to talk to Mother and Father next, so I have no idea when they'll be free. And I guess to Julius, and I can't warn him. They can't. No one can."

"Your brother's a clever man, Galen. You know that. And you say he didn't do it."

"Now she's put the thought in my head. I didn't know him really well before the War. Just the ways a younger brother knows his older brother. All looking up to him, and the sun shining, and him glowing, and nothing solid, nothing real."

Martin tossed another rock, and this one faltered, hitting a boulder oddly and bouncing to a stop. "That's not a thing you can fix. We can't go back, can we?"

"No." Galen frowned, rolling another pebble between his fingers, thinking. "Laura talked to me a bit about her sister. We were talking about something." He tried to figure out how to put it. "She resented her sister, for getting to travel and do things she couldn't. It made her angry and shouty in her head, she said."

"And?" Martin leaned forward a bit.

"She didn't like feeling like that." Then, more softly, he added. "I don't like feeling like that either."

"You too? Me three." Martin shook his head. "Fine lot of us we are."

Galen had to smile at that. "At least we're not alone with it?"

"You should have invited her down here with you. We could have squeezed three in."

"I - um. I upset her a bit. Fussing at her. She needed to be alone, she said. And that you had looked upset." Galen grimaced. "I only thought about you, not her."

Martin tossed another rock, and another before he said, "Ta for that. Being out here, away from it, that's a help. I can probably go in and face dinner. In a minute."

"What can I do once we do?"

"Be charming. Keep conversation going. The local islands, maybe. Did Captain FitzRanulf say if they had any idea about Basil?"

Galen shook his head. "Not that she told me." He then added "I've been trying to place her. Family."

"You don't know every family out there."

"Well, the Fitz, that usually means someone somewhere in the line was a bastard. If she's part of the First Families, that'd be her immediate line. Her or maybe her father. If she's something else, it could mean other things. Aunt Silvia might know, she was trying to place her."

"Important things?"

"I'm wondering why she was the one sent here. She doesn't much seem to like people with property."

Martin tossed another rock, a bigger one, more the size of his palm, and it made a satisfying deeper sound as it bounced against the larger boulders. "I didn't see that part of her. What made you say that?"

"She was very polite with me, courteous to a fault, but that sort of punctilious politeness that is keeping score."

"Only you, my brother, would use the word punctilious in a sentence like that."

Galen grinned. Ah, that was a definite improvement. "I am as I am."

Martin frowned, then said, "Do you think she's competent?"

"Oh, yes. Dangerous like a knife, but competent."

## TWENTY-EIGHT

### SUNDAY EVENING

Dinner had been nearly silent and terribly awkward. Galen and Martin had come back, together, ten minutes after everyone else had sat down. Well, everyone but Cassian and Parnell Amberly, who were still being interviewed. Together, which seemed odd, somehow. Surely that wasn't the usual practise?

When the meal was done, Attis and Silvia drifted off with barely a comment, and it left Galen and Martin looking at Laura. She ducked her head. "I'm sorry for earlier, Galen. I didn't mean..."

Galen waved a hand. "We're all unsettled. Look, I should go see to things. Especially if mother and father are going to be talking longer. Space for the Guard to sleep."

"Can't Blythe do that?" It slipped out of Martin, and Laura rather thought the comment startled him, that he'd made it out loud.

Galen just looked at him, and shook his head minutely. "Feel free to use the parlour. Or the guest sitting room upstairs. I'm sure no one will bother you."

Laura looked from one to the other, then said "Martin?

If you don't mind, I'd rather not be all on my own? Unless you need to help Galen."

Again, that fraction of a shake of Galen's head. Martin picked up easily. "Oh, I'm glad to keep you company. The sitting room?"

Laura nodded. "Let me stop by my room."

Martin nodded, and took himself off. Galen watched him go, then said, very quietly. "I've some things to do. He knows where to find me if I'm needed. I'll make sure Agnes brings up some tea."

There was something so delicate there, and fragile, that Laura could only nod. No other response was possible. That done, she turned away from him, picking up her skirts slightly to climb upstairs, then ducking into her room to change into something less formal. She picked out one of the nicer at home dresses she'd got this past year, a little warmer and more comfortable than her dinner frocks. She gathered up a light silk shawl to go with it, and then crossed the hall to peer into the sitting room.

Martin had already snuck in, she had no idea how she didn't hear him in the hall, but he had claimed a comfortable looking easy chair. "The couch? And Agnes is glad to start the fire, if we want. There's a bit of a chill."

"Oh, I'd hate to put her out. There must be a lot more work for them. More people, staying longer, plus the Guard."

Martin nodded slightly at this. "Considerate."

"Is it normal for people to be questioned together?" Laura wondered if Martin knew more than she did. Well, he probably did about many things, but possibly also this.

"Sometimes. I think it depends on the specific wedding vows and bindings? Or the situation. Or they might have started separately, and continued together. Something like that."

It wasn't much help, but it was something, and at least he'd taken the question seriously. Laura considered, then claimed the side of the small sofa nearer to Martin. "So you are the one to keep me entertained? Where is Galen going?" It was terribly improper and pushy to ask, of course, but he had been acting quite oddly.

Martin seemed about to answer, only then there was a slight knock on the door. "Tea, sir."

Laura raised his voice. "Come in." And there was Agnes, with a tea tray, and a selection of cakes.

"Miss, if you need anything, please ring. Oh. You changed, I'll see to your evening frock, too, and make everything ready for bed, if you'd like."

"Thank you. I can't imagine it will be a late night."

Agnes bobbed, and ducked out of the room. Once she was gone, Martin cleared his throat. "I'm quite sure Galen is up to see Julius again. Or at least sitting on the stairs trying to decide if he ought."

"Oh." Laura wasn't sure what to do with that. "Why are you so sure?"

"You encouraged him to go talk. He did. It went quite well, considering. That sort of thing makes people want to do it again."

Laura nodded. "And you?"

"I think it's a good thing. I'd brought it up, more than once, and Galen put me off. We ...." He paused. "We have our roles, you understand? I can only push so far. After that, it's, well."

Laura nodded then said, "Is he all right?" Then, suddenly, it hit her. "You're not all right." She was rewarded, if that was the word for it, by Martin's eyes going wide with surprise. She fully expected him to wave it off.

"You're very observant."

"It's one of the few skills I had any chance to perfect. Or as much as I've perfected any skill."

Martin considered that, tilting his head. "Unless you've another topic, I'm curious about that, your experiences. If you're willing to share."

Laura frowned. "Why?"

"Because I like understanding. Because there are things no one talks about. The Naples Scourge. What it was like during the War. TB sanitaria."

Laura grimaced. "I'm not sure what I think of that as a collection."

Martin leaned back, spreading his hands. "I'm not wrong, though."

She shook her head. "No, you're not. What, why do you want to know?"

"Because it affects an awful lot of people. Tuberculosis. And I know that part." His voice got soft.

"Who?"

"My mother. She got better. My sister. She didn't. Much older, we weren't." He stopped and tried again. "She died before I got to know her. Only there's this space, where she ought to be."

Laura nodded. "But not a sanitarium?"

"No. We didn't have the money with my sister. And she got bad, quickly. With my mother, they found a thing that helped enough, fast enough. She stayed at the Healer's Temple in Trellech for a month, but the air there is all right. Not like London, where we were with my sister."

Laura closed her eyes, trying to figure out what to say to that. "Should I begin with finding out? Or where I was?"

"The beginning. Finding out. If you don't mind?" Martin's voice was very gentle, now.

"I was twelve. Thirteen. And I got a bad cough, at school. After we'd moved into our own rooms, so they mostly improved the sound charms a bit, so I wasn't keeping anyone up. And Schola's damp, and especially that fall. Beginning of third year. But then I kept feeling worse and worse. It's an awful feeling, damp in your lungs, making it feel like you're breathing mud, and yet everything also gets very dry. And then there was the blood." She shivered once, and Martin immediately stood, rather instinctively.

"May I sit with you? If, if you want to continue, that is."

She looked up, then nodded once. "I came home for winter break, and my mother took me to Trellech, to the healers. I'd only just seen drops of blood, you understand. Nothing obvious. Everyone gets colds. I didn't know enough to know what it was, and I guess none of my teachers noticed. There were some difficult people in my year, and a crowd who took up all the space in the room."

Martin settled next to her on the sofa, offering a hand to her. "And you're not that sort. Even if you'd been in the prime of health, you'd not be taking up all that space."

Laura smiled at him. "No. Exactly." She let her eyes close again, this was easier if she wasn't looking at him. "The healers frowned and tutted, and then they talked to Mother, where I couldn't hear. And when she came back, she said I was going to need to go somewhere to get better. She and the Healers would figure out where would be best, and I should just rest."

"What about your sister? Or your father?"

"Oh, they were off on a trip, she was already out of school. We'd been supposed to join them, but."

"But instead, you went elsewhere."

Laura nodded. "To Switzerland, originally. The air is thought to be very good there. There is a whole..." She searched for words again. "A whole culture and tradition to them. A very rigid system." It was as if she was back in the moment, she could smell the sharp cleansing herbs and medicine in the air and taste the tang of them mingling.

"When I got there, I was thoroughly examined, and it was embarrassing. They made me stand, and they took me for one of the new doctor techniques, the things called x-rays? They don't exactly have the Silence there, but you couldn't talk about magic, it just wasn't done. And I didn't really understand much French or German then. No one bothered to explain anything to me, they just talked over my head."

Martin squeezed her hand. "More now?"

"I had plenty of time to learn. But my vocabulary isn't expansive. Food. Social pleasantries. Talking about books or music." She glanced down at their hands, then said "It was overwhelming. But they explained to me, in very small words, that I was to rest. Do nothing but rest."

Martin frowned. "That seems, very, I don't know. Limiting."

"Oh, trust me, it is. And all the nurses bustling around cleaning things, every time you looked. You had your time to lie in bed and rest, and then a time to walk slowly, or be pushed, to a bed on the balcony in the clear air. Then back to your bed inside. If you did well, eventually you were allowed to read, or sit up."

"It sounds..." Martin sounded horrified. "It sounds like a slow death. The cure."

That made her close her eyes and shudder, and she couldn't think of what to say.

# TWENTY-NINE

## SUNDAY EVENING

Martin was not sure any of this was a good idea. This was a woman Galen was interested in. Who liked his friend. Who was the sort of woman whose family could send her to sanitaria for years. But here she was, trembling, and he was so close.

He squeezed her hands again. "You don't need to tell me, if you don't want to."

Laura looked at him, for a moment, absolutely square on and certain. "You asked. You wanted to know." And oh, that challenge, he could not resist that challenge.

He ducked his chin, acknowledging both her certainty and his weakness. "Then do go on, please."

"It wasn't... " Laura paused, but this time she was gathering herself, looking for the right words. "There were three things that were particularly awful about it. The first was people died. Regularly. You'd go to sleep and wake in the night, and they'd be wheeling someone away. You didn't get to say goodbye. You weren't even allowed to miss them out loud."

Martin sucked in a breath. "That's. That's inhuman. Inhumane. What did they expect you to do?"

"They expected, so far as I can tell, that it would be like sailing on one of the great liners thrown together with people. Where you'd promise to keep in touch, and you'd never see them again. As they were gone, you'd forget."

"But you didn't." He was sure of this.

"No. I see their faces, sometimes, when I go to sleep. You know how people hear a voice calling their names? I hear a voice calling theirs. Women, mostly, that's who was on the ward of course."

Martin winced. "So you have your own ghosts. Memories."

Laura nodded. "That was the first awful thing no one talks about. The second is how restricted things were. Months and months of doing nothing more than lying in bed. Surgery or treatments, sometimes, that hurt, that ached, with nothing to ease it. Every movement you made judged and measured and tsked over."

"That seems awful too. Feeling like you had no privacy."

"Exactly." Her eyes lit up, like he'd understood something. "I still have problems having a maid around. I mean, I'm better than I used to be but when I'm somewhere someone might come in, I - I never properly relax."

"Huh." He had to think about that. "That's like some men from the War. Always expecting another shell to land."

Laura tilted her head, looking at him. "You mean that? Seriously?" He couldn't tell if she was upset or pleased.

"Yes." He would take her seriously, he had to. There was no other decent way to take the gift of her trust.

"People don't. No one. That it's like having been in a bit of a War."

"Even your sister?"

"She's a little better. Her husband thinks there's a difference but a similarity. Enough I don't shout at him. Shouting's not good for him." She paused for a bare instant. "Too much like shells. It's not kind."

"I like that you're kind even when you're upset." It came out of Martin in a little burst, something from the heart.

Laura smiled at him, for just a moment, then said, "Then I'll tell you the third. It will make you think the worse of me, but you should know, the truth is a thing."

He wasn't at all sure what she was going to say.

"Being somewhere like that, there are all these people who have power over you. The big ways, treatments and so on. I was young, and a woman, they thought I didn't know anything, they didn't ask what I wanted. But it was the little ways that were worse. Who got dinner first. Who got the sponge bath from the nurse with gentle hands. Or a gentler one from a nurse with rough hands. Whether you got a choice in your meal, or got to eat it while it was the temperature it should be. All sorts of things. Music choices, books read aloud, things to look at."

He wasn't quite following some part of this. "Why would I not like that?" He could only ask.

"Martin, I became the kind of person who'd do the things people liked. So they'd treat me well. Whatever that meant."

Once she'd said it, she sat there, her hand in his but no longer clasping, just resting. She'd gone completely still, as if she fully expected him to pull away, to want nothing to do with her.

He squeezed her hand, threaded his fingers with her

unresisting ones. "You were in a terrifying place, fighting your own war."

"You didn't fight." She winced, as soon as she said it.

"Not the Great War, no. But I've had my share of skirmishes. Enough to recognise a veteran properly. And you had plenty of people telling you your battles didn't count. I'll not do that."

When she opened her eyes again, there was something starlit in them. "Oh." She said. "Oh."

He cupped her hand in both of his, and said, "I'm doing my best."

Before he could do anything or say anything further, she leaned to kiss him. It was a gentle kiss, not the sort of feminine attack he would have expected from Senara, or some of the other girls at the party. Rather, it was feeling him out. Exploring.

He couldn't move. Anything he might do here felt wrong. To kiss her back, to explore her, was to betray Galen. To pull away would break his heart. He wanted more time to think, and there wasn't time to sort out anything he was feeling.

She did not press him too far, not so far he had to make a choice, but pulled back, before she murmured, "Thank you." Then, suddenly, briskly, she said. "I've made quite a few horrible choices, since." It was as if she was forging on, like fires were burning at her heels now.

Martin was baffled, completely turned around. He opened his mouth and no sound came out, until he finally managed a bare "Um?"

"The goldwasser." The word came out crisp, a little hint of a broad A, as it would have been in German. "I wanted all the things I hadn't been able to have. Travel. Enjoyment. Pleasures beyond counting. Men."

This did not make things easier for him. "Um?" He tried it again, because again, anything he said would be wrong.

"There was a young man. A relative of Mr Morland's. The man I was working for." Her voice was faster now, tighter. "He was the son of one of the families making the goldwasser. He helped distribute it. He's in gaol now. For some time to come."

This at least gave Martin somewhere to start. "Did he hurt you?"

"Not like you're thinking. But he, I let the dreams get in the way of sense. Over and over. Until something snapped. Until he turned from someone who was a pleasant dream, a fantasy outside the walls of the sanitaria. And he turned into one of the people I had to please to stay safe. To not be hurt."

The words came to a stop, as sudden as if she'd fallen away, off a cliff. She put her free hand to her mouth, looking suddenly distraught. "I shouldn't have. I didn't mean to."

Martin took a deep breath. One of them would have to be sensible here. "Breathe, please. Do you need a bit more tea?" It was a weak offer, and she waved her hand without saying anything.

It gave him enough space to figure out the next thing. "Galen would understand. I understand. I can help explain it, if you need me to?" He wasn't sure he wanted her to take him up on that, he couldn't imagine that conversation, but he'd try. For both their sakes.

Laura shook her head. "I believe you understand. But I wouldn't ask that. That's not kind."

"And you try to be kind." He was feeling his way with this now.

"I spent so long not feeling kind. Now, I might not feel it, but I can act it. It feels better than the other choices."

"Galen said you said you felt all angry and shouty."

"That's why I told him to go away. I'm hopeless when I'm like that. Like this."

"Don't send me away." Martin felt like if she did, something would be wrong for the rest of his life. He wanted desperately to ask about the kiss, and he couldn't. "Tell me what will help?"

He watched her close her eyes, not letting his hand go, watched her take her time, thinking. They sat like that, unmoving and just together for a full minute, by his count of the ticks of the clock on the mantle.

Finally, so softly he had to lean forward to hear her, she said "Tell me things you've learned."

# THIRTY

## MONDAY MORNING, EARLY

Laura woke very early the next morning, before dawn.

The evening before had ended poorly, with Galen's parents coming to make sure she was all right, interrupting her conversation with Martin. By that time, she and Martin had moved apart again, had more tea. They had been chatting over things he'd learned in his reporting, some of it horrible, but more stories about having hope.

Madam Amberly had been exceedingly disapproving, coming close to sending Martin away directly. Instead, he'd stayed just long enough that Laura could gather herself, then slipped away to let Galen know his parents were looking for him. That was much more important than whatever minor help Martin could give her.

Madam Amberly had set to, immediately, asking how Laura was, prying at what Martin might have told her. She was fishing for something, but Laura couldn't tell if it was personal, possibly about Martin getting in Galen's way, or something else.

It had given her a headache, all of it, and she had

retreated to her room after, letting herself fall into a restless sleep.

Now, though, something was bothering her. A nagging thought, at the back of her mind, insistent. Like a midge stinging in the summer.

She didn't bother ringing for Agnes. Polite young ladies, or even polite spinsters, did not get up before dawn and go wandering around the houses they were staying in. But she could dress herself, and did, before she slipped downstairs to go walk through the public rooms, trying to remember how things were the night of the party.

She had been in here, then dancing, then in the conservatory. She didn't go into the conservatory now. It was marked off with some of the wards that the Guard used, things that glowed a sickly red in the early light. Instead, she sat on one of the long couches in the ballroom, and thought about it.

It had been easy, during the party, to be rushed around, to let other people control the space. Senara, but also the group of women about Laura's age. Married, most of them. Successful, by most people's standards, matched to young men of good breeding.

Senara didn't fit that mould. But neither, she realised, did Basil.

She closed her eyes, thinking about it. About the patterns she'd heard. Senara flirting, being the centre of attention, drawing eyes and movements. People circling to be near her, whether or not they were intrigued by her. Some had been attracted, moths to a flame. Others had wanted to be close enough to gossip and chatter about how scandalous she was.

But where had Basil been?

Laura tried to remember. He'd danced, a little. He'd

danced once with her. She stood, trying to remember how that had gone. It felt ridiculous, standing there, one arm up, one as if around his waist, but it helped her think back. A step, two steps, a twirl...

She heard a slight cough behind her, and whirled around.

"Captain FitzRanulf."

"What are you up to, Miss Penhallow?" It was quiet, drawling, the sound of a cat about to pounce, entirely confident the prey would not escape.

Laura shifted, standing more evenly, hands behind her back. "Thinking." She tried to keep her voice calm.

"Down here?"

"I was trying to make sense of something at the party." No reason to hide it.

"Oh?" It was a weighted, heavy sound.

"I was trying to remember where Basil Wilson was. I danced with him, other people did too. But I am not sure where he was the whole night. I wasn't paying particular attention to him. Other people might not have been as well."

"It is very curious about him, yes."

There was just a hint of something in the reply, that made Laura lean forward. "You've found something."

"You, Miss Penhallow, are a witness, if not a suspect." Captain FitzRanulf's tone was harder.

"And I could be more useful about what I saw if I had an idea what might be relevant." Two could play that game.

The captain frowned, then took a step back. "Walk me through the Thursday and Friday, would you? With a particular focus on Basil Wilson, I have a better idea about the sister."

Laura took a deep breath. "He had much better

manners. They got here later than expected, I'm not sure what the holdup was. And they came down to supper just before the gong. Senara was awful, she ignored Madam Amberly entirely, and that's just not done. Do you see? Not everyone understands the social rules."

The captain waved a hand. "I do in fact understand the nuances. Was it the subtle rudenesses, or the obvious ones?"

"Oh, quite obvious. She didn't even greet Madam Amberly properly, used her nickname, just swept up Galen to talk to, to ask about what was outside the windows. It was well dark by then."

"And Galen was supposed to be paying attention to you. Were you jealous?"

No, Laura had not been, but putting that sensibly was a challenge. "Galen and I were - are - getting to know each other. I like him as a person."

She stopped, then decided on honesty. "I don't need to marry. Not like I did a few years ago. I'd not choose someone who couldn't be courteous. Kind. Looking at other people, that's one thing. But neglecting the person you're supposed to be with, to do it, that's a different thing, and not one I want to be around. Or attached to." It came out much more muddled and childish than she wanted, but it was how she felt, so at least it was honest.

At the end the captain nodded. "Interesting. So we can assume you were paying close attention to the details. What did Basil Wilson do?"

"He rather melted into the background. I didn't catch much of the supper conversation, but I got the sense he and Attis Tipson disagreed rather significantly about some business matter? Which makes me wonder, the servants said that Senara's clothes had been altered, what if they didn't have as much money as they wanted to look like they had?

If the business deal had to go through or something was going to happen to them, that might be why Basil was so intense about it." She paused. "Carillon said they had influential friends, but maybe they also had influential enemies. That's just speculating."

"It is," said the Captain. "Did you hear the details of the conversation? An informed speculation would be more help."

"They were down at the end with Madam Amberly."

"What was the seating?"

"Mr Amberly at the head, me, Galen, Silvia Tipson, Basil Wilson, Madam Amberly, Attis Tipson, Blythe, Martin, Senara."

"A little unconventional, yes? You should have been at the top left, not top right?"

Laura looked up, and blinked. "I'd assumed the goal was to put me closer to Galen. Unconventional, but very much in keeping with the goal of the weekend."

"I gather they have been quite free in the chaperoning?"

"I am not a debutante, and I've appreciated not being treated as one." It came out a bit sharper than Laura meant.

"Is it the sort of place where that's an excuse for more in private?"

Laura blushed, remembering both sets of kisses, and she hoped that was answer enough. There was a long pause, then Captain FitzRanulf nodded. "I can measure from that. Some space, but not - extensive privacy."

"Ma'am. Captain. Just so."

"Who did Basil spend time with at the party?"

"There was a group of women a bit younger than I am. Twenties, mostly, some married, a few not. He danced at least twice with Glenna, once with most of the others. Unremarkable. So much so that I don't know where he was for some of it. Eventually, Galen escorted me into a back corner of the conservatory, where it was quieter. I'm afraid I sometimes find the bustle of a large party exhausting."

"Did you see Martin dance with Senara?"

"The tail of it, yes. She was very intent on something. I thought I saw Basil at the end of the room, but I'm not certain. Near the punch, I think he was drinking a good deal, and not just the punch. There were a lot of people, and he - blended in. Dark hair, neutral dark clothing."

"Mmm." Captain FitzRanulf made an entirely noncommittal noise.

"Beg pardon, Captain. But has there been any news of Basil? It's rather worrying, thinking... well, all sorts of things."

"We hope to have some soon. And a bit more news about the portal." She paused, then said "Have you felt unsafe here?"

It was a blunt question.

"Unsettled, a few times. But I think all great houses creak a bit in the night, don't they? And families, communities, they have their own customs and ways of doing things. If you're going to visit such a place, things will be done in particular ways. The fact the Amberlys are here, that they rarely travel, the considerations for Julius." Laura shrugged slightly. "They are odd, but not upsetting."

"And you have not felt pressured unduly?" There was something entirely disapproving lurking somewhere.

Laura blinked. "I thought I'd made that clear, ma'am. Galen and Martin have been entirely appropriate. While it's clear Madam Amberly would like to see Galen suitably married, she has exerted rather less pressure on that front than many people I've met who feel that way about their sons."

It was silent for a good minute, before the Captain nodded. "If you say so." She sounded entirely unconvinced, but Laura got the sense it wasn't precisely about the case. Which meant, likely, it was about whatever personal matter Carillon had got himself tangled in.

Laura brushed her skirt for a moment, trying to decide whether to ask a last thing. Nothing ventured, nothing gained, so she asked, "One question, Captain, if you don't mind. I presume you know my brother-in-law, and more than casually?"

There was a long pause. "Yes. He suggested I might have a suitable eye for this problem. And you did give him some excuse to meddle."

Laura gestured. "Whatever this was, it needed something more than the nearest Guard. Guard Trevallen seems very pleasant, ma'am, considerate, but I know that there's different skills in the Guard, even if I don't know the nuances. This needed someone who would understand what was expected, in a situation like this, and what wasn't."

That made the captain nod once, briskly. "Good morning, Miss Penhallow." She turned on her heel and strode off.

Laura could not decide if that was good, bad, or some unknown state.

# THIRTY-ONE

## MONDAY MORNING, EARLY

Galen was startled to find Laura already down in the breakfast room. He had thought he would be the first up, if rather under-slept. Martin had pulled him away from the conversation with his brother just in time last night, to spare his parents throwing eight kinds of fits. At least eight.

He nodded at Laura, who did not seem particularly conversational that morning, both of them eating quietly. She accepted another cup of tea, then he did. Only when the plates were cleared did he say "A walk, perhaps? Or would you rather stay in?"

She paused, looking at him. "A walk. And a bit of conversation?" There was something hesitant, and he was certain he'd done something wrong again, or she'd figured out some failing he hadn't noticed.

"A shawl, then?" He could be gracious. He would be gracious.

She smiled at him and let him sort out making sure she had a warm layer. They walked in silence, away from the house. He realised only halfway there that he was walking toward the little ledge where he and Martin sat.

"Are you all right?" he offered, eventually.

"Oh. Not ill. Thinking. And there's something, something we should talk about. Discuss. Together."

"Not an ultimatum, then?" He tried to pass it off as a joke, and it went rather flat.

She shook her head, and reached to take his hand, and squeeze it. "You're very sweet, Galen."

That, he was not at all sure what to make of. They were at the wall and stones above the ledge. "There's a little ledge and hollow there. It's dusty, you probably don't want to sit, even if you wanted to climb down, but we can, I mean, the view's very nice here too?" He was babbling. In the dictionary, next to the word, was his picture.

She hesitated. "Sit up here, perhaps? I'm afraid I didn't put on good shoes for scrambling this morning."

Galen nodded, looking around and finding a reasonably flat pair of boulders, sitting on the less comfortably shaped of the two. Then, of course, he was not at all sure what to say.

Laura swallowed, then said, "You're a very kind man, Galen, smart and caring and thoughtful. And I like you a lot, as a person."

He could hear the 'but' coming, though he just nodded.

"I'm just not sure we'd be a good match." It came out rather softly, so much so he had to lean forward to hear against the wind. It made him shiver.

"Any particular reason?"

She reached out, took his hand. "You're loyal, and you're thoughtful and you're kind. And I'd like very much to keep being your friend. But I think you and I, together, we'd end up stuck somewhere. Here. Cumbria. And not really doing much. Not making the world better, like you want." She stopped, looking out at the ocean.

"I don't know if I can do the things you want, socially. You saw how the party tired me out. And people have opinions about Father and Uncle Kenver. About my sister and her husband. I didn't finish school, and I don't know a lot of the right people. I'm not clever." Her voice ran down at the end of the comment.

"Oh." He swallowed. "So it's nothing I've done?"

"Oh, no, nothing like that. I thought you were really brave, talking to your brother. I'm glad you did. But I think..." She pauses. "You need someone who can inspire that more often. I know a bit about sorting things out with a sibling you've not talked to for ages. But that's not a problem you're going to have again, I think."

Galen blushed. "It was, it was really grand last night. Until Martin came to warn me. We were sitting in his laboratory, and talking, and he was showing me things he'd been working on. A whole series of magical paints, for materia work, based on some of the modern chemistry, but with the proper magical associations. Or there's this thing he's been working on, to help avoid infections, distilling some of the properties of particular kinds of moss."

Laura smiled at him. "Ah, just like that. Seems you're not going to let anyone stop you doing that, are you?"

Galen shook his head. "I don't know why I didn't. I mean, I do. But it wasn't a good excuse. So I'm glad you came, for that."

"Does he have an idea what happened with Senara? I mean, did you..."

"He told me a bit. For the Captain's ear. He told me last night she'd talked to him, at length. She was up late, I think."

"I was thinking, this morning. The Captain found me in the ballroom."

"Was there a problem?" Galen didn't like the sound of that.

"She asked me what I was doing, and I said I was trying to sort out Basil. There wasn't any news of him, at least any she would share with me. Was she awful with you?"

"No, quite polite, really. Especially once I passed on the information from my brother. Martin had a bad time."

"He looked it. When - when you went off after him."

"Martin's got dragged in for questioning before. This was mild, as it goes, from what he said, but he's got memories of when it wasn't."

Laura frowned. "That's not fair. Because he's not from that sort of family."

"Exactly. He doesn't have the protections I do. That's why we work well together. Even if we get in trouble, they let me out fast, and then I can help him. But it's rough on him. And not fair it's always him getting the hard part."

Laura pulled one foot up, looking thoughtful. Galen thought she looked gorgeous, her hair ruffled like that, but no, she was not for him, she'd decided.

"I think you need someone like Martin to marry. Not the getting questioned by the Guard part, specifically, I mean. But someone you can do that kind of thing with. Take different parts. Use your skills, use different skills. Different backgrounds."

Galen got the increasingly strong sense there was something else she wasn't saying. "You think I should find someone then?"

"Oh, yes. I don't know who to suggest, mind you. But I'll think about it. Maybe you can meet me in Trellech, or

London, go to a museum or a show or something, and we can talk it through more?"

"Me and Martin?"

That made her flush, and that rather clued him in. She looked away, then back at him, and said "I'd like that." She swallowed, then said, very carefully. "I kissed him last night. I don't know what he thinks of it? I think he felt he was betraying you. Or going to hurt you. And he said he'd explain it to you, but that would be really unkind."

Galen sat, his thoughts churning. He couldn't speak for a minute, then said, "Was it something you liked? If it weren't for - me being in the picture?"

She blushed, darker, and couldn't speak, just nod.

"Did he like it?"

"Maybe? We changed the subject, after I explained something. We were talking about things I'd learned in the sanitaria. Awful habits. Some experiences with the goldwasser."

Galen looked out toward the ocean, noticing a sailing ship, maybe two of them, coming from one of the other islands. "Oh." he wasn't quite sure where to start with that. "It didn't upset you, though?"

She looked at him, leaning forward. "That's what you worry about?"

"Well. You've said that you think we wouldn't suit. And that smarts, but I think you're right. Or at least I'm sure I'll agree you're right when I've had a chance to go lick my wounds and think about it. So we can work around to being friends properly."

She smiled at that. "And?"

"Well. If you and Martin wanted to, wanted to see each other. He deserves someone excellent."

"I am sure I'm not excellent." Laura leaned back, one hand on the rock behind her.

"Oh, you've done rather a lot. Shown up, been sensible, been persistently pleasant, even with people getting murdered. And being extremely rude and overbearing before they were, besides."

Laura waved a hand. "That's not ... she was a bother, but people shouldn't get murdered for being a bother. And she couldn't really hurt me. Didn't have the right leverage. It rather irritated her that she couldn't, did you notice?"

Galen considered that. "Has anyone told you you have rather odd standards?"

"Usually they don't say it out loud. They look at me, and hmm and go somewhere else. It works particularly well when they have glasses, you know." She mimed someone peering over reading glasses at Galen.

"Does it bother you? It bothers me, not doing the right thing."

"Well. It depends on what the right thing is. And why it's the right thing. There are all sorts of rather ridiculous social rules, aren't there? And some of them have some reason behind them. Like the one about covering your shoulders, if you're in a certain social circle. Because people can try to hurt you, and most of the things that would casually hurt you don't work well through cloth. But there are others, like wearing white shoes in certain seasons, that are just - silly. And some in the middle, like rules about chaperones."

"You clearly don't require one. Quite able to set your own boundaries."

"Not everyone listens to them. And I understand why the concept is there. But it's a different world than it used to be. I mean, the world is always changing."

Galen shook his head. "This is why I like talking to you."

She smiled. "Well. We can keep doing that. I suppose we should get back, now. And look, I'll tell your mother, if you like. So you don't have to."

Galen was sure his relief was like a lighthouse beacon. "You really would?"

Laura nodded, then offered her hand. "Come on. Escort me back, and I'll see if I can sort that out."

# THIRTY-TWO

## MONDAY, LATE MORNING

As it turned out, Madam Amberly was lurking in the parlour when they came back in. Galen leaned in to kiss her cheek, and said "I'm just going to see if Martin needs anything, Mother."

Which was what Laura had suggested he do, near enough. It did not make anything easier. His mother opened her mouth, then closed it with a snap, and said "Are you sure you wouldn't prefer to join us, Galen, dear?"

"I think Laura would like to talk to you privately, Mother."

Madam Amberly couldn't precisely argue with that. Not that it made what Laura needed to do any easier, and she frowned at Galen as he left. But he was doing what he needed to do, and of course Martin did need checking on.

"Well. I suppose." Madam Amberly turned back to Laura, and said, "Come sit, Laura, please, make yourself at home."

Laura sat, though that was not the most fortuitous phrasing. "Are you doing all right, Madam Amberly? This must be awfully difficult for you." She sounded like something out of a children's book, but it was the right thing to say.

Madam Amberly's expression eased a little. "Aren't you kind to ask dear. Sylvia's been a great help to me. She tells me you were kind enough to talk to her."

"She was very curious about - well. I suppose she told you about the goldwasser."

"Such a disgraceful thing. Though of course, most of the people involved weren't from the best families. And I suppose even the best families have a black sheep or two." The prevarication was rather intriguing to listen to, Laura thought, even if she didn't agree with the underlying theory. "You're all right now, though, she was clear on that."

"Oh, yes. It turns out it wasn't the drink that was dangerous, but how they made it. Which is done and over now, thankfully." She didn't want to talk to Madam Amberly about how good it had made her feel. This was not a woman who would admit to understanding addiction, even if Laura suspected Julius had had his own battle with it at one point.

"And the healers checked everything out?"

"Oh, yes. My brother-in-law was very insistent."

Madam Amberly tutted slightly. "He does have a reputation. He keeps getting involved in unseemly situations. That party, during the engagement, and there's other stories. That bit about him agitating for review of the application process for the Five Schools. And wasn't there someting about - oh, something distressing about military research."

"Oh, yes. He's quite respected high up in the Ministry, I've gathered. Including the Guard. And he has strong opinions about banning gas manufacture for war use." Laura thought it was entirely sensible, honestly, but there were apparently a lot of people who were convinced there would be no more wars. Carillon was much less certain on that point.

That got a bit more tutting. "Did he have a hand in sending this Captain to us?"

Asked like that, Laura couldn't outright lie. "I think so, yes. He didn't tell me for certain, but - he does worry about me. And my sister worries more."

"Hmmm." It was very non-committal. "Are there reasons they should be worried?"

"No." Laura tried to make her voice as clear and firm. "I'm a grown woman, and I appreciate their care and their help, but I don't need leading reins." And even if Parnell Amberly thought Galen needed them, he didn't either. Not that Laura could say that.

"It must be a difficult transition for your sister. From your - modest home, dear, in Lanyon? One of the papers ran a spread."

"It's lovely, but not large, no. It was my father and uncle's childhood home. And I grew up there, of course, and Lizzie."

"I suppose that does have an effect." She sounded entirely unconvinced.

"I've spent a lot more time at Ytene, and at Hawk's Breath, Carillon's other large estate, the past year or so. Enough to have a sense how complex they are to run, but I've learned a bit from Lizzie. And of course, each estate like that is its own place. There was that large party at Hawk's Breath over the summer, and the way the staff there do things, quite distinct from Ytene, of course, the whole building's different."

"Larger?"

"Georgian." Laura said. "Ytene is much older, as an estate, back to the Conquest. They've built on wings and all, but it's centred around the original great hall, still. And Hawk's Breath was set up for entertaining entirely differently."

"I gather there was some difficulty?"

"Nothing Carillon couldn't manage - I gather he was almost expecting something at the time? He doesn't talk to me about that kind of thing, though."

"That sort of discretion is admirable. And a woman who understands there are things to fuss about and things to leave alone does well as mistress of a large estate. The servants will have their particular ways, dear, and you must always know which ones are worth putting your foot down about."

That was not helpful for what Laura actually needed out of this conversation, but she nodded. "I've found the way you manage the staff here very thoughtful, Madam Amberly. Agnes has been very helpful, and the other staff - well, I've barely noticed them unless they needed to ask me something. And it must be more challenging, here, where even with the portal it's a little remote. You must need to do more planning in advance."

"Oh, yes, thank you, dear, so few people appreciate the effort it takes. Cook is experienced, of course, but we need to think ahead about what foods we will need, when the ferry boat comes around with the heavier stock, or the things that might spoil in the portal."

"That must be quite a challenge. And of course there are storms, and so on. Have you had other troubles with the portal, before this?"

"The portal? Oh, no. Dear Cassian uses it quite regularly, he goes into the city on business several times a week. Sometimes he stays overnight, of course. It's never given us the least trouble before, though it's still quite new. They said it took a little while for them to settle in, but we've had no trouble with it. I do hope it isn't damaged. Do you have a portal, dear?"

"There's one in the village, in Layon. A pleasant walk from our house. And there's one at Ytene, but it's not open for public use. Security, I guess."

"Well, one wouldn't want all and sundry tromping through whenever they liked, that's quite sensible." Laura managed to stifle a laugh. If that was what made Madam Amberly finally decide to approve thoroughly of Carillon, he'd find it hilarious. She would tuck that away for next time she needed to distract him.

"Where was Hawk's Breath, again, dear? What part of the country?"

"Cumbria. Not so far from yours, perhaps? A day's ride? It has a beautiful view down into the lake valley. Ancient orchards, and a small folly. But I suppose most places with enough land have a folly."

"Oh, indeed. We've thought of building one here, but it would need to be done carefully, to be useable after storms. And other than Galen, we don't spend much time outside. Blythe burns horribly, can you imagine? And I don't like how the sea air makes my skin feel."

"That would be uncomfortable, yes, of course. And you have the lovely conservatory here, more sheltered."

"How very kind of you to notice. That is my particular pride, or it was, until this awful thing."

Laura nodded, and murmured. "Very unfortunate it was there." She drew Madam Amberly out with a few comments about the plants, which filled a good five minutes. Some were kept for medicinal use, a salve she favoured. Some for scent, and some for the quality they gave the air, or the way they could be used in vases in the rooms. After an extended discussion of the varieties of ferns, Laura paused and cleared her throat. "Madam Amberly, I - there's something I should tell you."

Madam Amberly raised an eyebrow, but clearly got the sense that something important was happening. She straightened her shoulders, inclined her head, all the little postures of someone exerting their status more clearly.

"Galen has been a very gracious host, Madam Amberly." She paused. Better to be blunt, but not too blunt. "I - he's a fine young man. But we've talked, and I've told him that I don't think we'd make a good marriage. I know he wants to see to things on the other estates, and he cares about the causes he's learned about through the Dwellers. And I don't think I'm the right person to help balance what he needs there."

It was not an answer Madam Amberly wanted, nor was it one that made sense to her. She blinked several times, then settled on the all purpose response, "Pardon?"

Laura cleared her throat. "He's a lovely young man, and I like him as a person. I hope as a friend. But I think we'd make each other unhappy, married. Make each other less."

"You haven't exactly had a wide selection to choose from." It was a very sharp retort, and Laura had to force herself not to wince.

"No, Madam Amberly. But I would rather be picky and remain a spinster than make someone less than they could be. He deserves better than that. He's a fine and thoughtful young man, a credit to you. I told him I'd be glad to think if there are people who might suit him better."

"Was it that Martin? Suggesting something else? You were talking with him last night. A terrible influence, dragging him into this Dweller nonsense." Madam Amberly's voice was sharper, with an almost nasty edge. “I wondered if he was...”

Laura broke in, rude as it was, keeping her toe as even as she could. "Martin is also a fine young man. Of different temperament. He's a good and loyal friend to your son, they're very good for each other. It's been a pleasure to get to know them both. And you have a lovely home, you've been a most thoughtful hostess."

"Hmph." Well. Laura could not do much with that. Disgruntled matriarchs would have to sort themselves out. She ducked her head, and said "Should I give you a bit on your own, Madam Amberly?"

There was a long pause, as if she could not decide which choice to make, then there was a "That Martin has a great deal to answer for. And you, young miss, may go amuse yourself somewhere else."

Laura nodded once, and fled as promptly as she could without falling over her feet.

# THIRTY-THREE

## MONDAY AFTER LUNCH

Martin took a deep breath, drawing his jacket around him and jamming his hands in the pockets. He made his way out the side door, avoiding everyone, including the staff. Someone had to go look at the docks and the portal, or at least that was what he would tell Galen later. He was the person who wouldn't be missed, now that he had been cornered by Captain Fitz-Ranulf for another round of interrogation. It had left him with a dull headache and a strong desire to be alone.

Once he got outside, it was foggy, and he could see the rough shapes of the larger islands, but not well at all. Just the land, and a few of the taller buildings near the shore. Not raining, at least, but the rain had probably washed any useful evidence away.

He should probably be more worried about people not missing, actually, rather than the puzzle of Basil. Not that he doubted Galen's loyalty one bit, no matter what the Captain had suggested. But the way the Amberlys had been treating him this visit, he was clear they'd prefer a great deal more distance between him and their precious golden son.

He wasn't sure what had changed. It would be one thing if he'd published a story that questioned their interests, or interfered with Galen's prospects in making a marriage.

Which he supposed that he had, but even Madam Amberly couldn't possibly know about that yet. And it certainly wouldn't explain her attitude the past few days, before that kiss, that conversation after the kiss.

He took a deep breath, turning to head down the winding path to the docks, glancing from side to side to see if anything was out of place, if there was some clue about Basil he could find to distract himself from the weight of the implications in the Captain's new line of questioning. The most recent round, she'd nearly spelled out that she thought the Amberlys were using him, even Galen. Especially Galen. He couldn't believe it, and wouldn't. Not about Galen, anyway. But now the thought was in his head and he couldn't escape it.

Of course, the chances he'd notice anything subtle were next to nil. It's not as if he had every stone and pebble memorised. He doubted even Galen did, though Galen spent a lot more time wandering the island when he was alone here.

Unfortunately, that thought led Martin into another uncomfortable realisation. Galen was so pleasant when he visited, but he'd only realised this time how isolated his friend must be. Two parents, both very specific in their attitudes and opinions. Blythe, who remained an enigma, and who was required to be Madam Amberly's shadow, near enough. Julius, locked up in the attic.

He wasn't even the one who'd got Galen to talk to his brother. That smarted, the slow burn of acid dripping, like when he'd helped Thomasina with some arcane bit of her alchemy. Not that alchemy wasn't all arcane. But maybe he was too close. Or too long a friend. It didn't matter. He had to keep telling himself, until he believed it, that it didn't matter who got Galen talking to Julius. It just mattered they were on the same side of the door for a change.

Still. It changed things. As long as he'd known Galen, they'd been like brothers, because Julius wasn't there. First he was older, and then he was at war, and then he was injured in ways Galen wasn't told about, was kept from understanding.

The Amberlys had refitted this place, and at some cost, he was sure, and then they'd just dug in, and made people come to them. Well. Not all of them. Mr Amberly went into Trellech several times a week for meetings and business. Both of them went for parties or events. But Galen just hovered, trapped, except maybe when he could join the Dwellers at some gathering or got an invitation to someone else's party. His parents didn't even like him being gone long enough for a regular session in Thomasina's lab, much as Galen treasured the chance when he got it.

He kicked a stone, watching it skitter downhill. Then he stopped himself from kicking another, in case it dislodged a clue. That wouldn't do at all. And he'd be a lousy reporter if he destroyed critical information. That's the kind of thing that got you mocked by your colleagues, even if it didn't lead to anything worse, like the Guard and Silence oaths. Which were already a certainty, and bad enough.

That made him shiver. He'd never talked to Galen properly about what happened, the times he'd been questioned. He was supposed to be good with words, but Martin had never known how to put the feelings into something he could tell anyone else. It was all about being cold and weak, and a catch in his chest, and hearing something that sounded like death that wasn't him, but was. It was an intimate fear. It was logical and illogical, all at once, and he couldn't shake it once it got into his head. Not for weeks, usually.

He supposed, thinking it over, that it was like taking a cup and spilling out all the life and beauty and joy that was in it, and leaving it empty. Lurking. Lurking was an excellent word. Waiting for something worse to fill it up, or rust and mould or whatever it was that was awful. There wasn't anything like that emptiness, he couldn't begin to explain it. It was just there until he managed to fill it up with something better.

Most of the time it wasn't a problem. It wasn't unless he had to take an oath by the Silence, and feel that looping around him, pulling him down like an undertow. It had only been four times, in all his life, and he didn't want a fifth. Not right now, when he wasn't sure if he'd have work come next week, or if he'd have to move back with his mum and dad, kip on the sofa, keep out of the way. He didn't want it, desperately didn't want it, and there was a dead woman in the shed who made sure it would be otherwise, her and her mysteriously missing brother.

It might not come to the sofa. There might be room with the Dwellers, or one of them could put him onto day labourer work, much as he hated it.

It rather depended on whether Galen was still talking to him, probably. After all, Martin had kissed Laura, and Laura, she liked Galen. Martin could tell that. Whether it was the kind of liking turned into marrying, well, that was another question. But she liked Galen enough not to want to hurt him. And what had Martin done? She'd kissed him, and he'd not pulled away. Hadn't wanted to, even knowing that his brother was courting her. He'd held her hand, and he'd leaned close to her, close enough to smell her hair, the scent in it.

He was coming down to the docks now, which at least distracted him from his brooding. And thinking about Laura, who was not relevant to this immediate investigation. He had been down here before, he and Galen sometimes took the smaller sailing boat out. It was a pleasure to sail with two, where the larger one for bringing in supplies really needed three.

It wasn't that rare for one to be gone, but both were, and the little rowboat that sometimes got used for checking in around the island was pulled well up onto the rocky beach, a strong rope connecting it to the rock of the cliffs. Whatever boat the Guard had used must have gone on to other tasks, since there was nothing tied up.

Martin frowned, shoving his hands deeper in his pockets as the wind picked up. There was the dock, not very big, bobbing at the end of the steps carved into the stone. There were the rings for the boats. And there, there was something odd, that caught his attention. He made his way down the last step, careful not to slip on the stone, before stepping onto the dock, hearing the wood creak.

He walked all the way to the end and there, caught between two planks, was a length of rope, one end still tied to one of the rings. He couldn't see the other end, but this didn't look as if the rope had come undone. It wasn't trailing out into the ocean like it might if the boat had pulled it apart in the storm. Even if something had come undone, surely it would be the end tied to the dock. Instead there was a length disappearing underneath.

He kept well back from it, so that he could swear he hadn't touched it, and he was stepping away when he saw Guard Ames coming down the path. "Sir, Guard Ames?"

The man paused for a moment, then moved quite swiftly down the curve of the path. "Away from there, please."

"I haven't touched anything, sir. Glad to swear so." Saying that often reassured people.

"Hmmm." It was non-committal. "Show me your hands." The command came out briskly. Martin held his hands out. They were dry from being in his pockets. "What did you find?"

"There is a rope there, and it does not look as if it came loose in the ordinary way of things. Wedged between the planks, five feet from the end of the dock, right side."

"You are very precise." It seemed that Guard Ames could not decide whether he approved or not. "You are the - journalist, then?"

"Yes, sir. They do pay me to notice things." When they paid, but that wasn't a problem for the immediate moment, and sinking back into those ruminations would help nothing.

"Stay there, please." Ames continued forward, leaning to peer at the rope, then casting a light charm, and setting the ball of light a foot above the rope, in order to - do something. Martin wasn't sure what. There were other movements, not measuring the rope, nor touching it, but something about the position.

Five minutes later, Ames looked back over his shoulder. "You should go away now."

"May I take a message up for you?"

"Goodness, no. Captain FitzRanulf knows her work." Ames sounded decidedly offended.

"Send down a flask of hot tea?"

There was a long pause, and the wind picked up again.

Ames glanced at the sky, and nodded. "If that is possible, yes."

Martin took that as his cue. "Sir."

He walked back up the path, at a good pace. When he reached the side path to the portal, he looked down to the dock. Ames was still hard at work on the rope, not looking up to the house, so Martin ducked off to look at the portal. He had even less sense of what might be different here, but he could still have a look.

So far as he could see, in the overcast light, there was nothing unusual about the portal. Nothing had been carved into it, nothing seemed to have been taken away. There were stories, in the sort of boy's own adventure magazines that were very popular with schoolboys, of people tossing a particular powdered stone at a portal, and disabling it. Or some particular potion, dashed upon the roots. He could see no sign of any of it, and frankly, it was foolish to expect to.

Which meant he should stop by the kitchen and get a flask sent down for Ames and tell Galen and Laura what he hadn't found.

# THIRTY-FOUR

## MONDAY AFTERNOON

"Martin, come, please." Galen had claimed the parlour and the fireplace. He'd expected to have to deal with his parents, but they were up in their sitting room. He thought. He wasn't sure what he thought of their absence, actually. "We're staying out of the way. You look," He paused, and tried something different. "Dweller at the Forge, how is the fire?"

Martin shrugged, a sharp little movement. "Ready for tempering. What are we doing here?"

Galen considered that, and felt that was at least some improvement.

Laura smiled at him. "Come sit here, it's warmer. Tea, as you like it." They were sitting at the card table, the tea things between them, as if the less cushioned chairs would signal to everyone else a sense of appropriate distance.

Galen watched his friend, the complex expression, a mix of guilt and pleasure and uncertainty. Martin looked at him, and Galen immediately said, "It's fine." He put a weight on it, hoping that his brother would take the correct meaning, about Laura and everything. "And she's right. Get warm, please. We were trying to figure out what we know, and what we don't know."

"Someone cut one of the boats at the dock free." Martin said, sinking into the third chair. "Thanks for the tea." He drained about half the cup immediately, then set it down.

Laura was looking at the cards that were laid out on the table. She picked up the deck, and started thumbing through them. It seemed like she wasn't paying attention, and Galen said, "That's something. What else do we know?"

Laura responded, not looking away from her hands, "Did we figure out more about why the Wilsons were here in the first place?"

Galen shook his head. "Aunt Sylvia said - going into lunch, I heard her - that Uncle Attis didn't like the materia deal that they were proposing, and father did. I don't understand the details though, why it would be a bad deal." He frowned. "No, she said it was - improbable? Something about it didn't make sense. She was trying to talk Uncle into explaining it to the Guard, better than she could."

"That's queer." Laura sounded decidedly distracted. "And the rope, you said, Martin. Was there anything else?"

"Guard Ames came down not long after me, and he shooed me off. I looked at the portal, and didn't see anything out of place, but I suppose I wouldn't. I mean, unless it were quite obvious." And then he asked, his voice a little bolder than Galen could dare. "What in green magic are you doing, Laura?"

She looked at Martin for a moment, smiling, and then back down. "A couple of weeks ago, I was at a party, and they had a card reader there, as an entertainment. And there was quite a queer reading." Laura waved at the cards. "I was just thinking, if we laid the people out, like we did with the cups and saucers, about the space, maybe something would make more sense."

Galen raised an eyebrow at Martin. This seemed a tad ridiculous. But Martin just shrugged, and said "I don't think either of us have a better idea. Do you, Galen?"

"Um. No?" He had to admit he didn't. "Do you know the deck meanings?"

"I'm not an expert, but enough to be going along with. Again, reasonably approved activities for recuperation, so long as one wasn't actually using energy. And the cards are beautiful."

"So, where do we start?" Galen couldn't help leaning forward a bit. Whatever else, this wasn't trudging through the same information the same way, over and over again.

"Here." Laura slid a card of a woman in a bright red dress, bound and blindfolded, with swords stuck into the ground around her, point down. "Eight of Swords. That's Senara."

"Bound?"

"Oh, something had her entirely tangled up, don't you think?" Laura sounded very certain of this. "She was trying to find a way out of something. Maybe that's why she wanted to come here, to see if Julius was a way to cut herself free." She frowned. "I feel sorry for her, maybe."

Galen could not help but remember Julius's comments about absolution. He did not say anything about it, he wanted to keep something of his time with his brother to himself, yet, but he nodded a small agreement.

There was an awkward pause, before Martin said, "So which card is Julius?"

Laura frowned. "I mean, normally you'd expect one of the Apprentices, or something of the kind. Or possibly the Magician, for his alchemy?"

"Isn't there one about sacrifice?" It came out of Galen's mouth before he could stop himself. Laura looked at him, blinking, and it was as if he had to continue. "Julius told me, told me last night, that he knew Senara was spying. That he - he got himself sent where he could help," He swallowed hard. "So it would be him trying his best to stop it, not someone else. Knowing it probably wouldn't work."

"Oh." Laura's voice was very soft. "That's very brave of him. Then and now." She thumbed through the deck, pulling out the card of a man hanging from a tree by one foot, red shirt, blue hose, and with an infinitely peaceful expression on his face. Galen hadn't seen his brother's face in a decade, but the expression in the eyes was the same, and the blonde hair had the same wave. He had no idea how his mother could play social card games with this deck.

Laura must have caught something of his roiling emotions, and she reached out to cover his hand for a moment, before she said. "Who else?"

"My parents?" Galen was not certain he wanted to know what Laura would pick. Or Martin.

She considered, thumbing through, pulling a card out, then pushing it back in. "I think your father wants to be the Emperor, all expansive joviality. But I don't think ... I think maybe he's the Lord of Pentacles." She pulled the card out.

"Your mother, that's easier. She was talking about how she set up the conservatory and gardens, how much she loves green growing things. That's the Lady of Pentacles." She moved the cards around, putting Senara to the right back corner, in the conservatory, Julius's card by his attic, and the queen and king together in the ballroom.

"I'm not sure I want to ask this, but what about us?" Martin's voice sounded distant for a moment, and when Galen looked up, there was a little trembling.

"This is the same card that came up in that reading, a few weeks ago. Though that deck was a man and two women." She turned over the Lovers. The Howard deck had a woman, attractive but not stunningly gorgeous, standing between two men, one young and handsome but poorly dressed, one richly adorned, but with a sharp unpleasant face and a look of distaste. "But that's not the right thing at all, is it?" She then pulled out the Apprentice of Swords. "This must be you, Martin. See, there's the pen."

"And an owl, but I suppose you can't have everything. And Galen?"

She tapped the card. "Part of me wants to say the Fool." Galen inhaled sharply, wanting to object, then he bit his tongue as she continued. "Not because you're foolish in the usual sense, Galen, but because you're at the beginning of something. You can feel it, can't you? Beyond all of this?"

He felt so sharply that this woman could see him this clearly and not want to marry him. And yet, she was entirely right. She then turned a card over. "Apprentice of Wands. See, there's your fox, in the corner, there. And the boar, too. Boar and fox are friends."

The way she put it made him smile, despite himself, and he nodded. "Fair. Very fair."

"Who else, then?"

Laura dealt out the Lady of Swords. "Madam Tipson. And this is Healer Tipson." Lord of Cups. They got their own places near the pentacles. And then she placed a few others for the servants, in their various places.

"And you?"

Laura shrugged, and before she could say anything, Galen said, "The Star."

Martin looked up at him, and grinned. "Oh, yes." And then they both had the same realisation at the same time, as

Laura drew out the card to look at it, of a golden-haired woman, dressed in translucent fabric, so that they could see every curve of her body, lit gently from behind and reaching up to appear to touch a star with one hand, water pouring from a jug in her other into a pool at her feet.

"Um."

"You flatter, both of you. You are very dear men." Laura's voice was clear and pleased, but she was apparently having none of their embarrassment, at least about this. "I can't decide about Basil."

"Do we think he did it?"

"Well. We know it wasn't us. And it wasn't Julius, I think we can assume that."

"But." The horror of it hit Galen all of a sudden. "Killing your sister. And it wasn't." He put his hand to his mouth, suddenly tasting bile. "He. He. He." Galen swallowed hard, and then took a sip of his tepid tea. After a deep breath, he could go on. "Aunt Silvia said it might have been a two-part poison. Which - means he decided twice he was going to kill her. Or at least thought about it. It wasn't a sudden decision, an act of fear or rage. Or making a bad choice on the moment because he was drunk."

He couldn't look up for a long moment, and when he did, they were both watching him, concerned. He took a deep breath, and said, "She might have been a traitor, but she deserved better than that."

They all heard the boots on the marble floor before anything else, then his mother's voice, ringing out clearly. "About time."

Captain FitzRanulf swept into the parlour, the other two Guards behind her, and Guard Trevallen immediately came to Martin and put hands on his shoulders, holding him in place. Martin grimaced, and Galen knew it was painful. He pushed back from his chair. "What are you doing?"

"I am taking Martin Taylor into custody." Her voice was even and steady, a woman with a clear plan and nothing to stop her.

"You have no cause." Standing there was taking all the bravery he had, he couldn't stand to look at his parents, either of them. Laura stood, taking a few steps back out of the way, he felt her more than saw the motion.

Ames advanced, casting some sort of cantrip that curled in deep sullen red coils around Martin's wrists that brought them together, crossing in front of him. Martin looked like he had collapsed into himself, a fit of quite reasonable despair that broke Galen's heart and hope.

"We will take him into custody, convey him to Trellech, where he may be properly questioned under Silence oath about his activities." Galen did not like the sound of that, not one bit, nor the part where she continued, "As he is a person of interest in this enquiry we cannot afford the risk of something happening to prevent him from testifying."

"Mother, please." He finally looked at his mother, but she looked smug and self-satisfied.

It was Laura who spoke, behind him. "I believe the law permits a statement of the evidence."

Captain FitzRanulf almost sounded amused. "Martin Taylor has stated he was in the room of the deceased, at the time of her death, for a meeting substantiated by no one else."

"Which means he was not killing her downstairs in the conservatory." Laura was insistent, her voice clear, pitched lower, not shrill and high. She saw something, he was sure of it, something that would keep Martin safe. He searched the Captain's face for a clue that would help him know what to do, not daring to look at Laura for a hint, and could not penetrate the wry and distant expression. She would not bend for someone like him. She did not like people like him, she'd made that clear.

Before Captain FitzRanulf could say anything further, they all heard the sound of more boots on the marble, and another Guard, one they had not seen before, pushed Basil into the room. "Captain, you requested we locate this man?"

Basil looked decidedly scruffy, unshaven and wearing a wool sweater with several snags and a battered oilskin coat over it that was far too big in the shoulders for him.

"Ah." The captain pivoted precisely on her heel, as if she had choreographed the entire thing. "Where was he?" She asked as if she were asking something as inconsequential as the flavour of the tea scones.

"On one of the small islands between here and Bryher. Looks like he went aground in the dark and couldn't get free."

"Quite. Take Mr Wilson to the library. Do not leave him alone. I will be along shortly." There was a satisfaction to her now, quite unlike when she had swept in to claim Martin, and it left Galen utterly bewildered.

She pivoted back, now looking at Martin again, but at a nod, Trevallen stepped back and released him, as if they had not just been on the point of accusing him of murder. "Martin Taylor, will you take an oath on your magic, on the Silence, to remain here, where you can be found easily, not attempting to leave the island, hide, or destroy evidence?"

Martin swallowed once, then took a deep breath. "I swear on the Silence I will remain on the island, where I can be found easily, not attempting to alter the course of justice, until such time as the current investigation is completed."

There was a slow smile Galen could not begin to interpret, then she said. "That is not what I asked, but it is correct. You are on your own recognisance, then." She made a pass with her hand in the air, and the dull red bindings disappeared, as if they had never existed save for a shift in pressure that felt to Galen like the aftermath of a storm. With that she swept out of the room. In the distance, they could hear Basil whining about how he was cold and hungry, and was this how they treated someone marooned on an island for days.

Galen didn't know what to make of the fact his parents disappeared without comment. It did not promise anything good.

# THIRTY-FIVE

## MONDAY AFTERNOON

Everyone leaving had at least given Martin a chance to gather himself. He felt awful, like he'd been pummelled in a particularly physical game of bohort, trod into mud and underfoot.

Laura's comment about fairness made him cough, and she turned to look at him, visibly worried. "Are you, no, you're not." She stopped, then said more cautiously. "You have experience, with your own wars."

He nodded, very slowly, barely shifting, like the movement could destroy him.

She reached out, and took his hand, not quite asking but giving him more than enough time to pull away. "Can you tell us?"

He'd expected her to say 'me' and that would have broken any fondness he had for her. Instead, he found himself falling down a deep well, the way she so easily included Galen. Included him. Galen settled back in his chair, entirely at ease, the relaxed pose he couldn't fake.

Martin took a breath. "She - came and found me. This morning." He paused. "She doesn't like your family, Galen.

At all. She was sure you were all hiding something. Protecting something."

Galen leaned forward. "Do you have an idea who? Or what?"

Martin frowned, thinking back. "It's not as if she told me," he pointed out. "She said things that implied your father. Your brother. Maybe you, or you helping cover things up. She thought for a bit you'd helped move things, but more people than just me said you hadn't."

Galen frowned. "Did she make trouble for Julius? Is he?" Then he stopped. "You'd tell me if you knew."

"I'm quite certain she talked to him. At some length, I think, but I don't know when. But I think she found him - frustrating? She would not drag him away, but she was certain something was going on, something wrong."

"This isn't some horrid gothic, with the roles reversed, what the books would say was a first wife stuffed up in an attic." Laura burst out with the comment. "I never saw the point of those, people notice when there's a whole area of a house no one goes into."

Martin blinked at her. "What did you notice?"

"Well, you told me about Julius." Laura pointed this out evenly. "It's not exactly a proper experiment. But I noticed how the maids disappear at particular times. Several times they told me someone would be along in fifteen minutes, something like that. Enough time for someone to run a tray to the upstairs part of the family wing and come back down. But too short for a lot of other time-consuming tasks a maid might do."

"But there are surely shorter tasks?"

Laura waved a hand. "Then they'd be along in a few minutes, not send someone to tell me the maid was coming.

It was as if it were a standard thing. Knowing how long it would take."

There was a knock at the door, and Millicent's voice, "Tea, sir." Galen got up to open the door for her, and she came in, set it on the low table near them, and disappeared again. Martin caught the way Galen glanced at them, then Galen said "I'll pour."

Laura blushed for a moment, then settled her hand more securely around Martin's, weaving her fingers between his. He blinked at her, then down at their hands, then managed to squeeze her fingers. He hoped it was reassuring. Having her there certainly was.

She swallowed, then said. "So. Yes. People might notice. They might not realise they notice? Many people don't. They see the signs, not what's going on below them." Then, she returned to the real question. "So she doesn't like Galen's family."

Martin nodded.

Laura chewed on her lip for a moment. "Galen's family in specific? Or families like this in general? Did it seem personal?"

Martin tilted his head, and then said, slowly. "I think in general. But that doesn't make sense, does it? Sending someone like that here?" He squeezed her hand again, mostly to feel her squeeze back, which she did.

Galen said, after a moment. "When she - when I thought she was going to take you away. I realised she wouldn't listen to me. She's not one I can be charming at."

Laura nodded. "No. She'll tolerate me." She considered, then added, thinking out loud. "And she's been pushing Martin. Martin, has it been her coming for you? Or has there been something about - worrying other people have it in for you? It'd be easy to make you disappear, if you stayed here when she left. Suspicious, but easy."

Martin shivered at the thought. "They wouldn't."

"They looked pleased enough to have you arrested. They don't know you very well. Or Galen. Sorry, Galen."

Galen grimaced, but said, "You're not wrong." Then he asked, "Do you think she was sent specifically because of that? Because she wouldn't just listen to the family?"

"Carillon didn't tell me who he was suggesting. So there are a couple of options. That she's not one of the people he recommended. But I think she is, from what she said to me earlier. Or that there's something else going on we're missing." She paused. "Or the world's gone completely haywire with no anchor in reality, but we can probably rule that out."

"Do you think that's likely?" Galen and Martin echoed each other, and despite the fears Martin still had, he grinned at his friend.

"It seems the least logical and most complicated." Laura considered, then reached for her tea. Martin found himself unsure what to do with his hands now, so he did the same. Tea was safe.

"Presuming she's here for a reason - because if she isn't, we won't figure it out - why?"

Martin sipped his tea, then offered, slowly. "There's a rather horrid idea. What if he thought you needed protecting? And asked for someone who would, who wouldn't be intimidated if you needed help? By all the money and the posh."

He watched Laura's expression shift, from thoughtful consideration to a moment of pure fury to settling down into something less terrible and exhausting. What she said was very short and simple. "Oh, probably. She was fishing for something like that. Blast him. He's a good man, but he sees the world a very particular way. Through a monocle."

"Does he really wear one?"

"Affectation." Her voice was still a bit flat, but there was a hint of amusement. "I do like him, when he's not being lord of the manor directly at me. Not lord of my manor, thanks awfully." She idly started cutting the remaining deck of cards, as if it provided a necessary distraction.

Martin had to snort. "All right." Then he sobered. "Assuming that logic, why was she taking me off?"

"On the assumption that if you were separated from Galen, it might be useful information about other pieces? And keep them from doing something dreadful to you, given the opportunity. And I think it's clear Galen's parents were doing their best to protect him. Julius, too."

Galen had been quiet for a good bit, but said softly. "You don't think they did something?"

Laura frowned. "I barely know them. And I suppose people do kill other people for what seem like pointless reasons. But your parents seemed quite normal, really? Considering?"

"Considering?"

She waved a hand. "Worrying about your brother. About you. I mean, going off to an island off the tip of Cornwall isn't a precisely sensible and practical lifestyle choice in the long run. But it's an understandable one, if what they want is to keep you all somewhere they know where you are, and safe." She paused. "Particularly - I don't know if you know there's rumours. That Julius is mad. Which would be another reason to be, to be away."

Galen scowled at that last. "You sound like you sympathise with them?"

"I was the reason my mother and father spent years

apart. Without me messing things up, Mother would have been travelling. Some of the time, anyway. And I watched my mother. Other people's mothers. Not everyone does it like that, getting all broody and over-protective, and all? But enough people do, when you've seen a few dozen people deal with horrible things."

Galen frowned. "Why couldn't they say so?"

"You didn't ask, for one thing. And they didn't want to talk about it, for another. We're all terribly British. Talking about what scares us, that won't do. It's protective."

Martin finished his tea and set down the cup. "Do you - does your brother-in-law know a solicitor?"

"Oh, I'm sure." Laura sounded very certain. "But if you can do the Silence oath."

"It's not being asked about this that worries me. It's what else they might ask. Before..." Martin couldn't keep going. "They threatened things. Held me for a long time. Without anyone knowing where I was. Or what was going on."

"Oh, well. In that case, I will stick to your side, and find you a solicitor, and bring you sandwiches."

Martin blinked at her, utterly bewildered now.

## THIRTY-SIX

### MONDAY AFTERNOON

The bewilderment didn't last. It was interrupted, by Galen's parents coming in from upstairs. "That Captain, she wants us down here. I can't imagine why." The Tipsons followed, though with less complaint.

"I'm sure she'll explain, sir." That was Guard Trevallen, standing rather implacably by the door. Laura thought he looked uncomfortable. He'd been ill at ease all along, but it was worse now. She caught him looking here and there, avoiding the eyes of the Amberlys. Something was up, or wrong, or going badly. She closed her eyes for a moment, thinking of the Captain, who she was, what part she was playing, and cut the deck again, looking at the card revealed.

The card's colour caught her first, deep purples and shadows set against a brightly lit figure, as if he shone with light. The breath went out of her in a sudden gasp. The Magician, with his power and his sleight of hand, stared back at her, surrounded by all the paraphenalia of Elizabethan magic.

Martin glanced at her, then at Galen, and Galen said

"Agnes, would you go fetch a shawl for Miss Penhallow, please?"

Laura almost objected, but the fussing filled in the space, and it was less awful than the way the Amberlys were eyeing her, and Martin, and Galen. Disappointment in Galen, something more complicated to her and to Martin. There was no conversation, and when Agnes came back with a shawl from her room, Laura accepted it.

The staff filed in, one by one, lining up, as if they'd been ordered to. Agnes ducked in at the rear, finding her her place next to Millicent with a furtiveness that suggested she was anxious about getting in trouble for fetching the shawl rather than queueing.

A moment later, Captain FitzRanulf swept in. "Good day. I do believe we have the beginnings of a resolution. Mr Wilson, there." Basil was shown to a chair near her, nearly within arm's reach. "And," She paused, turned, and then held the door. "Julius Amberly."

Laura looked up, blinking. She could see the same hair Galen had, that wave of blond, not quite curling, though cut rather shorter. But his face was behind a white mask made of rather matte ceramic, that showed just his eyes. He was wearing an old green over-robe, faded and worn at the elbows, over shirt and trousers and slippers. She could see him in the card that Galen had picked out, the golden hair and acceptance of his fate.

Galen sat up sharply. "Julius." And then more cautiously, a "Captain, ma'am?" before he couldn't figure out how to ask the questions he had.

"Here, that chair is fine." She pointed at one by itself, on Galen's other side, then paused just a moment. "I wanted you all here so we can sort this out. My plan is to make it clear what I know about this case, and then to take the relevant steps to charge and try the guilty."

Laura frowned, then realised that there was rather an implication that more than one person was guilty.

"Everyone settled? Good." There was a pause, then the Captain gathered herself, rather visibly. Invisibly. Magically. It was like she was pulling a cloak around her. "I declare this space held by the powers of justice and fair hearing." She made a particular gesture in the air, too fast to make sense of, then clapped her hands smartly three times. It ended with her hands clasping the opposite wrist in front of her for a moment.

Laura could feel a ripple of magic and then glanced at Martin and Galen. "May I ask, Captain, what that does?"

It turned the Captain's attention to her. The effort had taken something out of her, she needed a moment to get recover. But better that sharp attention be turned on Laura than Martin. Or Galen. Or Julius.

There was a slight nod, then the older woman said, "It creates an expectation of justice, magically, enforced by the Pact. It is not the same as a formal court, in that I can not enforce truth telling. I am not a magistrate or judge, nor lord of the land. But it should make it more obvious if people are not being as truthful as they should be." She glanced around, stern and focused, then said. "Let us begin."

They all shifted a little, the creaking of the chairs and sofas, the rustle of the staff who'd formed a tight line at the end of the room.

"You, Madam Amberly, and Mister Amberly, invited a house of guests to attend on you, some staying for several days, some visiting solely for the party on Saturday evening. Healer and Madam Tipson arrived on Thursday morning,

Miss Penhallow early in the afternoon, and the Wilsons nearly at supper time."

Madam Amberly nodded. "That is correct."

"Mr Wilson, when were you and your sister invited?"

"Oh, Senara had a meeting with Cassian a few weeks ago. I'd have to look at our diaries to remember precisely when and your people won't permit me to go near the rooms."

"As best you can remember." The captain's voice was clipped.

"Three weeks ago, the meeting. The invitation was ten days before. Short notice, but I gathered Cassian had just discussed the party with his wife."

"And your connection?"

"As I mentioned.." He sounded bored, more than anything, Laura thought. "Senara had known Julius previously." Julius barely got a nod.

"Julius?"

Julius spoke very carefully. "Knew her in the War. Never met Basil face to face. That I know." The sentences were short, clipped, a bit muffled by the mask.

"That you know?"

"Events. Large events. Paris. She kept," A longer pause, not driven by his slower speech, but looking for the right word. "Kept her own counsel."

The Captain nodded again. "And you, Miss Penhallow? Your invitation?"

"About a month ago. I'd met Madam Amberly at a gathering just before my sister and brother-in-law went on their delayed honeymoon trip. She extended the invitation by note a few days later."

"Did she mention the Wilsons?"

"No, I rather thought they were a later addition, but I wasn't told anything specific."

"And you arrived as I said?"

"In the early afternoon on Thursday. Galen and Martin came to meet me, the footmen were busy with some project for the larger gathering on Saturday. Putting up the lights and decorations, possibly."

"Did you know anyone here beforehand, other than brief social acquaintances?"

"No, ma'am." Laura paused. "By reputation, a little. But Galen and Martin are enough younger than I am that I wouldn't have known them through school circles. And my sister is older, so not her circles."

"Mr Taylor, you've known Galen Amberly for quite some time?"

Laura watched Martin shift uncomfortably as the focus moved to him. "Since we were at school, Captain. We are members of the same society, and I've been a guest here many times. Every two or three months, on average. We see each other at other times, of course."

"You are employed?"

"As an occasional journalist for several papers, on a freelance basis."

"And Galen Amberly, you are not employed, currently?"

Galen shook his head. "We've discussed some apprenticeship options, but have not quite found the proper fit. I've assisted Father in some tasks, but it's clearly not my forte." Laura frowned, since Madam Amberly had been quite clear she didn't consider apprenticeship an option. Perhaps Galen had been arguing for it against his parents' wishes.

"And you agree with Mr Taylor's statements."

"Oh, yes. He is one of my best friends."

"And your brother?"

Laura watched Galen's shoulders tense, the quick glance he took. "My brother and I have been - kept apart, since his injuries. We did talk, after this happened, and we regret that, but it's rather soon to say what will come of it." There was something self-protective in it, and Laura caught Julius shifting, his fingers twitching for a moment.

Captain FitzRanulf nodded. "Julius Amberly?"

The words came slowly again. "Have my wing. My lab, laboratory. My research. Don't see others. Guests come, sometimes. Ignore them."

Another nod, then a precise "Tell me about the gathering, Madam Amberly."

That got a precis of the invitations, how they went out. "I had planned it as a time for Laura and Galen to become better acquainted, though I gather that will not work out as I wished." Her tone was quite bitter, sour.

Laura tried not to wilt under the captain's focused attention. "Miss Penhallow?"

"Galen and I had a pleasant conversation this morning. I like him as a person and hope to continue the friendship, but we are not suited for marriage. He's been open and honest with me throughout."

"And Mr Taylor?"

"Martin as well. As I made clear to you from our first interview." She lifted her chin, trying to find a place between the fear and frustration she was feeling.

"I've heard about the Friday supper from everyone there, we needn't recap that, I think. And on Saturday, everyone had their own amusements until the evening gathering? When did the first guests arrive?"

There was a long pause, then the butler coughed and said, from the line of staff at the back of the room. "Half six, ma'am, in scheduled arrivals from different portals. The footmen were kept quite busy until nearly eight, when the last guests arrived."

"And there was dancing in the ballroom, people in the dining room for the buffet, and the conservatory for a quieter space."

Several people nodded.

"And there is no clear sense of who was moving where at any particular time, other than a few mentioned moments. You and Miss Penhallow took a break from the dancing to sit in the conservatory, didn't you, Galen Amberly?"

"Yes, Captain. She was tired, and I went to fetch drinks and refreshments, then we sat and talked."

"Did you notice anything out of place, when you were there?"

"No, ma'am. But of course, people were coming and going, their own conversations. I saw Blythe several times, back and forth."

There was a slow nod, as if Galen had missed something, then a long silence.

"Blythe? Do you have anything to add?"

Blythe had faded into the background, she always did, but she shook her head slightly. "Captain. No." Laura couldn't decide if that meant there wasn't anything more, or if it was something that Blythe had said in private, but wouldn't dare in front of the elder Amberlys, upon whom she depended.

# THIRTY-SEVEN

## MONDAY AFTERNOON

"And Mr Taylor, where were you toward the end of the party?" Captain FitzRanulf's voice seemed mild, but Martin could hear the steel underneath it. She might as well have drawn a sword and held it to his throat.

"Ma'am." He paused, gathering himself as best he could.

"Explain what you told me in our interview. The first one."

He couldn't help shivering for just an instant, the instinctive flinch.

"I was out on the terrace, and I heard a group of people talking. About the age of Julius or a bit older, somewhere between Galen and his parents. They were talking about people at the party, including Senara, and there was some gossip that she'd known Julius during the War."

"Do you remember who that was?"

"One of them was named Orion. That's no particular help, but he mentioned hearing it from Perry Lawton. I don't know Peregrine Lawton, but I believe his sister was around our age, Galen."

Galen nodded. "Married several years ago. One of the Iseults in our year." There had been rather a fashion for the name.

The captain nodded. "I can follow up on that, thank you. The name is a help. Did he say anything else?"

"That it was quite early in the War - he thought early 1915, just after everyone realised they wouldn't be home for Christmas. He remembered both of them, flashy, spending a lot of money. He commented she dressed up nicely, and it was well before most Americans were anywhere near the War. I got the impression they stood out."

Captain FitzRanulf nodded. "Mr Wilson, can you confirm the time frame?"

Basil looked irritated, but he nodded. "We were in Paris then, yes. And quite active socially, with officers posted to the city. Well behind the front lines."

"And then, Mr Taylor?"

"Orion said that then they sent Julius to the front, and Senara disappeared. That she turned up a few other places, he'd heard - London, Trellech, maybe Russia and Egypt. He sounded like he wasn't sure."

"Julius Amberly?"

There was a rumbling sound from Julius, then a "There is more to the story." And then a "I chose to go. I was not sent." There was a sound from his mother like her teeth snapping shut. He continued as if she had made no noise. "The rest. Official Secrets Act."

"Not for open discussion, then. Will you come and make proper evidence in the appropriate space?"

There was a long pause, then Julius slowly inclined his head. "With proper provision."

"Did your parents know about that, your relationship with her?"

Julius paused again, as if not sure how to answer that. "Not when she was invited."

Cassian Amberly leaned forward, and the captain caught the motion. "Do explain, sir." It had a little weight of force behind it, the first time she'd really used the magics she'd established. Martin knew that it could be fought, that mild compulsion. They were not bound by the Silence to speak, but they also all knew it would end there sooner than later. Lying now would make that later accounting much worse.

There was a pause, enough for it to be clear Cassian was weighing his options. "Senara and her brother approached me at the offices in London, trading on her closeness to Julius. At the time, she played it as wartime comrades, rather than something more intimate. That their paths had crossed in Paris, they had become friends, moving in the same circles."

"And Basil?"

"He did not say much, then or later, on the topic." There was a faint shimmer, Martin could feel it more than see it, of something not quite right. He frowned, but then Cassian was speaking again. "She asked if I could invite them for a few days, they had conversations they preferred to have in a more sociable setting."

"And you did?"

"I confirmed with my wife we had additional space and then extended the invitation. I expected it would be some sort of business proposal. I was willing enough to consider something of the kind, though I might not commit to the project."

Captain FitzRanulf nodded. "And when they arrived?"

"It became very clear they had some other sort of goal, but not precisely what it was. I became quite suspicious of Martin's interactions with her."

Martin went still. He had a sudden understanding of the mouse pursued by a falcon.

"You made that quite clear. Not your sort." The captain's voice was an upper class drawl, now, instead of her usual crisp pronunciation. Just for long enough to make it clear it was deliberate, before she continued. "Mr Taylor, if you'd describe the rest of the evening?"

Martin took a breath, trying without success to stop his heart racing. "I'd heard the gossip, ma'am, captain, and I came back in to see what a little boldness might do. I was curious. And I am a journalist, that kind of ripple, there's often a story there. Even if it's not a thing I can write about directly, it's like one of those mazes you can set to different pathways. There may be options later, because I learn a thing now."

"Do you always act the journalist at private parties?" It came out in a very neutral tone, so much so Martin was certain she was aiming at a specific reaction.

"I cannot stop being myself, Captain. I am thoughtful, of course, about what I turn into a story where I was invited in friendship. In this case, I thought there might be a later story about the Wilsons that would avoid the Amberlys."

The captain nodded. "So, you approached."

"I asked for the next dance. Senara told her brother to go dance with one of the young women. She wasn't very good at names, I think, she said Gemma instead of Glanna, and she called me Mark."

There was a short pause, and a "Oh, I see what you mean. What did you talk about it?"

"We focused on the dance, and she commented on my

strength. I move a fair amount of paper around. I'm not a bad dancer, though I don't care much for it, and she asked why I wasn't married." He shrugged. "I pointed out I'm not from the right sort of people."

It didn't hurt any less when he said it himself. Once upon a time, he'd thought claiming it would make it easier. It just made it different.

"What did she say?"

"That she wasn't the right sort of people. Not just American, though that's a problem still in a lot of more traditional families. But not from money, not fashionable, and I got the impression more than a little shady. I asked how she'd got an invitation, and she implied she'd made some sort of arrangement with Mr Amberly, past connections." He paused, then swallowed. "She said that if I came to her room, after the party, half an hour after everyone was asleep, she might tell me something useful."

"And what did you do?"

"I told Galen - both of us were unsure what she was up to. And it worried us."

"Did you tell anyone else?"

"No, Captain. Though I learned later that Laura heard me. Enough to see me open the door, then look around, and come back."

"What did you see?"

"Senara's room, clothing all over the place, but she wasn't there. I didn't hear anyone else nearby, not her brother, not anyone."

"Would you have heard anyone?"

"If they had been in Basil's room, or maybe Laura's. The house is solid, built to withstand the wind."

"So you would not have known if they were downstairs?"

"Not in November, with the windows closed, and some of the shutters." Martin was very clear about this. "The weather was turning, after all."

"What did you do next?"

"I looked around - as I said, I may have touched a few places, but I didn't handle any objects."

"For the record, we did confirm that." The captain's voice was now deliberately neutral.

"But we saw him go down the hall." That was Nell Amberly. "We saw him. You should arrest him. Again."

Martin looked up and then had no idea what to say. He wanted to yell and scream and shout, and that wasn't the right thing. He heard Galen inhale, near him, and turned his head, waved a hand, and felt Laura take his other again.

Captain FitzRanulf said, mildly enough to make it a warning. "You will have a chance to speak. In a moment." She paused for just a breath, then said "You are able to swear to what you did in court, Mr Taylor?"

"Yes, captain. I did not see Senara after I left the ballroom, with Galen. I could hear her behind us, still laughing and dancing."

"Excellent." Another measured pause, then she said, "And you, Julius Amberly. Did you see Senara at any time during her visit?"

Julius inhaled, an uneven and uneasy sound. "She came to speak. Saturday morning. Early. Knocked on my window."

"Your window?"

"There is an," He paused. "A walk. Outside. There."

"What did she want to say?"

"I do not know." Martin could tell the words were something of an effort. "I refused to hear her out."

"Why, may I ask?"

"Knew what she'd done. Spied. Turned traitor." He gestured for a moment at his face. "This. Deaths. Much more." He paused, and then offered, deliberately. "I had myself assigned where she had spread treachery."

It took a moment for that to sink in for everyone, that Julius had known and put himself at risk anyway. Madam Amberly put her hand to her mouth, looking white and shocked.

Martin could barely make sense of it, before there was a flurry of noise from the elder Amberlys. "You don't know what you're saying, Julius, that awful woman." That was Nell Amberly, and then a louder insistent bellow of Cassian, over her. "Stop talking, Julius, for the love of magic, stop talking."

Julius couldn't make himself heard over them, and Martin saw his lips close, behind the gap in the mask. The cacophony continued, for thirty seconds, then a minute, both of them pleading for something that made no sense.

# THIRTY-EIGHT

## MONDAY AFTERNOON

Captain FitzRanulf gave everyone a moment, then turned to Cassian and Parnell Amberly as they began murmuring to each other, just loudly enough that Laura was sure they were talking about Martin. "Did you have something to add, Madam Amberly?"

The murmuring stopped dead, then Madam Amberly said, "Aren't you going to see sense, and do something about that terrible young man." It was a demand, not a question.

Galen stiffened - Laura could feel how he shifted on the other end of the sofa. Martin had gone quite still, again.

Captain FitzRanulf settled onto her heels, something that seemed deliberate, as if she were settling into a saddle for a long ride, so she'd take the bumps and jars of the journey entirely in stride. "Do explain, please?"

"Well." Given the opportunity, Madam Amberly didn't seem to know how to begin. Then it came out, as if the magics on the space were pulling it out bit by bit, like unrolling a ball of yarn. "We've never been entirely happy with Galen's association with Taylor. And since the strike this summer, it's been worse. Never any idea when we'll have to get our solicitor to see to things for Galen, or what will turn up in the news. There was that remarkably unflattering shot, it's been a horror trying to figure out how to get a respectable young woman here."

Laura raised an eyebrow at this last part, then glanced at Galen to see how he was taking it. Rigidly, more or less.

Captain FitzRanulf inclined her head, then looked at Martin and Galen. "Context, please?" It was brief, but surprisingly not abrupt in tone, a request rather than a demand.

Galen coughed, and said "The Dwellers were involved in providing aid related to the Miner's Strike, and then the General Strike. It was..." He glanced at Martin. "It mattered to both of us, but Martin was more in the midst. Getting people's stories, sharing them." He stopped, then added, quickly, before anyone else could speak, "I am quite sure my parents are referring to a photo from when the general strike got going."

Captain FitzRanulf nodded. "Anything else?"

Madam Amberly sniffed, displeased. "And Taylor goes skulking around downstairs with the servants, making trouble and stirring things up. Not at all the done thing."

A woman who had to be the cook tutted, "Well, I never." and Laura saw one of the footmen lean to say something to the other.

Martin looked up, then said, much more quietly, "I went to ask how things were. And help feed the stove and keep-cool box. I was sure no one outside the staff would think of it." It had a rigorous stubbornness to it that Laura found she wanted to reward.

She said, "And we learned Senara had ruined her stockings, I guess we know now that must've happened when she went to bother Julius. She was dreadful to Millicent about it." That made the woman next to Agnes look up, with a quick flashing smile, before the housekeeper glared at her and she subsided.

That brought the Captain's attention right back to her. "Tell me what you told me, in your interview, Miss Penhallow. About your actions, the three of you, since the murder. In more detail, please, in case you happened to find anything relevant." She did not sound like she expected that to be the case.

Laura was glad she'd specified. "Martin is correct that we wanted to see if there was additional information. Not interfere, but we were worried, all three of us, that evidence would be altered."

"Was there a particular reason?"

Laura frowned. "It just seemed like no one was taking that part of it seriously. That it was a spot of fuss and bother but everyone ought to treat it like another instance of her being terribly rude." Madam Amberly sniffed, loudly and pointedly, but Laura kept on. "The Amberlys decided to move the body before anyone could investigate. And I agree, the conservatory would be complicated to manage, but they didn't even try. They moved - they moved Senara even before we knew a boat wouldn't be getting across for a day or two."

"Did you say anything about it to them?"

"Of course not. I'm a guest in the house, and honestly, I was rather in shock, myself. And I didn't really - I knew something wasn't right, I've been around a lot of people who died. But I couldn't pin down what it was until now."

She added, mostly to enjoy seeing the expression on Madam Amberly's face, "Madam Amberly, you inquired earlier about my health. What I said was true, I'm considered quite cured now, but I spent a decade in TB sanitaria."

The shock on her face was worth the way it made her shiver to say. And then she felt Martin squeeze her hand, silently, and she squeezed back, and knew she'd at least given him a little more hope.

"Is there anything else, Miss Penhallow?"

"Once we started thinking about it, I think we were all worried - the three of us - about making sure more evidence wasn't lost."

"Do outline what you found."

"We took a good close look at the conservatory. We didn't touch anything, of course, or go into the chalked off area, but we did have a look at everything we could. There was a pot of powder, hidden in one of the planters, the second from the right by the back door. And there was a spot on one leaf that seemed - unreasonably oily. A big leaf. Near the place where the - bench she was in was. Um. If you were facing that space, to the right, just past the marks for the end of the bench."

"Ames." The name rang out sharply, and they all heard a prompt. "Yes, Captain" before his footsteps went off toward the conservatory. "Describe the pot of powder, please."

"Small, about this size." Laura indicated the size, about an inch across. "About the same depth, with a gold lid. I'd have thought something more like an ointment, that container, but it was a powder. Something like a loose eye powder, perhaps, though mostly empty."

That got a very thoughtful sound. "Was it still there when you left the conservatory?"

"Of course, Captain." Laura did her best to make it clear she was offended at the idea that they'd move it.

"A container of that description, also about half full, was found in back of one of Mr Taylor's dressing table drawers. He denies touching it." She paused a beat, and then added,

"And the various enchantments Ames performed made it clear he was telling the truth."

That got a shocked gasp from the senior Amberlys and a look from Madam Tipson that made Laura suddenly suspect that Galen's aunt had known about and not at all approved of various actions. She saw Captain FitzRanulf make the same calculation, at least.

"Is that a usual sort of investigation at this stage, Captain FitzRanulf?" It might be foolhardy for her to press on this point, and yet she wanted to drive it home.

"There is no usual in a murder investigation, Miss Penhallow. We do our best to investigate all possible leads, without making assumptions."

It was of course the necessary thing to say, but Laura felt the reality had not come anywhere near that statement. The Captain had been awful to Martin, rather awful to a lot of people, and she was being terribly high-handed still. Laura tried to figure out what to say next, and she got as far as "Captain" when they heard footsteps coming back at a rapid clip.

Ames came in, holding up a glass jar with a green leaf clipping in it. "Captain." There was a slight click of his heels, and rather more formality than he'd shown in leaving.

"Report, Ames." Her voice was clear, direct, but there was a little bit of drawl here, just the hint of a predator who was herding her prey. Laura could only hope she had the sense to see it wasn't Martin.

"I found a leaf as described, it has been clipped and preserved according to the usual protocol. I have not of course done any significant testing, but it appears to be the hypothesised reagent. There is nothing to suggest it is not."

"Go deal with that, Ames, then." He nodded sharply, and disappeared back out the door before anyone could say anything. Captain FitzRanulf turned back to the assembled group, and looked decidedly pleased. "Thank you, Miss Penhallow. Now, Mr Wilson."

"Yes?" Basil was doing his best to sound as if he had no troubles in the world, and was failing utterly. Certainly, his charm was not a sort that worked on Captain FitzRanulf.

"You were found, shipwrecked, having fled. What did you think you were doing, precisely?"

"I thought," Basil tried to sound aggrieved. "I was stuck on an island with a peasant who had killed my sister, and likely didn't have much good will for me."

"Mr Taylor?" She raised an eyebrow. "Careful about the names you call, Mr Wilson. I am rather more a peasant, technically, than Mr Taylor." Laura got a glimpse of Silvia, a look of delight at something that comment confirmed. Something about the captain's background, probably.

"Look at him!" Basil's voice got high pitched. "You can tell he's not a proper sort. And I heard Madam Amberly say she regretted inviting him, no matter how difficult it was to make the numbers of the dancing."

"Mr Wilson." The captain's voice was sharp. "Answer, please." Laura could feel the little pulse of the magic enforcing the command. "Are you afraid of Martin Taylor."

"Yes, of course." He sounded aggrieved anyone might not be terrified of Martin, who was sitting on the sofa, one hand in Laura's, the other in his lap, looking down. "Big man like that, that sort of background, they're prone to violence, and now I hear he's involved with subversive activities and strikes besides?" He gestured at Madam Amberly.

"Has he harmed you in any way?"

That got a sulky sound, as if he wanted to answer differently, then Basil said, "No."

"Has he threatened you?"

The same noise, then another, "No."

"Why are you afraid of him, then?"

"My sister, my poor sweet sister," That got an odd noise from Julius, who stifled it before anyone managed to look in his direction. Basil continued, "Someone must have lured her away, on her own, to do something to her. And I fled because a man who could do that, could do anything." There was a little pulse in the magic, the kind of thing that suggested something askew, but Basil seemed clever enough to skirt it.

"Quite." Captain FitzRanulf's tone had become very dry. Laura could hear Madam and Mr Amberly murmuring again, but not what they said. "And why were you here again?"

"Oh, that was largely Senara's business, she oversees exports that we handle. She is - oh, she was, far better at opening up new markets than I was. I'm much better on negotiating the details, of course."

It was the smarminess that put Laura's back up, and she suspected neither Captain FitzRanulf or Madam Tipson approved.

Basil continued, "I assumed she was meeting someone here. Beyond the early discussions we'd had with Cassian, of course. It wasn't clear to me who, and there were - shall we say, a limited number of possibilities." His eyes lingered on Galen for a moment.

"So." Captain FitzRanulf cut in. "You are saying that you believe that it was Martin Taylor who threatened your sister, Senara, after the party. That the evidence is their interactions, and the oil and powder - one found by Miss Penhallow, the other in Martin's rooms. And Mr Taylor was the reason you fled, headlong, with no preparation or precaution."

There was a long pause, and Laura almost wondered if he was fighting against the truth charms, but then she realised the phrasing was all about what he was saying, not what he actually believed. It seemed unbelievable the Captain would be that sloppy in her questioning.

Worse, she could feel Martin, beside her, going more and more rigid. She glanced at him, and his head was down, and he looked utterly dejected. That was what convinced her. Keeping hold of his hand, she lifted her chin. "Captain FitzRanulf."

The captain glanced over at her, and something in that look, the way it was calculating, the way it was using the power she had to have other people dancing, made Laura furious. If it had been before, in the sanitaria, she would have folded, and hated herself. But now, well, the goldwasser had done some good. She wasn't going to do that again, make that same mistake.

She would speak, and act, and trust there'd be an afterwards that was better for it. If those doctors with false smiles were the Magician, then so was this woman, the cards had implied, and she would not put up with it anymore, even as rising to the confrontation sucked her breath away again.

"You know better. You are making people in this room miserable who did nothing wrong. You are letting others speak untruths, and you know they are. You must. I insist that..." She tried to remember, in stories, there were words you could use. Carillon knew the words, she'd heard him talking about it. But they wouldn't come to her mind, nor to her tongue, and finally, she said. "I insist you act with the judgement of your position."

Captain FitzRanulf said, and her tone was falsely mild, "Are you interfering in this investigation?"

"You're playing bohort somewhere in your head, with someone who isn't here, about being the cleverest at solving puzzles. But you're forgetting, you're playing with real people." She gestured at Martin, with her free hand. "You've said yourself Martin didn't touch that powder. He can't have done the things that man accuses him of. And yet, you're letting it go on. To make yourself look clever." She shook her head, her hair coming out of the bun at the back, she could feel it fall down past her shoulders. "Do better. I demand you do better."

Something in that, some small part of it, brought the captain up short. She took a deep breath, then she looked slowly around the room, starting with Martin, then going to one side, then back, then the other, then back. Finally, Captain FitzRanulf nodded slightly. But she didn't say anything.

A loud murmur broke out, nearly everyone in the room save Martin and Laura and the captain trying to talk over each other all at once. The Amberlys were so far undone as to be nearly shouting over each other, about how it had to be Martin, it simply had to be. Galen was trying to say something. But Laura couldn't even hear him, there was so much chaos.

# THIRTY-NINE

## MONDAY AFTERNOON

There was a sharp "Silence," in full-throated command voice, and the entire room stopped and looked at Captain FitzRanulf, who had stood up, hands out.

"Madam and Mr Amberly. Why are you so insistent that Martin Taylor is to blame? He has said here clearly that he had no opportunity to kill Senara Wilson. He was, in point of fact, in her bedroom upstairs, witnessed by four people, including yourselves, at the time she likely died. He did not touch the vial containing the lethal reagent."

The Amberlys spluttered and Martin ventured a breath. Laura squeezed his hand, and he tightened his fingers in hers.

That was a mistake. Nell Amberly caught the movement and launched into a new attack. "You are a shameless woman, nearly as bad as that, that American hussy. Coming here, oh, people had warned me it was a mistake to invite you, but I thought you'd appreciate the opportunity, and there you are, with that Martin. I was willing to overlook things, you, you bit of nothing."

Captain FitzRanulf cleared her throat, and said "Madam Amberly, if you do not restrain your tongue, I will do it for you." Her voice had turned from neutrality into something sharp and coiling. It would be utterly fascinating to observe if Martin were not in the midst of his world collapsing around him. As it was, it felt rather like a cobra getting ready to strike and not caring much where the fangs landed. Possibly he was between a cobra and a rattlesnake, given how Basil had been glad to help things along.

Laura did not move her hand, though he could feel her pulse racing, where the base of his thumb pressed against the vein in her wrist.

Julius said, after a moment, "They thought to protect me."

It did not surprise Captain FitzRanulf, Martin saw that instantly. She nodded toward Julius and said, "Go on."

"Thought I did it. Mad in my pain. So the stories go." He spoke carefully, slowly. And with, Martin realised, what must be considerable growing pain, as he turned to watch. Julius's eyes narrowed, his hand was clenching at the arm of the chair. "Was not me. Was not Martin. Was not them." He paused. "Was not Blythe."

"They thought to protect you. By setting up Martin. They should know better." The captain was dismissive now, despite the spluttering that followed. "Galen Amberly, do you have anything to add?"

Galen was white-faced, quiet, trembling. Martin knew that look, when he was working so hard on doing the right thing the right way there was no space in his head for anything else. Galen took a breath, then said, as carefully as his brother. "I know it was not Julius. Nor Martin, nor Laura. Not me."

"Who do you think it was?"

Galen frowned. "The only person it could have been is Basil. If it was not suicide."

"It was not." The words came out clipped. "Your rea..." At that moment, Basil lurched from his seat. Captain FitzRanulf spat out a Word of Command, that echoed for a moment then crumbled into dust in Martin's mind, so there was no memory of it. From the way she used it, she'd used it before. "Hold him." That was an order to the other two Guards.

They pinned him down, binding his hands in front of him with sullen red charms that Martin remembered too well. He reached for a moment, rubbing his wrist, feeling the ache again. It didn't hurt, precisely, but the feel of something inimical to his own magic, suppressive, controlling, too heavy. He felt Laura squeeze his hand again, and found she was looking at him, uncertain and wide-eyed.

"Do you wish to explain yourself, Mr Wilson?" That was Captain FitzRanulf, entirely in control of herself and the situation.

He nearly spat at her, and she shook her head, almost sorrowful. "Some people don't have the courage of their convictions," she said, as if addressing an invisible audience. Laura's comments about her making herself look clever clearly had not stung her enough to make her stop. "I will explain, then."

She leaned back in her chair, and said "From evidence gathered thus far, it has become clear to me that Senara Wilson deliberately sought an invitation to this house for reasons of her own. Evidence presented suggests that she had some role in espionage during the War. It is not currently clear what her goal was, whether it was to gain additional information or whether it was to make some apology for her actions. On Saturday morning, she sought to visit Julius, presumably the reason for her seeking an invitation to the house, since she did not do so openly."

There was a silence, but no one spoke until Captain FitzRanulf continued. "She must have revealed her goals to Basil at some point. He became certain that she would do something that would cause both of them a great deal of trouble. I believe it will be easily proven in full court that Basil encouraged his sister to linger after others retired to bed following the party, and then poisoned her."

Silvia Tipson offered, "The young people wondered if it was poison. I wondered myself, captain."

"You have expertise in the area, I understand. What are your thoughts on it?"

"That he may not have decided to kill his sister until something happened. He applied one part of the poison earlier, I suspect, but not the second part, the catalyst, that made it deadly." Martin watched her, how the woman who sometimes seemed a little foolish, all family relationships and genealogies and card games, turned serious. "If he had simply wanted to kill her, there are easier options. More sure, less complex to acquire."

"But the method he chose makes it clear it was premeditation?" The Captain wished to draw this out, she obviously knew the answer.

"Oh, I can't be certain without access to testing - her skin, her clothing, any other relevant materials. That leaf you found, thanks to the young people. But I would suspect so. It would be easy enough to do, she was careless about leaving her shoulders bare. He would certainly know how to take advantage of that."

Martin swallowed, then asked, carefully. "Was it her speaking to me that caused it?" He wondered now if perhaps, after Julius refused to speak to her, Senara had hoped to use him to get whatever she wanted known out into the world.

Basil made a muffled sound, unable to speak. The captain took a long look at him and turned her attention back to Martin. "Possibly. You were - more of a threat than others might be. Perhaps he worried that you would convince Galen to give her access to Julius, or to their parents. He does seem genuine in his fear of you, Mr Taylor, as we all observed from the charms. We will find out under full examination."

Martin let out a long breath, then said "May I ask what now?"

"There is a boat coming from the mainland. We will take Basil Wilson with us. You all will be required to testify at the trial." She paused, considering. "Madam and Mr Amberly, we offer you the opportunity to take an oath on the Silence. Swear that you will appear for the trial in two days, and we will permit you to remain here and arrange your household. I expect there will be consequences for you both, for interfering with the investigation and framing an innocent party. Martin Taylor, I would advise you to consult with a solicitor. You are not in any legal difficulty, but you do have some choices about how to proceed that would benefit from advice."

Martin suddenly felt entirely unsure of what to do. "Ma'am?"

"I am certain Miss Penhallow can make a few suggestions." That was dryly amused.

Martin swallowed, not sure what to say. He blinked up, feeling entirely flat-footed.

In the pause, Captain FitzRanulf added, "And, for the record, my apologies, for the ill treatment. You -" She paused, considering her words, and it made Martin listen even more closely. "The Dwellers have a reputation, that is true, and have made my life confoundedly difficult, more than once, and quite recently." Martin was sure that was something related to the strike. "But you conducted yourself honourably and with an admirable forthrightness. I thought to make sure you were safely away, but I should have found a better way to arrange it."

Martin nodded, slowly, then managed, a careful and distant reply. "That you think well of the Dwellers, or at least no worse, is something." He couldn't forgive her, not exactly, but at least if she were the one he had dealings with down the road again, it might go better.

Captain FitzRanulf nodded, then inclined her head to Laura. "My best wishes to your brother-in-law, by the by, Miss Penhallow. You yourself are quite free to go, but you will also be expected to testify. It will be a few days before the portal is mended - whatever Mr Wilson did to it requires some particular stones be replaced. I would advise you come with us by boat back to the Penzance portal."

"I will be letting my brother-in-law wait, I suspect. He's entirely up to his own plots, and I will need a little time to determine precisely what I want to say to him about this one." She took a breath, glancing at Martin, then nodding at Galen. "And Galen?"

Galen shook his head. "I need to consult with my parents." Then, carefully. "Martin, you shouldn't be on your own."

Laura said "We can sort that out once we're on the mainland. I have an idea or two." Then a "May we go pack, then? How long until your boat leaves?"

"Half an hour. If the staff could assist, I'll see to the oaths now."

Martin felt light headed, like the world was spinning.

Laura squeezed his hand, and said in his ear, "You're in shock. Go pack up your personal things, I know what will help. Will you trust me?"

"You, you understand?"

"Felt like this after - after things with the goldwasser. Go on. Pack. Meet me in the foyer."

She then slipped away, Agnes following behind her, promptly, as soon as the captain made a wave of dismissal to the staff.

Galen inched over, looking torn. "Are you - it's horrid."

"Will you be all right?" Galen didn't look all right. He was pale and trembling, and looked rather like Martin felt.

"They're my parents. I must - need to make sure they keep their oaths. Just a couple of days, then we can work something else out. I need to talk to Julius. And whoever else. Aunt Silvia's being very sensible, maybe she'll help. I hope she'll help." They glanced over, and she was speaking firmly to Cassian Amberly.

"You'll let me know?"

"Martin, you're my brother. You and Julius."

"They're your parents."

"That just means I know what they're like. Give me a day or two. I'll not lose you like I lost Julius."

Martin blinked at him. This was his chosen brother, and this was someone with a great deal more backbone than usual.

"Martin. Go let Laura do what she has in mind. I'm sure she'll take care of you. Remember, she mentioned she knew solicitors. And I'm sure she can - you know, tea and other things."

Martin shivered. "She, I..."

Galen's voice turned very gentle and got quite soft. "She told me you'd kissed. Laura's a fine young woman, but we're not a good fit for each other. I think you and she might make a go of it. And she's a good person. I'd like her as a friend. Or," A pause, and a careful. "My brother's wife. Go on. We'll talk soon."

Martin was still trying to figure out what to say to that, when Galen was called away sharply, to witness and take the oaths Captain FitzRanulf had in mind. Martin watched them gather, then slipped out of the drawing room to go see about his packing.

# FORTY

## MONDAY EVENING

Laura opened the door to the house, rummaging to get the light charm to work. "Here, come in, sit down. I'll make tea."

Martin looked awful, white and uncertain. He'd been near silent the entire way, the hours it had taken on the ferry back. From there, she'd shooed him off toward the portal, and then up the hill from the village on this end. It felt strange to be the person taking charge, but Martin was clearly unfit, and it didn't feel wrong to be taking care of him. Not at all.

"Here. Here's the table. Let me make tea, and we can make up a bed for you upstairs."

He blinked at her, but let her guide him to a chair while she put the kettle on. It must have rained since she'd left, there was that slight smell of damp earth from the garden outside.

"You - here?" It wasn't a very coherent question, but he must be curious.

"I've been staying in the New Forest, with Lizzie a lot - we gave our chickens away. But I'm here sometimes, too.

We like the house, don't want to let it go. Good memories, from when we were little."

"Not - not a bother?"

She shook her head, coming over and settling on the bench by the table, so she could take his hand. "Not a bother. And you shouldn't be alone. We'll sort things out. Tonight, though. Just here. Nothing to worry about."

She stood, kissed him on the forehead, and went off to find one of the shawls they kept. It was a ridiculous colour for him, a bright turquoise, but once she got it around his shoulders, he pulled it close and it seemed to help. When the kettle sang out, she poured the tea into two large pottery mugs. "There. Drink that. Plenty of honey. It'll help."

He took a sip, blew on it, and took another. "You're sure?"

"Tea helps. I'm very sure of that." She let him drink it, while she put together bread and a bit of butter and cheese. It was very good they'd put in the keep-fresh box here. She settled the plate in front of him, and waited as he near inhaled it, made some more, and waited while he worked his way through it more slowly.

"I - what?" That wasn't any more coherent, but she felt he was focusing a bit better.

"We tuck you into bed. We have a nice quiet day tomorrow. I can walk down to the pub and get a couple of proper meals for us. We have eggs and bread and cheese otherwise. We wait for that solicitor to write back. You read some books, or something. I read some books."

"So - simple?" He was watchful now. "Tomorrow, yes. No promises about the day after." She kept her tone light.

It made him smile, the corners of his mouth twitching up.

"Come on. Do you want to wash up?" He nodded, and

she took his hand, leading him upstairs to the guest room, and then going across to run the bath, laying out a towel and washcloth. "Nothing fancy, but the hot water's quite reliable. There's some old things of Uncle Kenver's around that should fit you. Let me find them."

Martin nodded, and when she nudged him into the bathroom, he closed the door and after a minute she heard the tap turn off, and then a little splashing.

First, she rummaged in the other guest room, the one her uncle always used. She kneeled and ran her hand along the sandalwood chest he'd brought home from one of their first trading trips. Then she opened it, finding folded clean pyjamas, a dressing gown, and a rather faded pair of slippers. She inhaled, the clean cotton and the sandalwood mixing. After a moment's thought, she placed them on the chair outside the bathroom, with a knock on the door. "Night things on the chair outside the door. I'll be in my room just down the hall if you need something."

She was, suddenly, not quite sure what to do with a man in her house. Oh, she had no worry he would overstep. And yet, having someone down the hall, who was not Lizzie. That was new.

In the end, she gave in to practicality. Back in her own room, she closed the door and gave herself a good cold water wash with a cloth and the basin. By the time he emerged, she was in a comfortable and sufficiently encompassing robe over a long nightgown. She heard him close the door to his room, then a few minutes later, open it again, calling out cautiously, "Laura?"

She poked her head out into the hallway. "Just down here." She set her book down and came out into the hallway. He was standing in the door of his room, blinking and visibly uncertain again.

"Would you, would you come sit? I just - I don't want to be alone right now." It was nearly impossible for him to admit, the way he looked down at his feet, at a spot on the floor, anywhere but her.

"Of course." She took a breath, steadying herself. "Here, let me take a minute, find a book I can read, and make another cup of tea. Do you want some more? There's mint."

"Mint." He nodded, and then he asked, as if he wasn't sure what the answer would be. "What sort of book?"

"What sort of book would you like? There's travel essays, Papa brought back a lot of them."

Martin closed his eyes. "You pick."

"You're out of ability to choose, aren't you. Right. I'll be back up in a few minutes." She turned, hearing him getting into bed, the creak of the springs, as she went downstairs. Making the tea and letting it steep took a few minutes.

It gave her time to rummage for the eggs and cheese and make everything easy to find in the morning. She would have to go down to the pub for anything beyond breakfast, but that was all right. It didn't look like rain.

The question of books was more complicated. In the end, she selected one set of travel essays. Her fingers lingered over one of her mother's favourites, a comedy of manners, but she thought that might be a raw spot. Instead she chose one Lizzie had loved and sent her, what felt like a lifetime ago. It was a rather charming tale of discovering a magical maze on a seaside cliff that changed the world around them each time they walked it.

Once the tea had steeped, she took it back upstairs, carefully balancing the tray and the books. She nearly dropped it, knocking on the door, but was glad to hear his "Come in?"

He was tucked into bed, looking tousled, and unsure

what to do with himself. It took her a few moments to set everything down. "Here, do you have a preference?" and handing the books to him. Lap tray here, with the tea for them both, pouring a cup each, offering him the honey jar.

All the fiddling gave them something to do, without the awkwardness of needing to speak about much more sharp-edged things. Finally, she moved the easy chair from the corner to the side of the bed, where she had both space and good light.

"Preference?"

"I don't know this one." He tapped the book about the maze.

"Lizzie sent it to me. It's rather charming. I suppose it's technically a children's book, but it's... well. Shall I read, and you can see what you think?"

He settled back in the pillows, cupping his hands around the warm mug. "I - yes. Please. If it's not a bother."

"Reading is never a bother. And I almost never get to read aloud anymore."

It was one of the few things she'd missed from the sanitaria. Once she'd begun to recover, she had been much in demand. She wasn't the sort of person who could do dozens of different voices or accents, but they had told her over and over that her voice was warm, encouraging. Maybe it would help Martin, now.

Once everything was in the proper place, for her to sip her tea when she needed to, she began to read. It took her a page or two to settle into the rhythm of the words. Then it took a few more to get a better sense for the character voices. By the end of the first chapter, Martin was leaning back, his eyes half closed.

Two more chapters, and she paused just long enough to remove the tray. He slipped down a little in bed, curling on his side, and just barely letting his hand shift on top of hers. It made turning the pages awkward, but it would be like disturbing a cat whose paws just barely touched your arm. Heresy and indignity and the height of rudeness.

When she next looked up, he had clearly fallen asleep, and to move might disturb that even more fragile balance. Instead, she took a breath, murmured the word that would extinguish the light, and settled in the chair to get as comfortable as its shape allowed.

# FORTY-ONE

## TUESDAY MORNING

Martin woke, feeling his legs and arm pinned. He inhaled, sharply, then felt the brush of hair against his cheek. Laura.

Had they, no, they couldn't have. Besides, once he got his eyes open, she was still in her dressing gown and night things. And above the blankets. He was just as clothed, and under the blankets. There was the chair she'd been sitting in, he remembered that. But how did she end up on the bed?

It was not a narrow single bed. He hadn't been in any state to notice last night, but there was space here for two, if they were willing to be close. She fit there, stretched along the edge, tidily, her head angled to rest perfectly on his shoulder. She was still sound asleep, or at least he thought so.

He must have been difficult to manage last night. Martin didn't remember most of it, it was all a blur. Coming through the portal, up a long slow hill he thought would never end, and then Laura making things warm and comfortable for him. He remembered her reading, though he could barely remember what the story was. A maze, and children, and he remembered details twined into the story, that mattered, how the author had the kind of observant attention to detail he particularly loved in books.

His hand tightened for a moment, and Laura stirred a little, then stopped, tensing up.

"'m awake." What did one say to the woman in one's arms and one's bed in this circumstance?

She took a deep breath. "You had my hand. I didn't want to leave you?"

Martin swallowed, then said, very softly. "Glad you didn't. This.." Then there was the flash of memory, of half-waking, some nightmare that was all sharp edges in his mind and nothing solid. "Did I wake you?"

"Once. Twice. A bad dream." She was clear about it. He liked how she didn't dance around.

Then he realised the awkwardness of things. That she was so close. "I'd like..." He couldn't find words. "I'd like a lot of things."

"How do you feel?" Laura's voice was quiet, but determined. About what, he wasn't quite sure.

"Better. The tea helped." He paused, evaluating. "I'm a bit hungry. But I don't - I don't want to move yet." It would be rather revealing. How he felt about her.

She shifted, very cautiously, like sharing a bed was not a thing she had much experience in. He supposed she wouldn't. Then, very carefully, she moved enough so she could see his face, and he could see hers, her hair tousled. "I'd like to kiss you. Again. Properly. When we won't be interrupted."

Martin closed his eyes and then said, "I can't, I want, but..." He stopped, this babbling was not doing anyone any good. Especially him. He opened his eyes again, trying to make it clear how confused he was. "I need to know what we're doing."

Laura smiled, and leaned to kiss his nose, once, lightly. "I like you. I'd like to see how that goes. Together. Is that all right? Is that too much right now?"

Martin blinked. Several times. "No?" It came out baffled. Not suave and in control at all. Fortunately she didn't seem to mind.

"I don't - I mean, my past experience isn't much, I don't know that I know what to do? But I'd like... I'd like to be warm. With you. Curled up. I feel right with you. Like we're doing things together." Emphasis firmly on the last word. "Not at cross-purposes."

It was too much, and in the end, all he could do was tug her closer to him, bringing her mouth closer to his. The kiss, a moment later, began tentatively. They were still so new to each other, learning what worked, what didn't. He'd had more experience than she had, that was obvious, in the way she tried different angles. But she was eager, even joyful about it, leaning into the touches and the brush of his lips, until they were both breathless, and he had to say, "Moment, Laura."

She ended up leaning on one arm, watching him, then something caught her attention, and he watched her eyes slip to his waist, and how the sheets were draping. She spent a moment, watching that, then the blush that rose on his cheeks, before whispering, "I - with you, I'd like more things."

"You're certain? It's not, you're not," He stopped and tried again. "It's not a thing I want to rush into."

"You rush into other things. Not this." She reached, touching his cheek. "Is it Galen?"

"No. He told me he thought we should give it a try. Not

that we had to, just that we might suit. And I think he might be right."

Laura nodded. "I don't want to rush you. But I don't want to let this moment run through our fingers, either."

"What's this moment, to you?"

"Warmth. Affection. Humour. The way your kisses feel, how I feel..." A tiny pause, she was searching for words. "They make me feel alive. Wonder what's around the next corner. It's been a long time since I had that."

It made him smile. "Ah, that I can do, yes. Not a lot in the way of financial stability."

"There's some options for that, maybe. Depending how things go. I can feed and house myself. You could stay here, if it came to that, and we suit."

He considered. "You mean that?"

"If it didn't bother you."

"Mmmm." He considered for a few seconds, and then shifted, moving to tug the blankets down on one side, the parts she wasn't lying on. "Would you - there are an awful lot of clothes in the way. Maybe we could start with a layer or two fewer?"

She paused, then nodded, visibly more nervous. "I've a scar or two. From surgery."

Martin shrugged. "I figured you might. Ribcage?" She nodded, silently. "It doesn't change my mind."

Laura looked away, and he caught something in the shyness. "It's not just that, though. You're worried because of the goldwasser?" She nodded, minutely.

"Oh, I'll be making sure you ask for what you want." And then he just settled back. "Not until you ask."

There was a moment where she was utterly still, and then she laughed, before sticking out her tongue at him. "You are impossible, Martin."

"Oh, not at all impossible. Very easy, in some circumstances. Once I'm sure you're eager."

The nervousness had broken, like a wave on the seashore, and she sat up, letting him move the blanket aside, as she shrugged out of the dressing gown. Her nightdress was cotton, worn smooth and comfortable, and clinging against her hip. He let his eyes trace what it showed of her body, and she said, "You'd tell me what you're thinking?"

"I'm wondering what your body is like, under that. Like the card, the Star, yes? You wear clothing well. Your poise. Your.. I don't know the right words. But I'm curious about your body, now. What touches you'll like. What you'll feel like against me." He paused and risked something much more adventurous. "What it will feel like if you allow me to slip inside you."

Oh, that approach got her, he won a sharp inhale. "Is that what you think of it?"

"There are all kinds of sex. And I've had a few rounds of things just about the body, the moment. Fast and fierce and all physical. But that's not what I want. Not with you, not long-term. I want to..." He reached out a hand, lacing his fingers through hers. "I want your desire. You choosing me to share it."

She shuddered, he could see it through her body, and he murmured, "Come here, stretch out." As she did, he began to undo his pyjama top. She watched, then her fingers shifted, moving to help him, to work her way down and he worked his way up, until there was bare skin and space to touch. She was uncertain, at first, as if afraid he'd scold or correct her, but the longer he let her explore, the more he grinned, the better she relaxed.

"May I, please?" Her gown would open a bit, let him get a hand to touch. It made her shy again, like a seal ready to dive into the sea from a rock on the shore. Then she propped herself on one elbow, loosened the buttons, and he began to let his fingers wander.

He took his time, pausing to kiss her, then to let one hand drift to her hip while the other petted and touched. It did not take long for her to be pressing her body against his side, arching in his fingers.

"You need to ask, love." The endearment slipped out.

She blinked at him, then swallowed. "What's next?"

"Whatever you want. But I was thinking, would you take your gown off? You can slip under the sheet if you're shy."

"And you?"

"Oh, I'll gladly strip whenever you're ready. But I don't want to scare you off."

Something in that broke the tension again. She ducked her head, and he wasn't sure what was going through her head, until she looked at him, again, grinning. "You're quite unique, Martin. You do know that."

"Show me." He was filled with all his desire, a surge, and all of a sudden he couldn't keep it back or contained. For a second, he was terrified it would be too much, would make her freeze up, or worse, flee his bed. The challenge seemed to have been quite the thing, though, because she sat up just long enough to wriggle out of the encompassing nightgown.

He got a flashing look at her body - trim, neat, fashionably small breasted, but entirely herself. The scar along her rib, that had healed badly. And then she was in his arms, kissing him intently, like she wanted to dive into him. She let her hands wander, helping him pull his own clothes off so he could kick them to the end of the bed in a clump under the sheets.

After that, there was no time for thought, just for the joy of exploration. Once she committed to it, she was a delight, not shy at all. She stretched out, when his hand stroked in a long line down her hip and her leg.

Laura turned to settle on her back. And oh, she purred. It wasn't always asking, but it was clear what she wanted. "Your hand, there, oh, yes." And then, when he slipped his fingers to the inside of her thigh, a "That, Martin, please." on the edge of something new.

Part of him wanted to curse the man who'd nearly scared her away forever. Part of him wanted to tell Galen what he was missing. But Galen wouldn't have found this, he was quite sure. Galen would have been too careful, too polite, too decorous. It would not be this, and the freedom she'd had buried inside her, waiting to dance with him.

By the time he slid inside her, she'd found her own pleasure once, slipping into it with a sharp cry of surprise. Once he settled into her, hips pressed to keep him deep, she looked at him, wide-eyed, and said "Oh." Just the one word, full of startlement.

Martin moved to kiss her, deep and slow, and then he began to move, helping her learn the rhythm, the ways their particular bodies fit. How it was to have someone focused on their shared pleasure. And then, what it felt like when he found his.

The aftermath, both of them relaxed and boneless, was even better. All trust and warmth and comfort, and a certainty he'd not thought he'd ever find.

# FORTY-TWO

## TRELLECH, LATE JANUARY 1926

"You're nervous." Martin drew her away from the portal, and then leaned in to kiss her, ignoring a wolf whistle from one of the carters nearby.

"Wouldn't you be? There's seeing Galen, and he's had a horrid time. And then meeting your friends. C'mon, we don't want to be late."

Martin settled her hand into the crook of his arm as they began to walk. "You'll be grand." And then, grinning. "You look grand." It had been a week since they'd been able to see each other, what with various family commitments. Now that was over, the world was getting back to its usual schedule, including the courts.

Laura snorted. "You have no idea how hard it was to pick out clothing." she said. Dressing first for a sentencing hearing in court, then to meet Martin and Galen's friends, that was tricky.

In the end, she'd chosen a dusty blue dress, with a more formal loose jacket over it for court. She'd topped it with a quite proper hat, and had a shawl that had been her mother's, with some gorgeous colour-shifting embroidery, tucked into her bag for the gathering afterwards.

"How did things go with your sister? And your brother-in-law? After I left?" He sounded very uncertain about that.

That just made Laura grin more. "Oh, very well. From my side of things."

"You giving them a piece of your mind - that's a thing a person could sell tickets to."

"Ah, some things are a command performance only. But we had a good time once they got through the obligatory fussing." She shook her head. "The gossip wasn't a lot of fun, but I will say Carillon shut that sort of nonsense down fast. People bothering me to ask about it."

Martin's voice was quieter. "What did you say? What did he say?"

"That the courts were still considering things, and they'd make their judgement, and asking me about it wasn't kind to anyone."

"That worked?"

Laura shrugged. "All right, and then he tossed half a dozen much more exciting things to gossip about into play." She shook her head. "Now, that I'd buy tickets for."

Martin snorted. "He's baffling. But I suppose he's baffling other people, to help you. That's something."

Laura nodded, and then they walked along just enjoying being together again, with an occasional gesture at a shop window. All too soon they turned into the square that held the main court building in Trellech, and climbed the stairs to walk into the pillared arcade, then into the courtroom. Martin spotted a couple of people he knew, and guided them into the end of that row, leaving Laura to nod politely, but with little time for introductions.

This was a different court room than Basil's trial, and

she was glad. There had been something decidedly horrid about the whole process. Compelled by the formal oaths, he had been all vinegar and nastiness about his sister's sudden change of heart. He was convinced that she'd been trying to talk to Julius to confess. Under the press of the magic, they'd heard a torrent that made it clear that he could not tolerate that kind of interference with his own goals - or his freedom. He had been unrepentant, and now he was dead, for the jury's decision had been extremely quick.

This courtroom was all wood panels and better light. Just as the court was about to come to order, she spotted Captain FitzRanulf slip into the seats for the Guard at the front. Galen was up on the other side, the family side. There was an older man, grey in his hair, sitting beside him who she didn't recognise at all. Julius was next to Galen on the other side, and right behind him, rather to her startlement, she spotted Blythe, in a blue dress quite different from anything she'd worn on the island.

Watching for a moment, it was clear Blythe and Julius were close, the way she leaned in, murmuring something. If there had been any doubt, it was gone as soon as Nell Amberly was lead in, with the glare she gave Blythe, like it was the greatest betrayal of them all.

The bailiff brought the court to order, the oaths were made, and the magic settled over them. It felt less uncomfortable than the trials themselves, where she'd had to take the formal oaths for testimony. She shivered for a moment, at how the touch of the Silence had felt, the way her lungs had contracted, how it had been hard to draw a breath.

"Ladies, lords, gentlemen, and all those assembled, we are gathered for the matter of obstruction of justice by Cassian Amberly and Parnell Amberly related to the murder of Senara Wilson. We have heard all the evidence, they have been questioned, and I will now proclaim sentence."

It was as if the entire room took a breath, anticipating.

"Our society expects that those with more advantages should use them wisely and well. In the course of investigation, it has been determined that Cassian and Parnell Amberly have used their position to limit their sons. They sought to use their influence to destroy the lives of at least two innocent parties, one of them their own son, as well as their interference with due and proper investigation of a capital crime."

There was a tiny pause. "In light of their choices, we have sentenced them to a restricted life. They may pick an estate of their choice to retire to, and will be required to remain there unless they are granted permission by the court offices. They may receive pre-approved guests and visitors, and may order items from elsewhere. However, they and their household staff may be required to submit to questioning under oath to the Silence at any time if there are concerns about their actions."

There was a low rolling gasp. It was one of the harsher penalties that could have been enacted. Martin leaned over, and said, "I wonder what else they found." More than Laura and Martin had known, certainly.

"Their current business interests and other properties will pass to their sons, both of whom have been found entirely blameless in all related matters. I have appointed an accomplished and experienced mentor to assist them in making long-term decisions about the properties and assets. He will serve for three years, with court review each year. Due to Julius Amberly's status as a wounded veteran, the court will also ensure his access to appropriate services." That was better news. Carillon had explained that it was possible they would fine or confiscate property as part of the punishment. She supposed they had, in their way, by passing it on.

The rest of it was formalities, laying out who the mentor was, which property they would be at, the timeline. All in all, it took fifteen minutes. Then the judge rose, everyone stood, and the court was adjourned. Martin leaned to add, "Galen will be along when he's signed the things he needs to sign. Shall we?"

The Dweller's club was a short walk away. There was a small gaggle of people walking with them, with Martin at the head. He'd said "Introductions when we can sit and relax, yes?" She recognised a few from his descriptions, but not many.

Martin lead her to a lovely Georgian home in a side street, three stories, and nodded at the staff member who opened the door. "The gathering space is all set, Mr Taylor. Miss Penhallow, welcome to the Forge. May I take your coat?" Laura blinked at him, she hadn't expected to be known. She nodded, slipping out of the coat and the jacket, then Martin drew her away into a large room, clearly designed for banqueting.

At the moment, the tables were pushed back to the walls, with a range of food and drink set out. There were groups of couches and chairs in convenient conversational circles. "Here we are. You can powder your nose in there." He pointed to the left side of the front of the room.

Laura smiled. "Practical. I'll just be a minute." The powder room was delightful, well appointed, and arranged with the kind of thoughtfulness that was far too rare. She drew the shawl out of her bag, used the facilities, and washed up. Then she took her place in front of the mirror and removed the comb that had held her hair up. There was something potent, magical, about letting her hair down. She took a deep breath and went out.

Martin had gathered a small circle of people around him, standing so he could see her emerge. He immediately held a hand out to her. "This is Laura Penhallow. Laura, love, this is Lydia Pyle, one of my fellow reporters. She's much better than I am at immersing in a story."

"Pah." Lydia laughed. "You have your own skills. And how's that going?"

"Ah, that's quite a thing." Laura slipped her hand into Martin's arm again. He'd mentioned he had something in the works, but not what. The way he was grinning, though, it was going very well.

"The Moon has agreed to take a chance on me. My series about services for veterans, and how they are and aren't working now. And then the follow up."

Laura asked, "Julius was willing, then?"

"Julius, and he found me a dozen other people who've agreed to interviews. It will take quite a lot of work. Building the trust, talking to the providers, figuring out how to shape it into a series. Five pieces, probably, but they might go to seven."

"That's grand, and that, that's important." Laura couldn't quite figure out how to say it better.

"They were interested in that idea about sanitaria life, and reintegration afterwards, too. Not immediately, but if this goes well, they'll consider it."

Laura ducked her head. "Oh, Martin." Then she did the only logical thing and shifted onto her toes to kiss his cheek. "Good."

More people came in, and Martin was then kept busy introducing her. The infamous Thomasina, who had an air of sulphur around her. Graham, another reporter, a little older than Martin, she remembered him from the reporting about the goldwasser. He gave her a polite nod and didn't bring it up, which she appreciated. Miriam, a woman with dark curly hair, and ink stains all over her fingers. Half a dozen others, who made a fleeting impression.

Half an hour in, she'd had enough of a drink to settle her nerves, and was figuring out who people were and how they connected to each other. There was a sudden silence, and she could see Galen at the door. The light framed him, and she leaned to murmur to Martin. "Love."

He nodded, and then said "Galen, my brother." His voice carried through the quiet.

She could see, everyone could see, how Galen instantly relaxed. He came over, and Martin dropped her arm, to meet him, hug him soundly, generous with his affection. They spoke quietly for just a moment, and then Martin led Galen back. "Let me round up a few things, Galen, for you." Galen nodded, but he didn't look away from Laura.

"You look grand." It came out uneven, and then he snapped his mouth shut.

"Galen." She leaned to kiss his cheek, not sure until the last moment it was the right thing. "It's so good to see you."

She felt him relax again, minutely, and then he took her hand. "You and Martin seem to be doing well? I haven't seen him this optimistic about his work for years."

Laura smiled. "Oh, that's all him. But I'm glad. And it's important, isn't it?"

"He had offers to write about what happened. The inside scoop. And he refused." Galen glanced over at where Martin was clearly searching for the best items from the tables.

"He's your brother, before anything else." Then, she risked. "And I hope I am your sister."

"Not formally yet, I gather? But I hope so." That was so fragile, that hope.

"We're giving it a few months, and then we plan to get a flat together. Down the road, quite possibly more but one big change at a time, yes? And there's still the family house in Cornwall. You should come visit, too. If you want."

"I'd like to see a different part of it. We're going to sell the house on the island. Julius and I decided, this morning. It should," His voice trailed off. "Something different."

"Do you want to go into the business?"

"I'm honestly not sure. That's what the mentor is for. They asked what I wanted to do, and I said I wasn't sure I knew enough. So they found someone. And oh, he's grand. He's had his own business, he comes from the same sort of family, he was a younger son. Inherited in his late twenties, his older brother was killed in the Boer War, in South Africa. So he understands. I was - I was worried they'd do something I couldn't figure out a way out of."

"And you have friends who would help, but maybe not know that specific part."

Galen nodded, eager now. "Exactly like that. He's given me things to read, and I think I can do something useful with it. Treat staff better, figure out how to build something worth doing. Mother and Father are taking one of the estates. Julius is getting space to set up a proper safe alchemy lab. With Blythe, of all things. She's come out of herself. There's someone who's willing to take him on for additional apprentice work, so he can do more complicated things. Maybe really useful things. Healing. My aunt and uncle are helping with that, the connections. He likes the idea, even if it's a big change."

"I'm so glad. A lot of hard work ahead, all round, but like you said, worth it."

Galen nodded and then went suddenly shy. "Yes. Um. So I know the Dwellers here, but not the other people. What should we do?"

"That's Lydia. And that's Graham, but I think you know him. But those are the only names I'm certain of. I think we stand here and look like we know what we're doing until Martin comes back and can do introductions again."

"A fine plan."

# EPILOGUE

## MARCH 1926, A FLAT IN TRELLECH

"Are we ready?"

"We are." Laura grinned at him and kissed his cheek. "I like that. We."

"You're sure about this?"

"It's a bit late if I'm not. We've already moved in together, sent out invitations, and in about a minute, various friends will show up on our doorstep. If I were going to have second thoughts, I should have had them ages ago." She paused, then added, grinning, "Especially given how many of them will probably ask when we're getting married."

Martin grunted. "You are being practical again." Then he added, amused, "We are getting married when you are ready. I'm quite clear on that."

"And you were telling me just this morning how much you appreciated my practicality. Twice. Once with the morning sex, once with the having tea ready to go." She left the other part, they were both comfortable with their choices, and didn't need to cater to those who weren't.

He laughed. "Both were true. And I do love it. Just it limits how much I can fuss."

"And then you put that toward writing fantastic articles and doing important investigations." His second series, about the sanitaria, had just come out. They had offered him a regular position at the Trellech Moon, focusing on stories about advances in healing, and all the ways healing arts affected people's lives. Plus, he hoped and suspected, some general news as well.

Laura looked around the flat one more time. "Everything's ready. Lots of seating, the food's ready." They'd got some from the staff at the Dweller's Forge, but Laura had made quite a lot of it. Fresh baked bread, biscuits, and then cheeses and beer and cider to go with it.

"Are we getting your family?"

"Oh, yes. But they promised just briefly, then they'll clear out of our hair."

"Still intimidating. Even your sister."

"She's grown into intimidation, yes. And they promised they wouldn't be the first here, either."

"This is all right for you?"

"This is grand. Very bohemian, but - that's what we want. A mix of people. In and out, your colleagues. Dwellers."

"And the people you're meeting."

Laura nodded. "I didn't think, until Lizzie suggested it, that I could be a help that way." What she was doing baffled Martin, but Laura had a real knack for helping people who'd been under long-term Healer care set their lives up again. She'd organise their papers, figure out what help they needed at home, coordinate visits with the healers and other specialists.

And then when they'd had that sorted out, she'd move on to someone else. It could be a week, it could be a month or more. She was on her tenth client now, and it was going brilliantly. She even had a waiting list a dozen people deep.

In his investigations, he'd found that too many people wanted to be condescending. To assume that someone who'd been very ill couldn't do anything for themselves. And oh, it was true many of them needed more help than they wanted to admit.

Laura just settled in and had a long chat over a cup of tea. She somehow got them to talk about what they hated doing, what they struggled with, what they felt guilty about. And then she'd help them figure out how to fix that in a way they could manage. Even enjoy.

The flat was the result. She'd needed a place in Trellech so she could be close to the Healing Temple, and the portals, she had had clients all over. It was cosy and comfortable, and she'd insisted on decorating it with a mix of styles, nothing fancy, nothing that felt uncomfortably posh. Rather like her family home in Cornwall, with pieces from everywhere.

A table from China, a stained glass lamp from America, pottery from Brazil. Cushions in jewel tones. And in their bedroom, which they'd only been sharing properly for a fortnight, the sandalwood chest her uncle had brought home. She'd said, with a grin, when she moved it in "The smell's quite a turn-on now, you realise."

He was lost in thought when he heard the knock. Not the first one, since Laura was already moving to get it. He followed and then grinned. "Ah, Lydia. Come in! You're the first, but I'm sure there will be other people along shortly. Coat rack here, there're drinks - you're cider, aren't you?"

Galen was a moment behind her. Laura got to him while Martin was finishing with Lydia's drink, drawing him inside so Martin could do the same. After the hug, Martin stood back, looking his brother up and down.

"You're a lot better."

"Still working rather a lot." Which was true, they'd not been able to see each other more than every couple of weeks for months. "But it's going well. Alastair will be along in a bit, he said he was looking forward to seeing you both." That was his mentor, and they had got close.

Martin would feel a little jealous, except it was so clearly what Galen had needed, and what Martin couldn't give him. Introductions to the people who would help the business, could teach the skills Galen needed.

"And he's pleased with things?"

"Oh, very. We're comfortably in the black for the year, and it should only get better. Father had been making some bad decisions." He paused, catching sight of Lydia.

She held up her hands. "Pax. Here as a friend, not as a journalist. I won't report anything you say here unless we agree to after."

Galen laughed. "Right. Well, my father had been making some rather short sighted decisions. With the business. It might have all come tumbling down like a house of cards, in a year or two. But Alastair and the people he's introduced me to, they think that's not at all likely now."

Martin grinned. "So that's good. Do we get to see a bit more of you, then? Laura was thinking we should set a regular night for dinner, now we can do that here."

Galen sketched out a bow. "I'd be delighted. So long as I don't have to bring a dinner partner. That may yet be beyond me."

Laura spread her hands. "Oh, our plan was to invite a likely set of people in rotation, and see what happened, actually."

The expression on Galen's face was utterly gobsmacked. Then he shook his head and said to Martin, "You do know what you've got into?"

"Oh, yes. Regularly. Don't argue. It's much worse if you argue. Plus, she has good ideas. And an excellent sense of people."

Galen was about to say something else, when a new crowd appeared at the door, and the conversation turned less teasing and more general.

IF YOU ENJOYED *In The Cards* and would like to read more of this series, please sign up for my mailing list to get all the latest news and fun extras. Your reviews (on whatever review site you use) are much appreciated, too!

As a thank you, you'll get *Ancient Trust,* a prequel novella about Laura's brother-in-law, Geoffrey Carillon, as well as how he came to know Captain FitzRanulf.

Learn more about Laura's sister Lizzie and her romance with Lord Geoffrey Carillon (with appearances from Laura) in *Goblin Fruit.* Galen gets his own romance in *Point By Point*

Read on for more historical details about this book and an excerpt from *On The Bias*

# AUTHOR'S NOTE

Thank you so much for reading *In The Cards*. I owe a particular thanks on this one to my editor and my early readers for helping me make the mystery plot stronger (and for cheering on Laura and her choices.) Any remaining errors are of course entirely mine.

If you're curious about the story of Lord Geoffrey Carillon and Lizzie Penhallow, or curious about the details of the goldwasser, then *Goblin Fruit* has all of those for you. Laura appears there as a secondary character.

It's likely quite obvious from this book that I'm a fan of more than just Dorothy L. Sayers when it comes to Golden Age of Mystery writers. I couldn't resist trying my hand at a **locked room murder mystery**. They're quite difficult to write, and keeping everyone straight took a lot of work. (Again, so much thanks to my editor and early readers for this.) Agatha Christie and all the others who contributed to this specific subgenre deserve a great deal of credit.

One of the threads through *In The Cards* is that Laura is a survivor of **tuberculosis**, a disease that killed vast numbers of the population. It is a bacterial disease, and you'll often see it referred to as 'consumption'. It's been around through all of human history - the earliest evidence of the bacterium dates back to bison in 17000 BCE.

However, as people moved to the cities, the number of people infected grew. Estimates in the 1800s suggest that one in four deaths was caused by tuberculosis, more so among those living in poverty or in crowded city conditions (since it is most commonly transmitted by droplets shared through coughing or spitting.) Even with treatment about half the patients died within five years. We didn't begin to reduce the number of cases substantially until the introduction of antibiotics. Unfortunately some strains of TB are now resistant to antibiotics.

The preferred treatment for people who could afford it was to go away to somewhere with fresh air and suitable nutrition and other support, in a sanitarium (also spelled sanitorium). As Laura describes, patients often had extreme restrictions on what they could do, and very regimented schedules. They were often in areas with particular kinds of air quality, notably mountains and seasides. (I grew up reading the Chalet School books, a series of British school stories which initially take place in the Austrian Tyrol, near a TB sanitarium.)

If you'd like to learn even more, I recommend *Spitting Blood: The History of Tuberculosis* by Helen Bynum for an excellent overview of both the medical side and the human side of the disease.

**Facial injuries** like the the one Julius suffered were regrettably not uncommon in the Great War. Even more regrettably, many families pressed those injured to hide away, or otherwise remove themselves from society. The ceramic mask Julius wears was one option commonly used, but a wide range of materials were used including cloth and metal. I first started thinking about this bit of history after reading Jacqueline Winspear's *Maisie Dobbs*.

~

**Tarot decks** also have a long and complex history. Some early decks have survived, others we know about, but they only exist in fragmentary amounts. Over the centuries, they've been used for symbolic representations for ritual and meditation, for divination, for religious purposes, and just for playing cards. *In The Cards* has a bit of all of these except the religious. The reading in the first chapter is divinatory, Laura plays Tarrochi (a game with many variations played with a Tarot deck), and then later uses the deck to represent the people in the house through the cards.

What makes something a Tarot deck, rather than a different kind of card deck, is generally considered to be the structure. Tarot decks commonly have 78 cards. These include 56 cards of the Minor Arcana, made up of four suits (like a playing card deck), court cards (most commonly Page, Knight, Queen, King), and then 22 cards in the Major Arcana, sometimes also called trumps, that represent various archetypal forces. The suits commonly represent the four elements - swords, wands or staves, cups, and pentacles or coins.

If you're at all familiar with Tarot, you're probably familiar with the Rider-Waite-Smith deck, based on the instructions of A.E. Waite, drawn by illustrator Pamela Colman Smith, and published by the Rider Company. This deck was published in 1909, and it seems likely that Smith was influenced by some exhibits of older decks at the British Museum earlier that decade, so my characters could be familiar with the deck. However, I found that the symbology (rooted in a particular line of Western esoteric and magical theory) didn't do what I wanted it to.

*In the Cards* references one well-known historic deck, the Marseilles, and two decks I made up. The earliest surviving cards of the Tarot de Marseilles were produced in the mid 1600s in Paris, France, but the symbology of the deck is a century or two older. This deck has scenes on some cards (the Major Arcana and court cards) but the other Minor Arcana are just pips or symbols. The Alpine deck, which gets referenced in passing, has some different images but roughly the same symbology, and is more popular in Switzerland and parts of France and Italy.

When I started *In The Cards*, I was intending to have the characters use the Marseilles deck, in part because I wanted the symbology of the Lovers card in that deck, which has a man choosing between two women, one younger and beautiful but poor, and one older but clearly well off, to set up Laura's choices in the book. However, as I got further into the story, it became clear I was going to need something that suited the world and the character needs better.

A lot of reading about older Tarot decks later, I decided the best way to go was create my own. I've read Tarot for about two decades now, so this is not quite as daunting as it might be. (I use Tarot mostly as a way to get a better grasp on elements of a situation and what I should pay attention to, but I have used it in other ways.) The more I looked at options, the more I realised I also wanted a deck that decentred Christianity in the implied symbology, and that played on some of the specific history of Albion.

(It's not as obvious in *In The Cards* as some of my books, but some people in Albion are Christian, but many are something else. Often that's religious traditions rooted in family lines like Ibis's commitments to Djehuty and Het-Heru in *Magician's Hoard*, and Carillon's family traditions that include a particular aspect of Mercury in *Goblin Fruit*, of those we've seen on screen. There are also many other religious represented in the magical community, of course.)

All these threads pulled me towards creating the Howard Tarot. The current form of the deck in Albion was commissioned by someone in the Howard family (a family of longstanding influence in England dating back to the Wars of the Roses) in the early 1600s. It is based on the symbology of an older deck used in the family since the early Tudor period.

I have not fully detailed all the cards yet, but there are a few I wanted to share here. Some of the cards are very similar to our known decks, but others have elements that are specific to historical events, or highlight different aspects.

**The Magician** depicts John Dee, court magician under Elizabeth I, or someone very like him, as a well-dressed Elizabethan man in a ritual circle chalked on the floor, with all the accoutrements of ritual magic. In a world with a variety of method of doing magic, this card takes on perhaps more of the meaning (also present in many decks) about not just being about magic, but about showy flashy forms of magic that may in fact be less effective than implied.

**The Heirophant** in the Howard Deck is Henry VIII, depicted around the time of his marriage to Catherine Howard (of the Howard family), in formal robes of state, showing rulership, but with an element of unpredictability or manipulation or threads of corruption that mean the figure is not necessarily serving the higher cause he claims.

**The Wheel of Fortune** gets mentioned by Laura early on, but she doesn't explain that the Wheel of Fortune in the Howard Deck depicts the Battle of Bosworth Field, where the first Duke of Norfolk, John Howard, died fighting with Richard III. The wheel itself has red and white roses, showing the rise and fall of power and the competing York and Lancaster houses.

**The Star** in many decks has a naked woman pouring water. In the Howard, the woman is reaching up, appearing to touch a constellation above her, but is dressed in gauzy fabric. The figure in the Visconti Tarot is also reaching up to touch a star.

There is no card for **The Devil** in the Howard Tarot, instead it is a card that is about fear, bondage to fear, and a lack of light, hope, or potential. In decks that are designed for magical work, the card actually is enchanted to reflect the fear that comes when you come close to breaking a Silence-held oath. (I'm still deciding on the name for this one, but I expect it to show up in a future book somewhere.)

**The Court cards** also have a slightly different structure. In Albion, the Lords and Ladies of the land have specific magical obligations, so they are the obvious candidates to replace "King" and "Queen". Likewise, apprenticeship plays a major role in most people's lives in Albion, as the transition between childhood and adulthood, so it's a natural fit to refer to the young active card as an Apprentice, rather than a knight. Child replaces Page quite naturally.

Finally, the **suits** are the same as in many decks, but they often reflect animals associated with particular Houses at the most elite of the magical schools of Albion, Schola. These houses are places where people live, but they also have their own lines of magical education and many people continue close connections in their house throughout their lives. In the Howard Tarot, Owl is associated with Swords, Boar and Fox with Wands, Salmon and Seal with Cups, and Horse and Bear with Pentacles.

Finally, the **Guard** are the magical law enforcement for Albion, with a number of divisions. This time, we get to see who deals with actual murder cases (relatively few and far between, as the magical population is numerically not huge, but there are enough there are people who specialise.)

*Ancient Trust,* a prequel novella about Laura's brother-in-law, Geoffrey Carillon, is available if you sign up for my mailing list. It explains how he came to know Captain Fitz-Ranulf in an entirely different sort of investigation.

You can find other stories with members of the Guard in *Wards of the Roses, Outcrossing, On The Bias* and *Pastiche.*

Learn more about Laura's sister Lizzie and her romance with Lord Geoffrey Carillon (with appearances from Laura) in *Goblin Fruit.* Galen gets his own romance in *Point By Point.*

The newsletter (https://www.celialake.com/newsletter/) and my social media accounts will have all the details about new and upcoming releases, and I hope to see you one of those places! Until then, happiest of reading to you.

Happy reading, and I do hope you'll join me for future stories of Albion.

www.ingramcontent.com/pod-product-compliance
Lightning Source LLC
LaVergne TN
LVHW050930080826
845145LV00001B/287

* 9 7 8 1 9 5 7 1 4 3 0 9 5 *